"Western readers have [...] the campfire, a writer who can tell a great adventure story with authority and wit. Welcome J. Lee Butts!"

—John S. McCord, author
of *Walking Hawk* and
the Baynes Clan novels

THE WANTED ONES

Just as Pa and I were discussing how to get our wagon out of the ditch, a preacher approached us and lifted his hand in greeting.

"May the peace of God be with you and your family, sir. Where are you headed this lovely day?"

"Goin' to Texas by way of Little Rock. Mighty kind of you to stop, Reverend."

"Might I give you and your family a blessing from Scripture?" the preacher asked, pulling out a well-worn black Bible.

"That's right thoughtful, sir. We'd be most grateful." Pa put his arm around my shoulders and bowed his head. Out of the corner of my eye, I saw Mother do the same. The Bible fell open in the minister's hands, as if to a favorite passage. He raised his right hand to the page as though to trace the lines he wanted to read. Instead, out of the book he drew a tiny pistol. An ugly smile danced across his face.

"What the he—?" Pa never got to finish his question. The preacher's first shot hit my father in his left eye. I pitched out of the wagon and into the water. Pa had landed at the water's edge and half floated there. I wanted to help so bad I thought I'd explode, but my limbs just froze.

long resisted a new voice around

LAWDOG

THE LIFE AND TIMES OF
HAYDEN TILDEN

J. LEE BUTTS

BERKLEY BOOKS, NEW YORK

LAWDOG

A Berkley Book / published by arrangement with
the author

PRINTING HISTORY
Berkley edition / November 2001

Visit our website at
www.penguinputnam.com

ISBN: 0-425-18218-5

BERKLEY®
Berkley Books are published by The Berkley Publishing Group,
a division of Penguin Putnam Inc.,
375 Hudson Street, New York, New York 10014.
BERKLEY and the "B" design
are trademarks belonging to Penguin Putnam Inc.

PRINTED IN THE UNITED STATES OF AMERICA

10 9 8 7 6 5 4 3 2 1

For my wife, Carol, who continues
to make my literary efforts possible

ACKNOWLEDGMENTS

Special thanks are extended to Michael and Barbara Rosenberg for believing in me. To Kimberly Waltemyer for making this all possible. And, finally, to the DFW Writer's Workshop whose knowledge, experience, and weekly contributions are evident on every page of this and all my other work.

Being a U.S. Marshal may appear to some to be a regular picnic, but we don't want any of it.

—*Fort Smith Elevator, 1884*

PROLOGUE

BY CHANCE, I stopped at Hardin's Grocery Store back in 'thirty-nine to buy myself a smoke. On the way out bumped into Caleb Spain. Arrested Caleb on a John Doe warrant a few years before I had to give up living by the gun. Hadn't seen him since. He shook my hand and thanked me. Said his two-year stay in prison put him on the straight and narrow. Said I'd saved him from a life of evil doings, probably an early death and eternity in a fiery hell.

It's strange how the past can reach out and grab you like that when you least expect it. Nine years after I saw Caleb I'd managed to get to a point in my life where no one ever recognized me anymore. Living at the Rolling Hills Home for the Aged, here in Little Rock, can do that for you. Kind of liked it that way. But being a retired killer in 1948 hadn't turned out like I expected. Course, I don't think being a retired anything ever turns out like most people expect. Then a guy I didn't know showed up at the home two weeks ago, and one name caused it all to come flooding back.

Carlton J. Cecil and I were slouched in chairs out on the screened porch. The July mugginess always kept us staked out under one of the ceiling fans—day and night. Our checkerboard acted as a prop to disguise the never-ending naps that plague people too old and too idle for much of anything else. Snapped out of a dreamy doze just when this well-dressed young man walked up.

He startled me enough to cause the ash to break off my neglected panatela. Senior nurse Leona Wildbank always said I'd set myself on fire someday if I didn't renounce what she called a "pernicious addiction." I steadfastly refuse.

"Which one of you gentlemen is former Deputy United States Marshal Hayden Tilden?" the youngster asked. He sounded bored. Like one of those people who think they know everything. Above his head the fan twisted the blue-gray cloud from my smoke into a miniature tornado.

"That old fart there. He's the one," said Carl, pointing a palsied ninety-two-year-old finger at me. He drew the ancient digit back to his mouth and gnawed at a newly discovered sprout on its nail with his two remaining teeth, then immediately snoozed off again.

"Mr. Tilden, my name is Franklin J. Lightfoot Jr. I'm a staff writer for the *Arkansas Gazette.*" The lad's suit and white shirt sparkled. His bright pink face glowed from a shave so close I marveled that any skin remained. Witch hazel sliced through the cigar smoke and tickled my nose. He was the cleanest man I'd seen since I arrived at Rolling Hills.

"Well, I'm right pleased to meet you, Junior," I said as we shook hands.

"You can call me Frank, sir." He leaned forward and stared hard like he wanted to slap me for being impertinent.

"Be glad to. Why don't you have a seat and tell the dozing Mr. Cecil and I what we can do for you this hot summer day, Junior." I adjusted myself further down into my wicker throne and watched as he pulled up a chair.

Didn't get many callers. Don't think Cecil ever had any. We'd both outlived almost everyone we ever knew. When you get to be as old as us, anyone who'll spend five minutes talking to you is a novelty. I've had days when I caught myself talking to the potted plant next to Maybelle Bryant's door. Been at it for almost an hour before I realized what I was doing. A red-faced writer from a local newspaper was like a Christmas package I couldn't wait to unwrap.

"Mr. Tilden, I've been assigned to write a piece on Judge Parker's court." He settled into a straight-backed, cane-bottomed instrument of torture rubbed fuzzy by decades of ancient, bony behinds. "During my preliminary research, I found your name linked with the capture or killing of some of the most infamous bad men Judge Parker's lawdogs ever tracked down, including none other than Saginaw Bob Magruder. Given what I've read, I think I could honestly say you made quite a name for yourself."

Pulled sagely at my beard and said, "Never meant to do it, Junior." The corners of his mouth turned down. "Just kind of happened, son. You know, I think most of us just kind of fall into things during our lives. My career as a man hunter for Judge Parker was like that."

"Well, Mr. Tilden, my editor thinks there's a market for the story of your days as a gunman. He feels the western novels and motion pictures of today portray a place that never existed. He'd like to publish your true life history, sir. Perhaps as a series of weekly chapters dealing with the various characters you arrested or exterminated. Wants to produce an authentic picture of your life. Not a soft-focus illusion like the autobiography Wyatt Earp and his wife put out. If it draws a large enough audience, might even be able to turn it into a book."

Franklin J. Lightfoot Jr. was something of a snotty twerp but buried under his superior-than-thou delivery I detected what bordered on a real interest.

There'd been other offers like ole Franklin's in the past. I'd just ignored all of them. Hadn't seen one in about ten years though. So I figured, well, I'll play along with this chicken wrangler and see where it leads.

"Right flattering, Junior. 'Course, I've forgotten a lot of what happened back then—some of it simply because of the passage of time. I mean, Lord almighty, I am eighty-eight years old. Forgot a good bit because it just wasn't the kind of thing I wanted to remember, but most because Judge Parker didn't want anyone to ever find out about it." Didn't want the boy to know that I could recall damned near every minute of my life. Figured I'd just string him along for a while and see what happened.

A befuddled look flickered across his face and he said, "I don't understand. What do you mean? What's the secret, Mr. Tilden?"

Blew smoke rings at the ceiling and thought about that for a minute before I said, "Junior, sometimes the bad things we do are like spots we can't fix on a hardwood floor. We just throw a rug over them and forget they're under there. A lot of what happened in the beginning, especially with monsters like Bob Magruder and most of what I did when I worked privately for the Judge, was like that. I performed a special kind of job for the man."

The puzzled look stayed with him for a bit. "My paper hopes you'll be willing to tell me about that period of your life—spots and all, black or white—even the monsters. Perhaps the two of us could pull back some of those rugs just mentioned and look underneath. Maybe we can tell a tale that'll show how silly those Saturday afternoon cowboys Bob Steele, Ken Maynard, Gene Autry, and the rest, really are." The seriously scrubbed boy was turning out smarter than I first thought.

Going to confess here I never expected to live eighty years. Don't think anyone ever does when they start out. Never figured on telling anyone my life story either. But eight more years on top of eighty can open secret doors in your past. Doors you always expected would stay closed.

So I asked myself, right then and there, what could it hurt? With General Black Jack Pershing, Rolling Hill's resident house cat, rubbing against my leg, I got to thinking. They're all dead and in the ground now, anyway. I'm the only one left, and this snot-nosed boy might actually be able to get the thing published. Now, wouldn't that really be something?

Sat across the checkerboard from him and sailed off into one of those instant fantasies—the kind which come over people my age with little or no encouragement. You know how you'll be talking to some old codger and they'll suddenly drift away from you. I could see the seventy-two-point block type on the front page of the

Arkansas Gazette . . . LAWDOG: THE LIFE AND TIMES OF HAYDEN TILDEN. Why not?

So I asked, "How do you want to do this, Junior? You want me to write it all down or do we just sit here and talk it over?"

"Why don't we start right now? You tell me how it began. Then tonight, make some notes. I'll come back tomorrow, and as many times as necessary, until you've finished."

"Well, in case you haven't noticed, I'm pretty close to being finished right now. My health hasn't been the greatest in the past few years. Bullet holes and age will do that, you know. Don't trust doctors any more today than I did back in 'eighty. And to be absolutely truthful, the story of my life finished itself almost thirty years ago. Country just grew out of a need for men like me. I didn't even notice it when it happened. Should've got a real big hint when those barn weasels in Wyoming hung Tom Horn. Didn't. Same thing will happen to you, boy. History will slip by, and you won't realize its full impact till years later."

He fished around in the pocket of his jacket, pulled a little pad of paper out, and licked the end of his pencil. "Just tell me what you remember," he said as he started writing.

Hadn't thought about my past for a long time. Amazed myself with how much came back when I went to scratching around in those little gray folds in the back of my brain. Tried not to let on to Franklin J. Jr., but the name Bob Magruder exploded in my head like a box of dynamite and reopened massive wounds on my heart.

1

"They Will Send You to Hell"

A GOOD MANY of the other old gomers here at Rolling Hills look back on their pasts like no other time in history compared in beauty or glory. I may be seriously rubbing up against ninety years old, but I can recall the years that included most of their lives. And I'm here to tell you it was a dirty, dangerous, and downright deadly time. Anyone who says otherwise is the kind of fool who'd intentionally pick a fight with a skunk.

I spent close to fifty years carrying a badge. It started in August of 1878 on the day Bob Magruder shot me in the face. That's about as deadly as you can get and what caused the scar on my right cheek that runs up to the bridge of my nose. My eighteenth birthday had just passed—so long ago. Still get furious every time I run my finger along the piece of hard, pink flesh he left behind.

My family's wagon had just creaked to a stop, because

of a tree across the Great River Road in Arkansas, when he appeared out of the darkness of the tree line. He rode a tall, coal black horse and dressed himself like a preacher. We could never have guessed his identity, how dangerous he was, or that three more just as bad hid in the bushes behind him.

My father waved as the stranger came closer. Papa was a man of little education and a trusting nature and didn't seem to notice the oddity of having a pastor just kind of grow up out of the ground in the middle of a godforsaken spot like Arkansas.

"Maybe he can help us with the tree, Hayden." He smiled and waved at the man in black again. The stranger acknowledged the gesture and kept coming.

From inside the wagon my mother said, "I'm glad you stopped, Jonathan. Rachael needed a rest from the jostling. Do you think we can get down for a few minutes?" She moved to a spot behind and between us and whispered, "What's a preacher doing all the way out here in the wilderness?"

He reined his mount to a stop on the right just a few feet away from Papa. Clutched to his chest he carried a huge Bible. The leather cover showed heavy use, and the gilt-edged pages had lost much of their luster. He again raised his left hand in a gesture of friendship, but the smile on his lips twisted and gave him a look contrary to his outfit.

"May the peace of God be with you and your family, sir. Where are you headed this lovely day?"

"Goin' to Texas by way of Little Rock. Have family in both places and hope to be as successful as my brother. He lives in the Cold River country of the great Lone Star State," my father replied.

"You've set yourself on a hazardous journey, friend. Arkansas and the territories still teem with wild animals and bad men. The woods are full of 'em. Both kinds."

"Well, my son and I can take care of anything that might come along. We've made it all the way from Cumberland County, Kentucky, with no trouble. But, just in case anything wayward takes place, I keep my trusty Greener down here in the floor." He moved his right foot and motioned toward the shotgun nested below.

"I don't doubt you are capable, sir, but you must be careful. Up the road a piece is Winchester Township. I heard just yesterday from friends that a terrible man called Saginaw Bob Magruder and his gang were prowling about in these parts. Story being circulated claims they're on the run from a robbery that went bad in Mississippi. I'd be on my toes if I were you."

Didn't like the look or sound of the man, but hated the idea of Papa and me having to move that tree alone, so I said, "Well, do you think you can help us with the tree, sir?"

He glanced at the leafless obstacle. "You can get around on this side." He urged his animal within arm's length of the jockey box. "There's more room than you can see from up there. But don't try to go left. That bar ditch is deep. It rained all day yesterday. Filled 'er full. You could throw one of your oxen in there and lose it."

I snapped a quick glance at the muddy canal. "Maybe we can make town before dark, Papa. Be nice to spend the night in a town."

Turned back just in time to hear the preacher say, "I'd like to read a little passage of scripture for you, brother. I think a message from God will help you on your way."

"That's right thoughtful, sir. We'd be most grateful for

your blessings." Papa put his arm around my shoulders and waited for God's grace. Out of the corner of my eye, I saw my mother bow her head and fold her hands in prayer. Couldn't see Rachael. She'd been sick with malaria for most of two weeks and didn't move around much.

The man in black transferred the huge book from his right hand to his left. It fell open as if to a favorite and often read passage. He raised his right hand to the page as though to trace the lines he wanted to read. Instead, a tiny pistol magically sprang from the book. An ugly smile danced across his face.

"What the h—?" Papa never got to finish his question.

The preacher's first shot hit my father in his left eye. Hair, blood, and bone splattered all over me. The second slug burned a bloody path across my right cheek and nose. If it hadn't been for the convulsive response of my father's legs, the man would have killed us both right then and there.

We pitched out of the wagon. I landed in the water. Went down and thought I'd never come up. Weeds clogged the ditch bottom and pulled at my feet. Must've been more unconscious than conscious for a minute or two. Maybe more. I came half awake, tangled under a clump of trash and twigs, on the far side of that swampy smelling trench. Heard the man in black again before I could see him.

"Get in the wagon, Benny. Hurry up. We don't have much time. Them ole boys from Mississippi might grow a piece of brain big enough between the ten of 'em to come back this way."

Cleared the mud and blood from my eyes just as he fired two more shots into my father's body. Papa had landed at the water's edge and half floated there. Wanted to help so bad I thought I'd explode. Parts of me just wouldn't move at the time. The shock of my father's death, the fall, and my wound partially paralyzed me.

I heard screaming. But it didn't seem real. It all sounded a long way off. Muffled for a while, then sharp and awful—the kind of awful that leaves no doubt when someone's dying. It took a while before I realized I knew the people doing the screaming.

A short man wearing a long, ragged military coat ran past the man in black and jumped into the wagon. The belt around his waist bristled with pistols and a huge knife. He stood there for a moment and spat tobacco juice over his shoulder. Then he dove into my mother's belongings like a man going swimming.

Furniture, pots, pans, and clothing flew from the wagon's back and sides like wounded birds going to ground. When he came up wearing one of mother's bonnets, he giggled and laughed like something crazed.

"See anything, Benny?" The man in black paced along the ditch. He stared at the stumps, grass, and floating logs. I knew if he spotted me he wouldn't miss again.

"Can't find that big Kentucky farm boy," he snarled. "Think I got him clean, but it'd be nice to put a couple more in him before we leave."

More squeals and giggles came pouring out the back of the wagon like a waterfall. "Preacher. Look. Look what Benny done found. Stupid greenhorn hid it under the boards jest like they always does."

The short man jumped from the back of the wagon and handed the leather pouch to his leader, then danced and twirled around the money after they dumped it on the ground. His half-witted brain probably couldn't completely comprehend what he'd discovered.

"Well, look at you, Benny. Fifteen brand spankin' new twenty-dollar gold pieces. Three hundred dollars. Damned fine take when you figure all we had to do was kill a stupid plow chaser and his family." The black-clad killer dropped the coins into the bag one at a time. He'd lied. Papa had put five hundred dollars in that bag.

Then he shoved the leather sack into his coat pocket, strolled to his tall black horse like a man on his way to Sunday school, and jumped into the saddle. "Go get the others and let's get away from here, Benny," he yelled.

"Don't think they's ready to go just yet, Preacher. You know they's never ready till the screamin' stops." He turned, cupped a hand over his right ear, and looked toward the spot in the trees where the man in black had first appeared. "Hear 'em?"

"Do as you're told, Benny. Go get 'em. We've got to get away from here right now."

Then the son of a bitch sat on his horse looking at my father's lifeless body, raised the Bible toward heaven, and said, "Blessed are the meek; for they shall inherit the earth. I regret your inheritance is this stinkin' Arkansas canal, brother, but I feel my needs far exceed those of a Kentucky sodbuster. Nothing personal. Come on, Satan, let's get gone." He put the spur to his huge horse and darted past Benny.

The little man yelled at the trees, "Come on. The Preacher's a-leavin'. Come on. Hurry up." Only the screams answered him from the darkness of the forest.

He stood in the road, hopped from foot to foot, scratched himself, and waited for the wailing to stop. He twitched and fidgeted, then vanished for about a minute and came back leading two horses and the biggest mule I'd ever seen.

The freshly fallen rainwater drained me of energy. Struggled to stay conscious. Got harder to do by the second. My concentration wandered all over Kentucky, Mississippi, and Arkansas. Then the quiet shocked me back.

Two men stumbled out of the woods pulling at their pants. They all resembled fearful men called Texians I'd seen on wanted posters tacked to trees along our route from Kentucky. Benny led their mounts to them. The man who rode the mule needed an animal that large. He stood every inch of six and a half feet and looked to weigh nigh two hundred and fifty pounds. They swung into their saddles and vanished into the muddy distance. Flew back into the woods like buzzards scared away from a meal by the appearance of larger, more powerful animals.

"Mr. Tilden, did you recognize Saginaw Bob Magruder or know he called himself the Preacher?"

"Well, no, I didn't know the man, Junior. Already told you that. Never seen Arkansas, Texas, or the Indian Territories. Kentucky farm boys weren't privy to their law enforcement problems. Go get yourself a map. Arkansas Post, not far from where Magruder murdered my family, sat on a swampy piece of bog just east of the Mississippi. Who could have expected an ambush in such a place by men like those? My family's slaughter was a classic example of being in the wrong place at the wrong time."

He mulled that one over for a while before he said, "You've described an awful scene, Mr. Tilden. I'm surprised you can remember it in such detail after all these years."

"What I've described so far can't compare to what I found in the woods, Junior." Pulled a red bandanna from my pocket and wiped away the tear.

Guess that open display of emotion surprised Franklin J. Jr. "After more than sixty years, it still affects you so deeply?"

"Till then I'd never seen anybody die, boy. My grandparents passed long before I got born. Magruder killed my father right in my face. It's not a thing you forget. No matter the passage of time. Took me almost two hours to crawl out of that ditch and recover enough to find and load my gruesome cargo into the wagon. When I located what those animals left of my mother and Rachael, I had trouble telling which was which. Only the clothing on the ground near their bodies gave away the mystery. Wept so much it could have refloated Noah's boat. Stood over those bodies and swore horrible, bloody vengeance. I've worked real hard not to think about that scene any more than necessary since then."

"What had they done to your mother and sister?"

"Won't tell you that. A gentleman doesn't discuss such subjects. You wouldn't print it anyway. The tender readers of Pulaski County would run you and your editor out of the state if I told you the whole truth of the thing. So there's no point. It's enough you know that men skilled in the use of a Bowie knife can render a human being damn near unrecognizable."

"I thought we agreed you'd tell me everything, black or white. Spots and all."

"I didn't agree to anything. I'm just telling you the story of how fate got me started as a lawman. Won't go into detail about the barbarity of my mother's and sister's deaths. That's my final word on the matter, Junior."

"All right. Okay. Can we go on? Oh—wait just a minute." He fished around in his pants pocket and came up with a small knife. Little shavings from his pencil filtered down to General Black Jack Pershing, who rolled over on his orange-striped back and swatted at them like they were pesky gnats.

Well, I left almost everything my parents owned in the road and pushed the oxen toward Winchester Township. Fell asleep. Exhaustion, shock, loss of blood—all of it finally caught up with me. When I woke, the wagon had rolled to a stop in front of a rough saloon. Burned letters in a primitive rough-cut board sign over the door announced it as "Hooty Gwen's." Got quite a reaction when I stumbled in and fell to my knees just inside the door. An unwelcome silence rushed around the place.

Then, a man at one of the tables along the right side of the room jumped up, grabbed my arm, and led me to his chair.

"Lord in heaven, son. What happened to you?" He helped me get seated and looked at my face.

"Man dressed like a preacher shot me."

He turned to the bartender and said, "Hooty, bring me a rag and some water. This boy's been shot." He poked around on my head for a minute. "My name's Robbie Bullard, son. What's yours?"

"Hayden Tilden."

He waved toward some men across the table. "That one's Chester Gober, and the other's Beaver Acorn." They both gave me a wide-eyed nod and acted like they wanted to hit the door as fast as they could.

A man who sat alone at the only other table stood and moved to a spot behind the one called Chester. He carried a large tumbler of whiskey and swayed slightly when he stopped. "Ain't you gonna introduce me, Robbie? I'm just as important as these spit wads. I got rights just like these others."

Hooty Gwen dropped a wet rag in Bullard's hand and placed a pan of water beside a bottle of reddish green liquid on the table in front of me.

"Sorry there, Chad. Forgot you were here. You've always been the quietest drunk in these parts, and it's easy to forget you're around. Hayden, the one about to fall down behind Chester goes by the name of Chad Luther. Most folks around here think that's an alias, but if you call him that he'll come to supper, when he's sober."

"You say a preacher shot you, son?" Hooty Gwen pulled a chair up beside me and dabbed around on the back of my neck with another wet rag. His bald head sparkled like a glass doorknob under the light thrown from a kerosene lamp hanging above the table.

"Yes, sir. Big man. Had three others with him. Short, tobacco chewing fella he called Benny and two others. They all dressed like Texians and carried pistols and big knives. I'll know them when I see them again."

The one introduced as Beaver said, "Damn, boy. You've just described Saginaw Bob Magruder and his gang. That little one was most likely Benny Stubbs. Other two was Azel Stroud and Cecil Morris. Worst kinda murderin' scum in these parts. They robbed a bank over in Ennis, Mississippi, couple of days ago. Killed a sheriff and some other folks in the process. You're lucky you're alive."

"Yeah, lucky," added Chad Luther. "You travelin' alone, son?"

"No. I left my family outside in the wagon." Bullard

squeezed my blood into the pan of water. "They're all dead."

The town's entire drunken welcoming committee jerked a nervous look at the door. "How many do you have, Hayden?" asked Chester Gober.

"Could you speak up, boy? I can barely hear you." Luther moved around his friend, stopped next to me, and frowned down at the wound on my face. "Lord almighty," he whispered.

"Three dead. My father, mother, and sister."

Hooty Gwen glanced at each face around the table. "We'd better send for Horace. If they's been murder done, he needs to know about it."

They all nodded their agreement just as Chester Gober jumped from his chair. "I'll go get 'im. You boys see what's in the wagon." He skulked toward the door like a man afraid the devil waited in the dark, peeked out for a moment, then disappeared.

Bullard dropped his bloody rag in the pan and lifted the lantern from its hook above the table. "I guess we'd better look."

"I ain't goin' out there in the dark to stare at folk murdered by Bob Magruder and his bunch," Luther whined. He took a deep swallow from his glass and added, "I-I'll stay here with the boy till ya'll get back."

Gwen and Acorn followed Bullard's light and were gone but a minute or two. Stunned and white-faced, they stumbled back in and immediately headed for the bar.

Beaver Acorn threw down a shot of something straight that made him shake his head. "I ain't seen anyone cut up that bad since Bosephus Chandler fell on the big blade down at Sheridan's sawmill."

Everyone stared at me like I was dead too. Things got

real quiet. I could hear the clock on the wall by the bar. Time just kind of stood still for about a minute. Then the door busted open and Chester Gober pulled a man who looked like a farmer in by the arm.

"Dammit, Hooty, this crazy boozehound jerked me out of a warm bed with some wild story about murder and robbery. If this turns out like the last dodge you and this swarm of barflies tried to pull on me, I'll have you all prosecuted the next time Judge McCord makes the circuit."

"Hayden, meet Horace Potts, the sometimes mayor of our little hole in the road," said Hooty Gwen. "Horace, this boy has three bodies out in his wagon. We've all seen 'em. We're pretty sure Saginaw Bob Magruder and his bunch did the killings. What are we gonna do about it?"

Potts looked at me like a man who'd just been presented with a plate of his own deep-fried internal organs. "Bury 'em," he squawked, and ran for the door like a scalded dog.

Well, I've got to hand it to that bunch of drunks. In the middle of a moonless night, they took me to what went for their local church, helped me unload my family, and placed them on its porch.

Slept in the wagon on top of boards saturated in their blood. Had a terrible dream. A skeletal apparition dressed like a preacher flew down from heaven. In each bony hand, a tiny pistol spat fire at me. Behind him, a three-headed dog snapped at his black horse's feet. I heard the shrieks of women I knew. Next morning at daylight, Robbie and the others came back and took turns helping me dig graves.

No undertaker tended my mother, father, or Rachael.

No preacher said words over them. They went in the
ground wrapped in blankets that once kept them warm
during icy Kentucky winters. I wasted no time over those
graves. The bullets that killed Papa and creased my face
caused an infection of my soul. Finding the bodies of my
mother and sister forced that infection into my heart. I
had but one object in life, as far as I could see—find the
Magruder gang and kill as many of them as I could. No
matter how long it took. No matter where they tried to
hide. They were dead men from the moment I threw the
last shovel of dirt on my family.

I ran from that graveyard to Winchester Township's
only mercantile and gun shop. A clerk named Westbrook,
wearing garters on his arms, bought my wagon and team.
That money, and the two bags Benny Stubbs had failed
to find, left me fairly well off. All told, it amounted to
almost two thousand dollars.

"Hold it. Wait just a minute, Mr. Tilden. Where exactly
did your father hide all that extra money?" Franklin J.
Lightfoot Jr. looked at me like a kid with his fingers
caught in a set of Chinese handcuffs.

"Oh, I'm right sorry there, Junior. Forgot to tell you
Benny Stubbs didn't come anywhere close to finding all
the money hid in the wagon. Papa stashed a bag in the
water barrel and another in a hollowed-out spot under the
seat. We set out for Texas with just over fifteen hundred
dollars. Benny found only five hundred of it. What with
selling the wagon and team, I had a nice little stake when
it all shook out. Bought myself a Winchester model 1876,
.45-70 hunting rifle with a thirty-inch octagon barrel and
extra sights, a used Colt's Richards Conversion, and two
boxes of ammunition for each. That rifle was one whop-

per of a big ole gun. Learned how to shoot one just like it from a friend back home named Clovis Hickerson. I could hit a sparrow at five hundred yards. What with some new duds and the weapons, I didn't spend all that much."

"What about a horse? Didn't you need a horse?"

"Of course I needed a horse. Mr. Westbrook told me that the best in town belonged to none other than the honorable Mr. Horace Potts, the low-life coward of a mayor who ran from me the night before."

"Did he sell it to you?"

"Well, he didn't want to. Let's just say when I left him standing in front of his barn I rode a fine chestnut mare named Thunder, and he had more money in hand than an Arkansas dirt farmer normally saw in two years. I still have the bill of sale. He wrote it on a page torn from his family Bible."

"Then what?"

"It took me about two hours to go back up the Great River Road and find Magruder's trail. But once I did I almost rode that big chestnut to death catching up with him. I hoped early on to find those cutthroats in the woods and kill them out of the sight of civilization and the law, but my luck didn't hold."

"So, you caught up with him and his gang?"

"I did. Took me almost three days, but I found them in that tick-riddled burg by the Arkansas River just south of here named Pine Bluff."

Franklin J. looked surprised. "My family lives there." He scribbled in his book some more. "I take it you counted skill as a tracker in your background?"

"Junior, *you* could have tracked Magruder and his bunch. Those arrogant jaybirds left a trail wide enough for a blind Sunday school teacher to follow. I guess they figured the posse from Mississippi had already given up on them, and no one in my family survived to give chase or tell the tale. They plowed along like a steam engine and a string of freight cars. The four of them tore down enough bushes and small trees between Winchester and Pine Bluff to build a three-room house."

I walked Thunder up and down all the streets and alleys of the rowdiest parts of Pine Bluff. Checked every hitching post for the Preacher's stallion and that big ole mule. Stopped three times and asked local loafers if they had seen four scruffy men, one on a large black horse.

Almost all of them laughed at me and snorted out something along the lines of, "Hell, boy, do you see anybody here that ain't scruffy?" or "Jesus H. Christ, might near everybody in this mud pie of a town is either scruffy or riding somethin' big and black."

There'd be gales of laughter from the dawdlers who sat on the benches or walkways. The laughing usually stopped when that .45-70 came out of its hiding place behind my right leg and nestled in the crook of my left arm. Sight of the rifle—in the hands of a six-foot-tall, raw-boned farm boy with a nasty cut on his face— sobered many an Arkansas drunk that night.

It took almost an hour, but I finally spotted the Preacher's mount. Biggest mule in Arkansas stood beside it. Found them tied in front of a saloon named the Dew Drop Inn. Appeared to me the establishment had at one time been a makeshift hotel, but now danced and laughed to the tune of lewd women and drunken men.

Tied Thunder's reins to a post near the back door. Checked both my weapons before I entered the building.

Wasn't much of a shot with any kind of handgun, but decided if I got caught in close quarters the weapon would be better than nothing. Pistol's action was so stiff and awkward I swore not to even try it unless all else failed.

Levered a shell into the chamber of the rifle and left the hammer back. Pushed my way through the door of the colored entrance. The din of noise and smoke engulfed me like a shroud. Steak sizzled on a grill in one corner. Hadn't eaten in a couple of days. My stomach started to rumble and complain. The smell of whiskey tickled my nose like cheap perfume.

Someone said, "Suh, you be in de wrong place. De white section be in yondah."

Things got considerable quiet when I put the index finger of my left hand to my lips, then raised the rifle and cradled it in the crook of my arm. I guess the only thing that could have inspired more fear would have been Papa's twelve-gauge Greener. But Magruder's men took it when they murdered him.

A set of bat-wing doors divided the black and white sections of the bar. Peeked over and searched from face to face for someone I could identify. Sitting at a table not ten feet from the front door, the mule rider pitched money on the green felt and shuffled cards around. A half-empty bottle of whiskey was perched near his left hand. A tiny silver cross hung from his huge Texas sombrero and twinkled like the evening star. My mother loved that trinket. Papa gave it to her on their twentieth anniversary. In the chair to his right, and slightly behind him, sat a restless and noisy Benny Stubbs.

He said, "Come on, Azel. Let's go get Cecil and find a place with some life to it. That gal I just left upstairs didn't have no more energy than a lightnin' bug in a pitcher of cream." Stroud ignored Benny and went on with his cards.

"The Dew Drop ain't showin' me much fun, Azel. You can gamble anywhere on Barracue Street. Let's get Cecil and go to the Hen House." Benny leaned forward and pushed on his friend's shoulder.

"Damn you, Benny. You want to go find Cecil, go. Quit a-punchin' on me. It's dee-stractin'." The Texan turned and swatted drunkenly at his friend's hand like it was a bothersome insect. "If you and Bob and Cecil want to spend your time with whores that's your lookout. I want to play poker right here, right now. Leave me be."

One of the gamblers—a man wearing a suit and a silk hat—lost his patience. "Mister, are you gonna play cards with us or pat-a-cake with your friend?"

The drunken Texas waddie took offense at being chastised. His right hand found the grip of the pistol strapped high on his side. "You shut your mouth, you Arkansas clodhopper. Play cards when I please. Talk to my friends when I please. You can keep your tater-diggin' opinions to yourself. Gotta lotta nerve thinkin' you can talk to a Texas man like one of your snot-nosed pullets."

The gambler lowered his cards and said, "Just ease up, friend. No one here wants any trouble. We play poker. Thought you sat down for the game. Your friend's making it difficult to concentrate."

"Well, you keep to your cards, smart mouth. I'll worry about Benny."

Stubbs gave everyone at the table a snaggle-toothed, tobacco-stained smile and went right back to his nagging. The other players immediately folded their hands, quietly headed for the door, and left the two surly friends alone

at the table. The Texians put their heads together and
began to whisper back and forth. When they looked up
again, the big ole .45-70 was grinning at them less than
ten feet away. Muzzle on that gun looked like hell's front
gate.

"Uh, could we stop here for just a second? I have a few
questions."

"Dammit, Junior. The first part of my story was just
getting going good. Grow a little patience, boy. Sweet
Jesus, you people who just can't wait from one minute
to the next for something dramatic to happen irritate the
bejabbers out of me. You ever given any thought to the
possibility that sometimes the going is as much fun as
the getting there? Can't it wait?"

"No, sir, it can't. What went through your mind as you
approached those men? Your thoughts, for instance. Did
you do a mental check of all the things a gunfighter
needed to watch for before the battle? Assess the light or
lack of it? Decide which man to kill first? Was it Stroud?
What I'm trying to get at here is a feel for whether you
did any of the things Randolph Scott, John Wayne, or
the heroes of all those dime novels always did."

"You said a few questions, Junior. You asked five of
them at once. If you'd shut up long enough you might
find out the answers. But since you can't wait . . . I'd
barely passed my eighteenth birthday when I stopped in
front of Benny Stubbs and Azel Stroud's table. My family's murders were the first I'd seen. Never killed anybody. Never even shot at another person. Only shooting
I'd ever done involved ducks, squirrels, rabbits, and deer.
That night I was about as handy with a rifle as anyone
who had to hunt to eat. But didn't have a pissant-sized

idea what I was going to do when the crunch came. Can tell you this: anyone who says killing a man for the first time comes easy is a primo liar or mad dog crazy like Magruder and his bunch. And any of them scribbling blackguards that write novels and think they're entertaining by making readers believe gunfights involved quick drawing, fanning, or killing numerous men with one pistol—and other such nonsense—never saw a real one."

I had my stinger out and was about to put bumps all over young Franklin's head. He squirmed in his chair.

"Take a breath, Mr. Tilden. You're going to seize up on me here if you don't calm down."

"Junior, only one thing set me apart from them others at the Dew Drop Inn and made me deadly. I'd already decided, when I stopped in front of their table, that they'd probably kill me. I walked straight up to those boys ready to die."

"You expected them to kill you?" The surprise on the boy's face carved deep creases in his forehead.

"Of course I did. Their business was robbery and murder. Mine was following a mule around cornfields. I knew full well my odds of survival bordered on a thousand to one. But didn't care. It wouldn't have mattered if they'd all four been at that table. In fact, I'd have preferred it that way. Having them all in one place at the same time would've been perfect, as far as I was concerned. But just for the sake of argument, if you'd been there and had time to bet on the outcome, who would you have put your money on?"

"The gunfighters, I suppose."

"They weren't gunfighters. They were thieves and killers—big difference, Junior. Those movie stars you mentioned earlier—and others of their kind—would have you believe that every man who carried a pistol back then was a gunfighter. That's a real knee-slapper. From the time I hired on with Judge Parker till I retired in 1930, I might have met a little over a dozen men could be labeled real gunfighters. But Lord almighty, Arkansas and the Territories overflowed with thieves and killers of every kind. Including Magruder and his bunch."

Benny Stubbs saw me first. He kind of glanced up from their whispering and got this goofy, squinty look on his face. Pushed his hat back on his head, leaned away from the parley, and pointed silently. His friend followed the direction of the finger and jerked back in astonishment to see the open muzzle of the Winchester.

Azel Stroud snarled, "What you want, boy?" My mother's silver cross jiggled from the brim of his hat.

Benny snickered. "I think you best put that big popper down 'fore you gets hurt or it goes off and hurts one of us."

Took one more step toward those bastards. No matter what happened I knew it would be impossible to miss from that distance. Pretty sure they realized at that very moment at least one of them was about to die.

A bartender behind me said, "Someone go get the law. Everett needs to stop this before this crazy farm boy does something foolish."

Fear choked me down to the point where I was barely able to croak, "Anyone who goes through that door tonight will be buried tomorrow. These men have the crimes of murder and robbery to answer for, and they'll answer to me. Boys, my father, mother, and sister are waiting for you on the other side. I'll send you to them for judgment. They will send you to hell."

Recognition flashed across Benny Stubbs's face. "Oh, I know you now. You're that big farm boy from Kentucky."

"I'll just be damned," whispered Azel Stroud.

He made the first move. His right hand darted under the table. Be willing to bet I didn't have to shift the Winchester more than an inch to my right before I pulled the trigger and blasted him into the other life. He managed to get the pistol out of his belt, but, as he slumped forward on the table, the muzzle shifted toward his friend as it discharged. Slug hit Benny's lower jaw and blasted the bottom half of his face into a bloody spot on the ceiling.

Benny made a strangled noise, kind of like *smurggle-storrfel,* and jumped to his feet just in time for my second slug to push his black heart out his back and knock a hole in the saloon's plate-glass window.

Now, to that point, I'd been uncommonly lucky. Stood there amazed by the outcome of the whole thing, while Benny flopped down into his chair and twitched. Movement reflected in the glass behind him spun me toward the landing above the bar. Cecil Morris drew as I turned.

He hurried his first shot. It grazed my upper left arm. I didn't even feel it. His second hit me in the leg. Felt that one all the way to my eyeteeth. If he hadn't been drunk I'm pretty sure he'd've got off a third and deadlier one. But as I went down, I swung the rifle out at arm's length. My only shot hit him dead center. He kind of crumpled up and sat down next to the newel post like he was tired.

I got sick and passed out. Woke up propped against the bar. A nice-looking man sporting a big handlebar mustache squatted in front of me. He rested my rifle across his legs and directed another man's actions.

"Just a little tighter, Tom. All we want to do is stop him bleeding." He put his hand on my shoulder and gently shook me. "You awake? Can you hear me?"

"Yes, sir."

"What's your name?"

"Hayden Tilden."

"I'm Everett Lovelady, son. I'm the Pine Bluff city marshal. The feller jerkin' around on your leg is my deputy, Tom Spires."

Everything about Spires looked square—head, shoulders, hands, and teeth. He flashed me a big gap-toothed grin. "How're you doin' there, Hayden?"

I told him I'd felt a damn sight better. He snickered. "Wish I'd been here when the shootin' started. They's a couple of people outside on the boardwalk almost got trampled by folks tryin' to get out of here and away from you. Most of 'em stumbled over that big ole mule you killed with the shot that went through the winder. You're the first mule killer we've had 'round here." He laughed. "You'll probably be in more trouble for killin' the mule than for killin' these boys.

"I knew two of these men." Lovelady sounded like he was instructing a class of Sunday school students on the evils of crime. "Sorriest folks on the planet. That 'un still sittin' at the table used to be Azel Stroud. Put him in jail twice up in Fort Smith. Last time I locked him up he'd almost beat a man to death with a stick of stove wood. The one up there by the newel post was Cecil Morris. His favorite pastime involved shootin' greenhorns in the feet till they couldn't dance anymore. Then he'd kill 'em. This other one is such a mess I don't think his mother would recognize him."

"Benny Stubbs," I mumbled.

Marshal Lovelady took a glass of water from the bartender and held it in my direction. "What'd you say, son?"

"Stubbs. His name was Benny Stubbs."

"Ah, yes. Well, you know, even his friends called him Benny the Idiot—crazy, stupid, and dangerous. It all makes sense now. I heard they were travelin' together. Strange they're so far east. Most of their mayhem takes place in the Territories. I've got posters on these men. You're gonna have a nice sum of money coming. 'Course, if that bullet you took managed to break the bone, you might end up losing your leg. That'd be a heck of a trade."

A bloody gurgle oozed out of Azel Stroud. Marshal Lovelady went to the table and leaned over the man. "Did you say something, Azel?" He listened for a moment and then said, "Wish you'd gone to Hot Springs, do you?" He put a finger to the man's neck. "An amazin' thing, Hayden. Your shot went through his upper left arm, came outta his chest over here, and lodged in the windowsill. And he still managed to stay alive—one tough ole boy. But thanks be to a gracious God, he's totally dead now."

2

"You Come Highly Recommended"

FRANKLIN J. LIGHTFOOT Jr. excused himself and shuffled off to the men's room. Carlton woke up when the boy's pad dropped on the table.

He looked around like an old dog trying to figure out what had happened. "You run that young feller off?"

"He had to take a leak."

He cupped his right hand over his ear. "Whadya say?"

Louder, I said, "He had to take a leak."

"Oh, yeah? Wish I could take a leak anytime I wanted. Ain't had that luxury in almost ten years. Never thought I'd miss bein' able to pee whenever I wanted to. My twelve-year-old doctor says my prostrate gland is bigger'n an Irish po-tater. Can't pee worth a damn. Just sit here and dribble."

"Go back to sleep, Carlton."

"Whaddaya mean he took a sheep?"

I yelled, "No, you crazy old fart. Go back to sleep."

"Whad'd he want anyway?"

"Wanted to hear about my life."

"I liked your wife. Fine woman. Can't imagine why a young feller like him would want to know 'bout her, though."

"Can't pee or hear," I mumbled to myself.

"Seen Leona lately?" He squirmed around in his chair and fumbled for the spectacles he'd left on the table.

"Nope, she hasn't made her rounds yet."

"Lord, but I do love havin' that big-boned woman rub my achin' back." He glanced behind me and then around the porch, looking for Nurse Wildbank. "That big ole gal makes me wish I was sixty again."

Every man at Rolling Hills finds Leona Wildbank just by-God-irresistible. Her Swedish beauty and reasonably good-natured disposition can melt the ice around the hearts of all us crusty old fuds like sunshine on fresh snow. Everyone needs something to dream about no matter how old they get. A looker like Leona's as good as any. I couldn't imagine what Carlton's dreams must have been like.

Well, he sat there staring at me for about a minute. A fantasy-filled grin crooked its way across his face, and his head dropped back down on his chest again. That's all it ever takes with Carl—one minute of near quiet and he's gone.

"Let's get back to Pine Bluff." Junior snatched his pad up and began scribbling again. "Tell me about Everett Lovelady and what your stay with him was like."

Took almost six weeks to get healed up enough so I could leave town. Everett contacted Horace Potts and determined the story about my family's murders was true.

He also discovered local drunks had seen Magruder sneaking out of town just after I shot Benny, Azel, and Cecil. Seemed he'd spent his evening in the company of a lewd woman named Jenny Compton.

Everett said, "Ole Bob always liked them young whores. Jenny's almost thirty, but when made up just right can appear to be closer to fifteen. Her sportin' man passed her off for fourteen. Lord, that's a heap of hilarity. Anyway, Bob believed it and was right in the middle of the act when you snuffed his pards. If I know him, he's headed directly back to the safety of the Indian Nations. He loves the place and don't usually get too far away from there 'less'n he just has to."

He talked as loud as he could while a horse doctor tried to pull the bullet out of my leg. I passed out anyway. Let me live in one of his jail cells while I recuperated. Most likable man I've ever met.

We were sitting in his office the afternoon he said, "Got word Magruder and his bunch have been identified as the ones who botched that bank robbery in Mississippi. Them posters I told you about on the three you killed are worth almost two thousand dollars. Should have the money in a day or two. You'll be pretty well fixed financially for a man your age."

"The money doesn't matter, Everett. You know that. Got to find Magruder. Going to attend his funeral just like I did those others."

"Hayden, I admire the sand it took for a man of your limited experience to face three known killers and rub 'em all out. Never seen anything like you gettin' out of bed two days later and hobblin' to see 'em planted. You've become something of a celebrity around here because of it. Borderin' on local hero and legendary gunfighter. I'd like you to stay here and work for me. You don't have to go after Magruder right now. He'll turn up in the Nations soon enough."

"He's been gone almost two months. If I don't get back on his trail soon, might not ever find him. Somebody else could kill him. Want to do the deed myself. Want to look him in the eye when he dies."

"Oh, you'll find 'im. Bob's never been one to stay low for very long. His kind always shows hisself again. I could list several of his murders just as vicious as your family's he did in the Nations. None of them kept him hid long. Besides, it's comin' on winter pretty soon. The Nations can be mighty rough in the winter. Bob'll get out there somewhere in the Kiamichi or Winding Stair Mountains and den up like a hibernatin' bear." He leaned his chair back on two legs and blew smoke from his cigar toward the ceiling.

"I know the weather's about to go south on us. And from what every loafer who comes through your jail says, things won't get good again until April. To hear Deputy Spires tell it, Arkansas and the Territories have some of the worst weather on the planet. But I have to go, Everett. You know I do."

"Yeah, well, maybe I can help you out some if you're determined to stay the course on this thing. I've never asked you before, Hayden, but how old are you?"

Ash from the cigar he gave me got thumped onto the floor. I lied and said, "Twenty-two."

Everett's chair snapped back down on all four legs. "Not sure I believe that, but I'll take your word on it. If you say you're twenty-two, then as far as I'm concerned that's the way of it. It don't matter much anyhow. You've already showed everyone around here you're about as much a man as you're ever gonna be. So I tell you what I'm gonna do. I'll write you a letter of introduction to Judge Parker, explain your problem, and ask him to take you on as a deputy marshal. It'll give you a job in Fort Smith and a base for your hunt for Magruder. How does that strike you?"

"I'm flattered, Everett. I do appreciate your help. More than I can say."

"No need to flush up on me there, son. I know how you feel. Know you won't stop till ole Bob is in the ground and you see it happen. It would be derelict on my part not to help you in such a worthy effort. Just remember, when you finish with this, there'll always be a place for you here if you want it."

Left Pine Bluff about a week later. Everett helped me finalize collection of the bounty on Benny, Azel, and Cecil. I needed to be on my way and the prospect of finding Magruder pulled pretty hard at me. We shook hands like family, and I put the spur to Thunder.

Stopped over here in Little Rock for one night. Bought passage for Thunder and me on a flat-bottomed boat going upriver. Little stern-wheeler named the *Jezebel*. Had an urge to visit cousins living here at the time, but decided against it.

The trip on the water must have been quicker than riding it. But it seemed awful slow to me at the time. A storm ripped up and down the river for a good bit of the first two days. Boat pilot spent most of his time dodging trash and new snags or tied up to the bank for shelter. We arrived a day later than I expected.

The three-day float wasn't a complete waste, though. It gave me plenty of time to think about what had happened. I'd started out a Kentucky farm boy on the way

to becoming a Texas farm boy. Searched my conscience
for that wide-eyed youth and discovered a grown man
who'd killed other men in a gunfight. Found myself in a
place I'd never planned on even visiting—in search of
another man to kill. But when I led Thunder off that boat
and settled into the saddle again, I felt completely at ease
with the new world ahead of me, and what I intended to
do.

Guess busy probably describes Fort Smith better than
any word I can think of. Place swarmed with every kind
of miscreant known to God or man—cowboys, river runners, railroaders, prostitutes, gamblers, transients on their
way west, and every other kind of worthless human riffraff imaginable.

The storm that delayed my arrival must've missed the
primitive burg. Streets appeared to be about six inches
deep in dust, and the stuff covered every flat surface
available to the eye. The town looked like an anthill after
someone stepped on it. People were walking and running
in every direction. Kids and dogs played in the streets.
In the only wet spot I could detect, a pig the size of a
Shetland pony had flopped down in an alleyway where
people had to walk. She refused to move in spite of
heated efforts to dislocate her by several of the children.
Piglets squealed and ran all around her trying to get away
from the kids. Out on the edge of civilization boys and
girls grew up quick and mean. Today they'd all be in
school, but back then wasn't much educating going on.

The weather had turned colder that morning. Stopped
at the first dry goods store I spotted. Tied Thunder to the
rack out front and pushed my way through the swarm of
people passing on the boardwalk.

Stood at the counter and kind of gandered around,

when I heard this young woman say, "Can I help you, sir?"

Hadn't been addressed as "sir" enough to know the question was pointed at me. Caught myself looking over my shoulder for the phantom gentleman. Had to smile when I realized my mistake.

She floated up to me like she'd appeared out of thin air. Blond-haired, blue-eyed. Looked like the angel pictured standing behind Jesus on the Mount of Olives in my mother's Bible. I felt like I'd been struck by lightning. For about five seconds I couldn't speak.

"Yuh . . . yuh . . . yes, miss. I . . . I'm in need of a leather coat. It—it's colder here than I expected." I stared into those blue eyes and knew I'd love her till the day I died. In less time than it took for my heart to beat once, I fell for her like a drunk who'd got his spurs tangled.

"Try this on, sir. I think you will be quite striking in it." She pulled a natural-colored leather coat from a rack in the center of the store.

I stood the Winchester against the counter and placed my pistol next to a gallon jar of pickles. She held the coat open as I slid into it, then she smoothed the wrinkles down my back. It had been almost two months since a woman had touched me. Little pricks of electricity ran up and down my spine and the hair on my arms stood up.

"Very nice," she said as she pushed me to a mirror standing against the back wall.

The image in that glass would have stunned my mother. I'd lost weight. The scar that ran across my right cheek still glowed pink with anger. Scraggly hair hung long against my collar. My rough farmer's pants and boots needed replacing. For the first time in my life, I felt embarrassed by my own appearance and a blue-eyed angel caused it.

I said, "I'll take the coat, miss. I'd also like to look at some new trousers and perhaps a pair of western boots." She tilted her head slightly and smiled as I handed her the coat. A flirtatious performance guaranteed to further my newly discovered infatuation.

For almost an hour, that beautiful young woman fussed and fretted over me. And, for the first time since the murders of my family, I felt like I could lie down and sleep without having nightmares. When she finished, the image of a man who might have lived all his life in the wilds of the Territories stared back at me from her mirror.

She'd covered my head with a wide-brimmed, tall-crowned, Texas-style hat. The leather coat was cinched close with a heavy, double-rowed cartridge belt. The butt of my .45 stuck out of the belt in a way that made it easy to pull with my right hand. My pants were soft and comfortable. The new boots came to my knees and sported a pair of heavy silver spurs.

"Well, miss, you have accomplished quite a change in my appearance. One I'm sure is for the better."

"My name is Elizabeth Reed, sir. You needn't call me miss."

"I'll try, miss . . . I mean, Miss Reed." She laughed at my fumbled attempt to please her.

The spurs chinked and sang as I followed her back to the counter to settle my bill. Since I now deemed myself a man of some substance, I didn't even bat an eye at the cost of my new garb.

She handed me the change, flashed another killing smile, and said, "Thank you, sir. Can we expect to see you again soon, Mr. . . . I'm sorry, you didn't offer your name."

"Tilden, Miss Reed. Hayden Tilden. Hope to visit you again very soon. Would it be possible for you to direct me to Judge Parker's court?"

"Easily, Mr. Tilden—just follow the crowd. There's another hanging in about an hour. Six more depraved men will find perdition this day. Once you see the gallows, Judge Parker will be nearby."

I removed my new hat, held it against my chest, and bowed slightly. "Good day to you, miss." Elizabeth Reed's surprise at my freely offered gallantry flashed in her eyes. Discovered later that such behavior tended to be the exception rather than the rule in that rough place. Started for the door, but my eye caught something important on the shelf behind her. I pointed toward the book.

"I'll take that too."

She pulled the heavy work from its place on the shelf, handed it to me, and touched my hand again as I paid her.

"You are familiar with the plays of Shakespeare, Mr. Tilden?"

"My mother introduced us. She read to me from the Bible and Mr. Shakespeare's writings every night when I was a child. She always said, 'Hayden, if you're familiar with these books you'll have about as much education as a Kentucky farm boy can expect. Read them. Study them. They can teach you much.' Before marrying my father, she lived in a lively and educated household in West Virginia. She shared all that knowledge with my sister, Rachael, and me. Compared to most, Miss Reed, I consider myself relatively well educated. I've recently been separated from her copy of Mr. Shakespeare's works. I will remember her when I read from this book." I bowed again, and rushed for the street.

Glanced back toward the store as I wheeled Thunder away. Elizabeth Reed was staring at me through the beveled glass of the heavy door. I touched the brim of my hat and tilted my head in her direction. She smiled again—and waved. That blue-eyed smile warmed me up more than the new coat she had hung on my back.

Followed a swarm of people to a gate cut into a rough stone wall. Empty cannon bastions and a serious state of disrepair led me to believe that soldiers had not been in evidence at the fort for some time. The stockade teemed with people. The crowd numbered in the thousands. I'd never seen that many people in one place in my entire life.

Vendors sold roasted corn, jerked beef, and every sort of keepsake imaginable to remind the buyer of the day's upcoming events. One man even hawked little hand-carved scaffolds decorated with tiny ropes and straw men. Spicy aromas of tobacco and liquor fought with each other to drown out the scents of food, people, and animals.

The multitude surrounded an enormous gallows. It appeared fully capable of dispatching a dozen or more men at the same time. Above the heavy timber from which six nooses dangled, a sign declared that skeletal framework as "THE GATES OF HELL."

"New in town?" A man dressed in shotgun chaps, sombrero, and Spanish rowels pulled his horse next to Thunder.

"Yes. And you?"

"Been here long enough to see two of these shindigs.

I'm on my way back to San Antonio from Dodge. Stopped in three weeks ago just in time to watch Parker send three ole boys to the Maker. There was a crowd then, but nothing like today. Hear tell from the locals this passel's about to witness the biggest hanging ever to take place in these parts. People from as far away as Texas, south Missouri, and Little Rock came for this one. Don't know about you, but I never seen this many people before. Looks like history, my man. We're about to become a part of history."

We moved up as close to the festivities as the huge crowd would allow and waited. About a minute later, a knot of guards carrying rifles pushed a path through the masses and led each of those destined for the hangman to his designated spot on the platform.

"All those men in front are deputies. A well-known murderer jumped off the scaffold a few hangings back. Almost got away. But the hangman, that Maledon, let him run a bit. Then he plugged the man dead at a hundred paces. Most amazin' pistol shot anyone in these parts ever saw or heard tell of."

Four ministers accompanied the condemned. They all read from their Bibles or prayed at the top of their lungs. Put me in mind of Magruder and how he'd approached my family at Arkansas Post.

My new friend said, "They'll read the death sentences for each of them, and he can make a final speech if he wants. 'Course, from way back here, we probably won't be able to hear much of anything that gets said. That'll be a shame. Last time one of the fellers did a fine job with his. Probably the best thing he ever did. He told all about the evils of alcohol, the perils of keeping company with fallen women, and the degradation of foul and un-

natural murder—real soul-shaker of a speech. Won't ever
forget it."

He rolled himself a smoke and pulled a bottle of whiskey from his saddlebags. "Care for a snort?"

"No, thanks."

"Trust me, mister. You're gonna wish you'd taken it
by the time this is all over. They're all standing on a
single trap. It's gonna be something to see all of 'em
drop at the same time." He pushed the bottle against my
arm.

"No, I'll see it sober. I don't want to forget any of it."

A man dressed in a suit walked up to each of the condemned, individually, and read from a large piece of paper. I couldn't hear anything but snatches. The word
murder got used a bunch. Near as I could determine
every man on the platform had killed at least one person.
Some more. One fellow who looked to be an Indian hung
his head when the sentence was read, but then started
singing and doing a little dance when the deputy moved
to his neighbor. The neighbor, a tall towheaded boy, wept
and had to be held up when he crumpled into a heap at
the sentence reader's feet.

Only three of them had anything to say. One, a black
fellow, must have made a fine speech. People in the first
row or two applauded.

Once the final man had his turn, a single minister
stepped forward and led the crowd in that old hymn
"Rock of Ages." A subdued quiet fell on the throng when
heavy bags were pulled over the heads of the condemned,
and the nooses cinched close to their necks by a thin,
bearded man with no hat. When finished, he walked to a
lever at one end of the platform, placed his right hand

on its leather-wrapped grip, and threw it forward. He didn't hesitate a fraction of a second.

A muffled zip caught my ear. Then a sound like a whip being cracked shot from the platform to the back of the gathering. The crowd sucked in a single breath when those men hit the end of the rope, and they moved back about half a step more when the sound of necks snapping like cottonwood limbs slapped them in the face.

The cowboy shook his head. "Eerie feeling, ain't it."

Some might find it hard to believe, but thousands of people can be in one place and not make a sound. In a matter of minutes that huge crowd disappeared like smoke carried off by a chilling wind.

I sat there on Thunder watching the men dangle. Two jerked and twitched for almost a minute. The silence that accompanied their passing shocked me far more than the noise and gaiety that preceded it.

After the crowd melted away, I noticed several buildings off to the left and slightly behind the gallows. I tied Thunder and presented myself to a clerk in the largest of them. Gave my letter of introduction from Everett Lovelady to him. Took a seat on a bench along one wall and waited almost two hours before anyone noticed me again.

A different clerk came to the landing on the second floor and called my name. He escorted me through a heavy door to an office dominated by a large desk. Behind that desk sat Judge Isaac Charles Parker. Tall, dignified, and elegantly dressed. He wore a dark coat, clean white shirt, neat tie, and gold watch chain. A mustache and small beard made him look more like a banker than like the most powerful judge in the country.

He motioned me to one of a pair of chairs. "You come highly recommended, young man. I have a good deal of respect for Marshal Everett Lovelady. I believe he would still be with me if it hadn't been for the numerous wounds he suffered in pursuit of evil men."

I took the cigar he offered from a box on the desk as he continued. "Tell you what this job involves. You won't be paid much. Six cents a mile traveled and two dollars for each man brought in for trial in this court. Sometimes these men have rewards on their heads, and that will be a bonus for you, but I can assure you no one is getting rich. Most of my marshals are able to make about five hundred dollars a year. You may supplement that amount somewhat by the fines you levy while on patrol in the Nations. I don't encourage such fines except where necessary, but some of the men use this power to make a little more. I don't like the practice, but I won't attempt to stop it."

He stood and moved to a curtained window behind his chair, pulled one panel aside with his finger, and stared at the grounds below.

"My marshals usually travel in groups. It isn't uncommon for criminals to band together and ambush them. We've determined it's unwise for them to travel alone. Make no mistake, Mr. Tilden, this is dangerous work. We lose an average of five deputies a year killed in the line of duty. I hope to reduce that rate, but at the moment the lawless outnumber us significantly. Every outlaw within a thousand miles runs for the Nations if he gets a chance."

"Marshal Lovelady warned me the job would be difficult, sir."

He turned back toward me, arched an eyebrow and dropped Everett's letter on his desk. "Our friend writes that you're deadly with that big Winchester. I don't like gunfighters as a rule, but know if you want to catch a dangerous man you don't send a Sunday school teacher. If you take this job, be completely understanding of the fact that I don't care for dead criminals. I want them in my court so they can see, feel, and understand the mighty hand of the law they have chosen to break."

I shifted the rifle in my lap. "I don't care about the pay. Don't care how difficult the job might be. I want the chance to find Saginaw Bob Magruder. Alive if that's how he sees it, but dead if he resists. I have reason to believe he's hiding out in the Nations somewhere. So, I promise to do the best job possible for you, Judge. But you must understand, sir, that my search for Magruder will always come first and I'll drop whatever I'm doing at the time for an opportunity to go after him. If that's agreeable, I'm ready."

He slapped the top of the desk with his palm. "By Godfrey, I admire your forthrightness and determination, Mr. Tilden. Stand and raise your right hand, sir."

Well, he made a little speech, and I said, "I do." It took about fifteen seconds. Walked me down the hall to another office with a brass plate on the door that read U.S. MARSHAL, D.P. UPHAM. Several armed and determined looking men stood when the Judge entered. He swept past them and pushed his way into an inner office. Returned with a shiny deputy U.S. marshal badge and pinned it on my new leather coat.

He led me to a man sitting in the corner. "Bix, I want you to meet Hayden Tilden. Sending him out with you this time. Hayden, meet Deputy Marshal Bixley Conner. I'm sure the two of you will get along famously." He smiled and left us standing there staring at each other.

Bix Conner held out a stubby-fingered block that

somewhat resembled a human hand and shook mine so
hard I thought my arm was gonna snap off.

"Mighty glad to have you along, son. We'll be pulling
out tomorrow morning. There are two other marshals,
and a jailer who drives the wagon, who'll be along for
the ride. I have three men named on warrants we'll look
for in par-tic-a-ler, and I usually carry a pocketful of John
Does just in case we need 'em."

"I could use a hot meal and a good night's sleep before
we start, Marshal Conner."

He pulled a long, thin cigar from his vest pocket and
lit it. "There's a fair hotel down on Towson Avenue
called the Pines. You can meet me out front of the courthouse at six, or we'll stop there for you on the way out
of town. Whichever you prefer."

"No need to look for me, Mr. Conner. I'll meet you
here." Started out the door before I realized he had something I needed. "I'd like to have one of those John Doe
warrants. Have someone in mind for it."

The stout little deputy looked at me for about two seconds like I might be crazy. Threw back his head and
laughed. "Oh, you bet. Here, I'll give you several of 'em
in case the man you want has any friends."

Stopped at Reed's Elkhorn Bank on the way to the
hotel and deposited all but two hundred dollars of my
newly acquired wealth. Rented a room by the month at
the Pines. Treated myself to a skin singeing bath, a haircut, and the biggest piece of beefsteak available at a restaurant next door named Julia's. The popularity of the
place forced me to sit near the window.

Finished my meal and excused myself from the table
just in time to bump elbows with the beautiful Elizabeth
Reed. She'd been at a back table, and I hadn't seen her.

Soon as she looked at me—and smiled—I did the typical male thing and got stupid again. The smell of her perfume reached out and grabbed me by the nose. Thought I'd pass out.

She said, "Why, Mr. Tilden, how handsome you look in your new coat and fresh haircut. I do believe I can detect the scent of lilac. I've always thought it quite nice to smell something other than tobacco, whiskey, or horses on a man." She smiled and traced the outline of my new badge with her finger.

My brain refused to recognize my tongue. Couldn't think of anything to say except, "Miss Reed, we meet again." Tried to bow, but we stood so close I could only nod my head. Then surprised the absolute hell out of myself when I mumbled, "May I walk with you a bit?"

"Of course, sir. But first you must meet my father." She turned and took the elbow of a man who stood behind her, talking with people at another table. "Father, I want you to meet Mr. Tilden. Although new to Fort Smith, he seems to have found employment. Hayden, this is my father, Jennings Reed."

The stoutly built banker shook my hand. "Good evening, Marshal Tilden. Good to see you again so soon."

Elizabeth looked surprised. "You two have met?"

"Your father helped me open an account this afternoon at the Elkhorn Bank. At the time I didn't realize you were related."

"Father plays banker. I run the store." She fluttered her eyelashes and took my arm.

We strolled in the glow of lanterns and candles that threw light from curtained windows. Our walk didn't last long. Elizabeth and her father lived on the second floor of their dry goods store only a few doors down from the hotel. Neither of them mentioned a Mrs. Reed. I decided not to inquire as to her whereabouts.

"Well, here we are." We stopped in front of the big door through which I'd last viewed her. She held out her hand and said, "We could meet again tomorrow, Mr. Tilden. Julia's at noon, if you'd like."

Her obvious invitation for a deeper relationship pleased and surprised me, but, of course, I couldn't accept. "I have to leave Fort Smith in the morning and be out of town for some time, Miss Reed. Perhaps we can dine when I return."

"I look forward to dinner with you then, Mr. Tilden. I'll read Shakespeare in anticipation of that day. We'll discuss *Romeo and Juliet.*" She smiled again and did a little curtsy. "Good night, sir." Her hand slipped from mine. She disappeared into the darkness behind the door. An hour later I could still smell her perfume on my fingertips.

When I finally closed my eyes that night, my dreams for the first time since the robbery were filled with something other than blood, death, and horror.

I walked with Elizabeth in a sun-drenched field that rippled like an ocean of purple flowers. A huge tree spread giant limbs and offered welcome shade. Three people waited there and motioned for us to hurry.

My father, mother, and Rachael sat on a checkered blanket. A picnic lunch was spread out over the blanket, and my sister sang a song I didn't recognize.

The coming morning pulled at me. As I raced back to consciousness, I noticed my mother had her arm around Elizabeth.

Sat up in my bed that morning with an ache in my chest I'd never felt before.

• • •

Franklin Jr. squirmed in his chair. "Incredible," he mumbled. He stabbed at the candy bowl with the stub of his cigarette and managed to leave a mashed-up, stinking wad of smoldering tobacco.

Carlton snapped out of his nap. General Black Jack Pershing jumped off his lap and flopped down in a hairy heap under the table. "If you're gonna smoke them things, fine. But when you finish, put 'em out. All the way out. Don't leave 'em layin' in there a-stinking like that. Nurse Leona Wildbank don't mind us smoking, but she can smell a stinky butt from LaHarpe Boulevard to the capitol building. And she'll knock a knot big as a goose egg on all us smokers if she finds that."

A finger that looked like a piece of kinked string shook itself in Junior's direction just before Carlton dropped back into his fantasy-filled dreams.

Franklin finished crushing his smoke. "I don't see how you old guys get through the day without having a seizure. Let's back up here just a little, Mr. Tilden. Do you expect me to believe you fell in love with Elizabeth Reed within minutes of meeting her?"

"Well, Frank, you can believe whatever you want. I'm just telling it the way it happened. People didn't live as long as they do today. You had to make hay when you could."

"I understand that, Mr. Tilden. I've just never been able to believe in love at first sight."

"Junior, I read the *Encyclopedia Britannica* at night. Helps put me to sleep. Found a table in one of them that said people in 1880 had a life expectancy of about forty years. An urgency to everything existed back then similar to what people felt during W.W.II. See, son, we knew living causes dying, and we wanted to do as much of that first part as we could. I loved Elizabeth. Loved her more than life itself. And it all happened faster than you can fire up another cigarette."

"All right, but don't you think it just a bit amazing that Judge Parker took you on as a deputy the way he did?"

"Why would I think that?"

"You had no law enforcement experience. You weren't a well-known gunfighter. Everett Lovelady's letter was all you had."

"Didn't need any padded résumé back then, Junior. I'd killed three vicious criminals, each well known for his skill with pistols and knives. Once the title *man killer* got attached to you, people looked at you in a whole different light. Owned enough of a reputation to ensure respect and any kind of job as a lawman I wanted."

"Did you feel even the least bit of discomfort before your first patrol with Marshal Conner?"

"I gave the whole thing some serious thought my first night at the Pines. Decided I'd go at the job with three simple rules. Lived by them for the rest of my life. First, I'd take the initiative whenever necessary, no matter the circumstances. Second, think before I acted, and third, take my time while thinking. I felt the deliberate man's chance of survival outweighed the impulsive acts of those who couldn't control their own behavior. Well, rubbing out three killers at the Dew Drop Inn had already proved that. Seventy years later, I'm convinced I was right. Anything else?"

"Several times you've mentioned dreams. You believed in dreams?"

"Still do. I can remember every significant dream I've

ever had. My mother's fault actually. She let a dying old woman who claimed to have the sight stay on our farm till she passed. Old lady could read palms, cast spells, and see the future. She predicted my life as a lawman. No one believed her at the time. She convinced my mother dreams were important. So, we talked about our dreams every morning at breakfast. To this day the first thing I do when I wake is go over my dreams from the night before. You should try it, Junior. Might be surprised what you'll learn."

3

"THE FIRST CHANCE YOU GET— KILL 'IM."

BIXLEY CONNER WAS leaning against a spotted horse and sipping on a cup of steaming coffee when I arrived at the courthouse the next morning. He handed me a tin cup filled with the same stout liquid and introduced me to the other marshals in the party.

"That 'un there is Quinten Moon." He waved in the direction of a short, thin man wearing two Smith and Wesson Schofield .45s and a gigantic knife. "The good-lookin' feller is Handsome Harry Tate, and the one pouring the stump juice is Johnny Peterman. Johnny cooks for us and pulls duty as the armorer and jailer."

I nodded in the direction of each man. They nodded back, drank their coffee, stamped their feet, and tried to get themselves awake. No one did much talking.

The man Bix called Handsome Harry was indeed a dandy. His clothing didn't resemble any of the rough duds of the others. He wore tailored leather breeches, a clean white shirt and tie, a fitted parka, and a fur hat that looked like a whole beaver sitting on his head. He favored a shoulder rig that contained a short-barreled sheriff's model Colt .45. A silver-plated scroll-engraved Peacemaker slept in a holster backward against his belly. The butt of the pistol pointed toward his right side. An image of a beautiful woman whose hair endlessly flowed around the handles decorated the grips of both weapons.

Peterman was the roughest of the group and, by action, seemed the oldest. He wore a hat that looked like it had been attacked by the beaver on Handsome Harry's head, a crude leather vest, a heavy homespun shirt, and boots that had seen better days. All appeared more than able.

"Come on, boys, we may as well get goin'. They's criminals to be caught, and all we have to do is find 'em," said Bix. He poured out the remains of his cup and climbed onto the spotted horse.

From inside his canvas jacket, he produced a piece of folded paper. "Hayden, today's the beginnin' of your education as a deputy U.S. marshal. What we're doin' out here is mostly police work. Cleanin' up stuff. Things rarely ever go the way we expect. So read over this stuff when you get a chance. We try to do what it says, but sometimes we just can't. When those times come, we do our best and hope it's somewhere close to the law."

Bold letters on the front of the pamphlet read, "Laws Governing U.S. Marshal and His Deputies." A document titled "Certificate of Commission" was nestled inside. I slipped them both into the pocket of my coat. Less than five minutes later, we ferried across the Arkansas to the Choctaw Nation.

Even as far away as Kentucky, people knew about the Indian Nations or, as some called them, the Territories.

More than once I'd heard my father say, "God and the law don't exist west of Fort Smith."

As I climbed aboard Thunder on the far side of the river, I said, "I didn't realize the most lawless place in the country was so close to civilization."

Bix laughed till he almost cried. I made a mental note to try and not say anything else that would bring unwanted attention my direction.

"Yesterday you said we would look for three men in particular, Bix. Who are they?" I wanted to erase any hint of callowness on my part as quickly as possible.

"We'd like to catch Gooch Bonds. He married a Choctaw gal so he could move out here legally and settle. They musta not got along too well. He took an axe and chopped her up pretty good 'bout a month ago. Yancy Pietrie borrowed his best friend's shotgun. When the friend wanted it back, Yancy shot him with it. Then there's that lovely fellow Dangerous Dave Crowder. He recently got drunk and cut off the head of an Indian whore he got angry with."

"My Lord. Don't you have any run-of-the-mill petty criminals like thieves?"

"We got every kind you can imagine. But the petty crimes kinda go by the board because they's so many hard cases out and about. By the time we start back to Fort Smith, we'll probably have fifteen or twenty of 'em trailing behind the wagon. All you have to do is show up where people congregate and you'll catch at least one of 'em breaking some kind of law. Some people live here legally. Most don't. They gather at the rail ends, stage stations, and ranches. You can bet that when we see just about anyone prowlin' these parts they're doing something evil."

His rambling answer hadn't included the name I wanted to hear most. "Have you ever encountered a man named Saginaw Bob Magruder?"

"Oh, once or twice. That's about as many times as anyone would want to run up against ole Bob. He's the kind Sunday school teachers use to scare kids. If that John Doe you wanted is for Bob, you don't really need it. They's posters out on him. I guess he's worth about a thousand dollars by hisself. He'd be a heck of a catch. But my advice is, don't even try to catch him. The first chance you get—kill 'im. According to posters I've seen, he's worth just as much dead as alive. I personally wouldn't want to try and get him back to Judge Parker's court. He'd most likely manage to kill you on the trail back and then get away. He's done it before."

Almost fell off my horse. "He's been caught and got away?"

"Oh, yeah. Once an old friend of mine caught 'im. Name was Godfrey Cox. Englishman who'd soldiered and fought all over the world—tough as a boiled anvil. Bob got loose somehow and nailed Godfrey to a tree. Shot him in four or five extremely painful, but not life-ending, spots. Left him to bleed to death—horrible way to die. Almost everyone you meet out here can tell you a story just as awful. Ole Bob is a bad one." He spurred his horse away and pulled up close to the wagon.

For the next few days nothing much happened. We stopped at some stage depots and ranch houses, poked through gullies, behind bushes and trees, but nothing turned up.

On the fifth day, any idea my first trip was destined to be the most boring and fruitless ever made into the Nations got put to a bullet-riddled rest.

We ambled onto a little hill that looked down on a patch of stunted trees just north of Winding Stair Mountain. The sounds of gunfire and yelling drifted up to us.

Dismounted and left the horses and wagon on the side of the rise away from the festivities. Crawled up to the ridge and laid on our stomachs to watch the show. Harry Tate handed me a long, collapsible glass that brought the disagreement close enough to get an idea of what transpired below.

At least ten people had a part in the shouting and shooting. I could see what looked like four men already down. One group of shooters had the safety of the trees, and the other was huddled behind a broken-down wagon and several dead horses.

Harry said, "We'll have to be careful with this one. Everybody out here hates us. If we go riding down on them without thinking this through, they'll all turn on us. You can bet those new spurs of yours on it."

Quinten Moon suggested we wait until one side or the other gave up, then make our move. "I don't see how we can get 'em all. I ain't never took on this many at one time. There must be ten of 'em down there," he grumbled.

You didn't need a crystal ball to know all the marshals felt uncomfortable with the circumstances as they stood. Bix Conner allowed as how the fight would likely end when the ammunition started to run low.

"Be willing to bet they're just about out now. Jesus, they've been shooting steady for the past thirty minutes. Most men carry plenty of ammo, but no one carries enough to keep up a shooting match like this forever," he said.

From all appearances the men already down had been

shot in the initial dispute. None moved or took part in the gunfight. Those who remained with the living poured vast quantities of lead into the air in an effort to kill anyone or anything that got in front of it. Their noisy blasting managed to do little more than put holes in trees, rocks, and the air at large.

Bix stared through the long glass for several minutes. "There's whiskey in that wagon. Some of them sons of bitches are whiskey runners. Lord almighty, I hate whiskey runners. One thing for sure, we can get 'em all for introducin' no matter what else shakes out."

Johnny Peterman took the glass from Bix. "I'd bet everything we make this trip that the group in the trees tried to take the goods from those under the wagon." He rolled onto his back and looked at me. "It happens out here a lot, Hayden. One group brings the goods hoping to make a boatload of money. Call that introducin'. Another group, nastier and more murderous, takes the stuff away from them. Trouble is, they all sell it to the Indians, and that causes a world of other problems."

The gun battle fell out exactly the way Bix Conner predicted. The shooting began to diminish after the passage of another half hour and soon stopped altogether. He and Quinten Moon circled around behind the stand of trees.

Harry pulled a sawed-off shotgun from its bindings behind his saddle. Peterman handed me his shotgun and took my Winchester to guard our backs. Barrels on both those scatterguns had been cut back to about an inch past the forearm. Peterman grinned and told me, "They puts out a sizable spread. Missin' with one of these blasters is close on to impossible."

Handsome Harry and I worked our way up to the

group under the wagon and waited for a signal from Bix before we moved in.

As we crept from rock to bush to tree, Harry whispered, "We'll get as close to the shooters as we can. They won't like the odds when they're looking down the barrels of these scatterguns."

A few minutes had passed when a voice from the woods called out, "I am Deputy Marshal Bixley Conner. I now have in my custody five men. You boys under the wagon throw down your weapons and raise your hands."

"Bullshit," yelled one of the men under the wagon. "Bix Conner hasn't been out of Fort Smith in two months."

"I know you to be John Baxter Pole," yelled Bix. "Put your pistol aside, John. I have men behind you, and if you continue on this course it might cost you your life."

I heard a heated discussion among the men under the wagon. Two of them acknowledged that the voice in the trees did, in fact, belong to Bixley Conner. One turned around just in time to stare up the double-barreled muzzle of my twelve-gauge.

He meekly dropped his pistol and shouted to his friends, "The marshals has got us, boys. Best give 'em up."

We rounded them all up pretty quick after that. Johnny Peterman shackled the whole bunch to a long center chain fastened to a steel pin on the side of the wagon. But the contrariety between the two groups became so heated, he had to separate them and put five on one side of the wagon and five on the other.

Bix beamed with pride at the peaceful outcome. "Once me and Quinten got into the trees and closed in on them boys hiding in there, they gave it up mighty fast. I think they'd seen all the gunfightin' they wanted for one day."

One of the whiskey runners, a sixteen-year-old boy named Shelby Cooper, told me the whole tale. "Me, John Pole, and Ruben Duckworth slept in the wagon. Papa and my brother, Clevis, were curled up underneath. Then this gang showed up—nine of 'em. They didn't see nobody but Papa and Clevis and figured they outnumbered us so bad we'd just give it up. We threw the wagon tarp back and killed four of 'em faster'n they could spit. Them left living headed for the trees."

"You also managed to kill six good horses in the bloody process," noted Quinten Moon.

The boy just laughed at him. "Yessir, we did make one hellacious, bloody mess. But, by Godfrey, we're still alive, ain't we?"

Bix fined the group all the cash they possessed for the various offenses he figured they'd committed. Altogether the ten living men and four dead ones had almost two hundred dollars on them. It amounted to about forty dollars for each of us.

The fines, mileage, and other compensation made Johnny Peterman happier than I'd seen him to that point. "This just might be the best week I've had since I started this dance two years ago. Maybe I can buy my wife a new dress when we get back."

Moon slapped me on the back and grinned. "You might be our good luck charm this trip, Hayden."

After Bix searched the bodies, he made the prisoners bury them. Late that afternoon, we headed southwest along the Kaimichi River toward a well-known watering hole Bix called Stark's Station. Our captives rattled along behind the wagon. Some of them had murder to answer for, and the others were thieves who'd witnessed the fracas. Bix figured he'd let the lawyers back in Fort Smith sort it all out.

Stark's rugged palace of swill squatted about fifty yards west of a sparkling stream named Sunfish Creek that emptied into the Kaimichi. The long, low log structure looked like someone chopped it out of a little mound of earth, threw some logs in the hole, then covered it all back up.

Bix stopped our party a good distance from the house for a discussion of what might await us inside the makeshift saloon.

"We're all familiar with this joint, Hayden. It belongs to Jamie Stark. She married a Choctaw named Benjamin One Elk Stark and started living out here about five years ago." He looped several sets of shackles over his shoulder, thumbed through his warrants, and pulled one to the top of the pile.

Handsome Harry rolled the cylinder of his belly gun as he walked up. "Yeah, she sells whiskey to anyone who wants to stop by and runs card games and such, too. We usually waltz in and fine her ten or twenty dollars, break a few bottles, and leave."

"I hope it goes that way today," added Bix. "But I overheard one of our whiskey runners tell his friend that Dave Crowder may be visiting. I'm a lot more concerned with that than any introducin' Jamie's doing. So keep your wits about you. Johnny and Quinten will stay with the wagon. I want you and Harry with me. Bring the shotguns."

The three of us walked the last hundred yards so as not to arouse the inhabitants before we got there. Bix went in first. I followed Harry.

It took a bit for my eyes to adjust to the poor light

inside that dungeonlike tavern. The single room was about thirty-five feet long and twenty feet deep. A makeshift bar, comprised of nothing more than some coarse planks sitting on barrel tops, took up the entire left end of the building. Rough chairs and tables sat in random spots around the rest of the open space. A large fireplace in the back wall overflowed with barely lit logs that popped and sputtered.

A tall, thin woman who had a face like a starving barn owl stumbled from behind the counter. She smoked a cigar about the size of an axe handle and greeted Bix like they were old friends.

"Why, it's Marshal Bixley Conner. Come on in here, Bix. Sit by the fire and warm your big ole self up some." She smelled like a wet horse, and her hair appeared to be falling out by the handful. "You boys want a cup of hot coffee?"

Bix said, "No, thanks, Jamie, we're here on business. We don't have time to socialize."

"Well, who're you lawdogs a-sniffin' around after this time?" She swayed to a stop so close to Bix her cigar dribbled ashes on his shirt. Didn't take a genius to tell she hated us for being there, but at least she acted friendly enough on the surface.

He grasped the woman by the arm and guided her to the far end of the bar. They spoke in tones so low I couldn't hear what they were saying. I eased down along the bark-covered wall to the other end of the building and took up residence in a corner near a table where five hard-looking men played poker. None of them even noticed me. They directed their collective attention at Harry Tate, who leaned against the doorjamb as though to block any prospect for a running escape.

Kept my shotgun nestled tight against my leg and made no display of it when I finally settled in the corner. But I noticed some uneasy movement at the table and eased the hammers back on both barrels just in case things started to get out of hand.

Bix glanced over in the direction of the table while Jamie Stark whispered in his ear. He smiled, nodded at the witch, and started toward the five card players. He stopped behind the biggest, ugliest man in the poker klatch.

"I have a warrant for you, Dave. Judge Parker has requested your presence in his court. You'll have to come with us." He dropped the paper on the table in front of the man, then moved away.

The burly brute, who had a face that looked like a map for the M.K.&T. Railroad, snatched the document off the table and said, "I doan thank I'll be going with you boys today." He dropped the warrant into a cuspidor on the floor and leaned back in his chair. He seemed totally confident in his decision.

Bix, who had drawn his pistols and held them behind his back, asked real friendly, "And why would you presume to think something like that, Dave?"

The big gambler motioned across the table toward a dark-skinned young man sitting there with his back to the wall. "Well, I want you do-right boys to meet a new and very close personal acquaintance of mine. This here is Mr. John Wesley Hardin."

I'd never heard of John Wesley Hardin at the time, but the name had a noticeable effect on Bix and Handsome Harry.

"That's a bald-faced lie. Rangers threw Hardin in jail down in Texas," Harry called from the doorway.

Bix took a couple more steps away from the table. Harry moved from the light into a corner by the doorjamb. The Greener rested across his left arm.

No doubt about it, that young fellow was the best-dressed man in the room, even better than Handsome Harry Tate. Under his gray suit coat, I could see ivory-handled pistols in leather holsters strapped high on his hips. He stood and, with an insolent sneer, pulled his coat back and pushed the pistols forward with the heels of his hands. The entire room held its breath. I could see that some of the other card players were shocked by the turn of events and wanted nothing to do with the episode unfolding.

You could've bobtailed the tension in that room with a pickled pig's foot from the jar on the bar. I kept waiting for something to happen, but Hardin just stood there and smiled. He still hadn't noticed me hiding in my corner.

Bix made this tiny little motion with the pistol in his left hand. That's all I needed to make my move. I brought the shotgun up and leveled it in the young gambler's direction.

Licked my lips and swallowed hard. My finger trembled on the trigger. As quiet and slow as I could, I said, "Our business isn't with you, Mr. Hardin. We have no warrants or posters for your capture. We know of no reason to keep you from your travels. Now, I don't want to kill you, but if you so much as blink I'll cut you in half and destroy at least three of your friends."

I admit it was bold talk and a mighty nervy bluff from a week-old deputy marshal who didn't have any idea what he was doing. But it worked.

Everyone at that table seemed to relax at the same time—almost like the wind taken from a sailing ship.

Hardin held his hands out and turned the palms up. The other men put their hands next to their cards and didn't move.

"Walk around the table on the side away from me. I'll guide you from the building, sir. I wouldn't want anything to happen to you as you continue on with your business."

Bix Conner looked stunned. I could tell Harry Tate wanted to laugh, but he realized they still had to take Dangerous Dave into custody.

As I put the shotgun muzzle to the neck of my new ward and pushed him toward the door, Bix brought his pistols out of hiding and snapped, "Stand up, Dave. It's time to go." The hammers coming back on Harry's shotgun sounded like popcorn cooking. The infamous Dangerous Dave Crowder raised his hands. Bix pushed Crowder's arms down and slapped shackles on him.

Soon as we stepped out the door, I took possession of my young gambler's pistols.

"Which is your animal?" I asked.

He indicated a roan mare tied in front of the house. "Mr. Hardin, there's a wagon to your right about a hundred yards away. I'll lead the horse while you walk in front of me. Don't forget what I told you inside."

He didn't say anything till I stopped him and Quinten took charge of his guns. As soon as he realized the finality of his position, his arrogant manner changed dramatically. He motioned for me to follow and led me a few feet away from the wagon.

"I am not John Wesley Hardin, sir. My true name is Noah Burns. I'm from Austin and have been told I bear a striking resemblance to the gunman. The marshal by the door hit the nail on the head. Mr. Hardin now resides in prison just outside the capitol."

I said, "Why would you tell such a tale and challenge a deputy U.S. marshal in so thoughtless a manner? Bix Conner would've shot you before you got one of those big pistols clear of its holster."

"The hard cases all over the Nations fear Hardin. They all know him as a man killer. I've used his reputation to get their confidence so I could take their money in poker. You can brand me for a card cheat, to be sure, but I'm not John Wesley Hardin."

He began to shake. The muscles in his face twitched. Terror had him in a mean grip. I felt sorry for the man. His cowardice overcame him while I watched. It's a sad thing to see a man lose his dignity like that.

"Get on your horse, Mr. Burns. As I said before, we have no reason to detain you. Get away from this place." I unloaded his pistols and pushed them into his war bag. "If I were you I'd think twice before I used the Hardin ruse again, sir. And remember this as you ride away: I'm an expert shot at up to five hundred yards with the rifle hanging on that chestnut mare. If I see you turn back, I'll assume you lied to me and that you intend more mischief. I won't hesitate to shoot you off this horse."

"You'll never see me again, Marshal." He nodded his thanks, put the spur to his animal, and shot away from Stark's Station like big yellow dogs from Arkansas were snapping at his heels.

Ole Bix levied his usual fines and broke a few bottles, and we turned the wagon back toward Fort Smith with Dangerous Dave Crowder and two of his poker pals in tow. Somewhere along the trail back to civilization, Crowder managed to spread the story of how I'd thrown down on Texas' most deadly killer and then run the man out of the Territories.

That incident got quite a bit of space in an 1878 issue of the *Fort Smith Elevator*. Fortunately or not, the report made no mention of the man's true identity. Everyone who read that article believed I'd done exactly what Dangerous Dave claimed when he told the world about it. I never made much of an effort to set the record straight. Far as I was concerned an intimidating reputation wouldn't hurt when bad men had to be confronted.

Actually, no one ever bothered to ask me about what really happened. By the time the tale hit the streets, Judge Parker and Marshal Upham had me back in the Nations again. Reporters worked pretty much the same way then as they do now. They would hear a story and if an editor thought it'd sell papers then that's what ended up getting printed. No one wanted to read that I'd caught a gambler named Noah Burns who couldn't have hit a barn door from ten feet with those big pistols of his. They wanted to believe Dangerous Dave's fairy tale about how I'd thrown down on the infamous John Wesley Hardin and then put him on a horse back to Texas.

That counterfeit killer started the Hayden Tilden "famous marshal" ball rolling, but Morgan Bryce turned out to be the real reason for any reputation that followed me back into Fort Smith after my first time out. Guess I'd have been well known for the John Wesley incident from then on, but ole Morgan was waiting for us on the road back to Fort Smith. And once the news of our meeting got spread around, lawless men all over the Territories started to think twice when they heard Hayden Tilden wanted them.

4

"On a Stroll to Sunday School"

"I DON'T REALLY know a thing about anyone named Morgan Bryce." Franklin J. snatched the pad off the table, rubbed around on the page with his eraser, and started writing again.

Carlton coughed, snorted, and pushed himself further down in the cushion of his chair like an old dog trying to get his bed in just the right order before lying down. General Black Jack Pershing rubbed against my leg, hopped up in my lap, and immediately fell into a purring snooze.

"Well, Junior, if you and I sat down today and made up a list with all the names of the most infamous men in the Territories, Morgan Bryce's would occupy a spot near the top."

"How much do you remember about the man?"

"Good God, son, I remember almost everything about the man. Some claimed he rode with Quantrill during the rebellion. Others said he liked to keep company with the James boys when they needed an extra gun and conducted their business outside the confines of Missouri. Harry Tate said citizens claimed to have seen him with Frank and Jesse anytime they were spotted here in Arkansas."

"Did you believe all those stories?"

"I didn't hear any of them until after we'd met. I had no reason to disbelieve them."

"Can you recall any more of his background? I'll have to check it all out, of course, but I'll take any information you can give me now."

"You can find most of what I'm about to say in the transcripts of his trial in Fort Smith. According to his neighbors down in southeast Arkansas, his career in crime started right after the Civil War ended. He hated the carpetbaggers who moved into the state, and most believed he helped in the murder of a detachment of Negro soldiers outside the little settlement of Macedonia in 'sixty-eight. Bryce family members buried the bodies and hid the horses. Union Army questioned people for a year and couldn't prove any of their suspicions. Mainly because Bryce's family threatened to kill anyone who talked."

"Why did witnesses come forward at his trial in Fort Smith?"

"More than ten years had passed, and most of his relatives had either died or departed for more lucrative areas of the country. Can't blame anyone for that. Arkansas might be the most beautiful place I've ever seen, but poor doesn't even come close to describing how bad off its people are."

"So, no one found out about the soldiers. Then what?"

"He went north and botched the robbery of a bank in the little Missouri township of Elk Creek. Stormed into the place under the false impression that Wells Fargo funds, being transferred from one part of the state to another, resided in their vault."

"False impression?"

"Couldn't have been more wrong. Anyway, he went flying into the bank in May of 'seventy and demanded all the money. Waved a shotgun around and carried several pistols and knives. Teller gave him everything in his till but couldn't persuade Bryce that no more could be had."

"What do you mean by couldn't persuade him no more could be had?"

"Bryce didn't believe him. Shot that teller DRT—dead right there. Five people saw it. Then he lit in on the bank manager. Gunfire brought a seventy-year-old man who acted as town marshal running for the bank. He got there just as Bryce killed the manager."

"Killed two people for no reason?"

"Yep and when he realized no one else in the establishment could throw money his direction, he started his escape. The town marshal, who spent most of his official time locking up a single drunk every Saturday night, called for the thief to stop and throw his weapons aside. Bryce pitched the shotgun at the old man, whipped out his pistols, and put four bullets in him. In the short space of five minutes, he'd managed to kill three people and all for less than a hundred dollars."

"And these murders marked the beginning of his career?"

"You bet. He ran for the Territories and raided back and forth into Arkansas, Texas, and Missouri for years.

Same as thousands of others like him. Rumors had him
spotted as far north as Ogallala and as far east as Memphis. He robbed small local banks, mainly. Usually managed to kill someone in the process. Over the years,
Judge Parker issued numerous warrants in his name for
robbery, murder, rape, forgery, mayhem, and inciting to
riot—just to name a few."

"Parker's corps of marshals couldn't find him?"

"Well, Junior, he kept several hiding places located in
different spots around the Territories. One of them, a
double walled cabin, sat on a hill not far off the trail we
took on our way back to Fort Smith. About a mile from
the hideout, Deputy Marshal Louis Poteete stopped our
little parade and asked Bix Conner for help. Bix, Quinten
and Harry had all investigated one or more of Bryce's
atrocities. They jumped at the chance to help with his
capture."

"How did you feel about going after a man like
Bryce?"

"At the time I didn't know any more about him than
I did about John Wesley Hardin. It didn't matter to me
one way or the other. I just saw it as a sterling opportunity to continue my education and a possibility for me
to make it absolutely clear that given the chance I would
act where others might not."

Bryce couldn't have picked a better spot to hole up. His
cabin sat atop the only hill beside a fast running creek
not far from a place now known as Red Oak, Oklahoma.
He'd dug down three feet in the soft soil before going
up with the walls. Occupants could stand upright and fire
from rifle ports between the second and third rows of
doubled logs. Gunfire couldn't penetrate the fortress, and

anyone trying to sprint up the hill from the sheltering timber below made a wonderful target, because all the trees and bushes had been removed.

Peterman said, "It musta taken him a year to move all that stuff. There ain't so much as a twig left up there."

"How long have you been at this?" Bix asked Poteete.

"There's twenty of us, and we've been blasting away long enough to feel we might need a new direction. You got any suggestions?"

They chewed it around for almost an hour and no one came up with an idea that even sounded like it had any reasonable chance of success. During one heated exchange, someone mentioned that we might be able to use a cache of dynamite available at a local sawmill.

I listened till I got tired of hearing them argue and said, "Get the dynamite. When the sun goes down, I'll snake my way up, plant it, and blow the door away. The concussion should give me time to get inside and do whatever has to be done."

"Who's this baby with the lightning bolt on his face, Bix?" Poteete sneered.

"I'm afraid I didn't think to introduce you, Louis. Meet Judge Parker's newest deputy marshal, Hayden Tilden. Hayden's the man what killed Azel Stroud, Benny Stubbs, and Cecil Morris in that little Pecos promenade over in Pine Bluff awhile back. You remember that one, don't you?"

The sneer bled off Poteete's lips. "Well, I'll accept your word that you'll do what you said, Marshal Tilden. It shouldn't take more'n an hour to get the dynamite."

"Wake me up when it arrives." I crawled under a wagon and pulled my hat down over my eyes.

I'd been lying there about ten minutes when I heard

Bix and Poteete whispering. "Didn't anyone think of this before?"

"Sure," Poteete replied. "But no one was foolish enough to volunteer for such a maneuver. Your young friend carrying the big Winchester's the first to say he'd actually do it. Hope it works. We've been here three days and two nights. I'm tired to the bone."

Knew what he meant. My first foray into the Nations had drained me. Needed a good rest. Sleeping on the ground and eating Johnny Peterman's grub for almost three weeks called for a bath and female company. Wanted to get back to civilization and Elizabeth. I'd known girls in Kentucky, but Elizabeth's crystal blue eyes came to me more and more often in my dreams. Got to thinking a life with her would be about as much happiness as any man could wish for.

Fell asleep, but didn't dream about Elizabeth. For some reason the image of my old friend Clovis Hickerson filled my reveries. Hickerson's Gun Shoppe in Wolf Creek, Kentucky, lured me away from my work in the field at every opportunity before I left Cumberland County with my family. Learned to care for and use rifles like the iron-framed Winchester sleeping beside me under the wagon. I'd never taken to farm work and would sneak away to study at the bench of the only gunsmith within fifty miles of home.

My father served in the Union Army. Mother said he never seemed the same when he returned. He refused me the pleasure of guns and kept only two in the house— his old shotgun and the Navy Colt he carried during the war.

As I lay under the wagon, I dreamed of how I could have had a beautiful rifle in hand when Saginaw Bob

Magruder appeared from the woods at Arkansas Post.

Learned everything I knew about weapons from Clovis, and he tried to give me his favorite Henry .44 the day before we left. My father wouldn't allow it. In my dream that beautiful repeater lay across my lap when we were stopped on the Great River Road, and Saginaw Bob died when he pulled the pocket pistol from his Bible.

Snapped awake just in time to hear Poteete ask Bix, "Are you satisfied this boy can do what he said?"

"According to the letter Everett Lovelady wrote Judge Parker, that boy rubbed out three of the worst types we've ever seen since I became a deputy, and I can tell you he handled a dandy who claimed he was John Wesley Hardin about as calmly as a man on a stroll to Sunday school."

Peeked from under my hat and watched him blow on a cup of steaming coffee as he glanced toward my makeshift bed. A few minutes later the sound of a horse galloping into camp rattled me completely awake. Bix came over and punched me on the arm.

"It's here, Hayden."

"This enough?" Poteete pushed five flame red sticks of explosives at me.

"One or two should do fine. Where are the caps and fuse cord?"

"Kept the caps in my shirt pocket. Didn't want anything to happen to them," said the runner as he gingerly handed them over.

"Anyone here got a watch with a second hand on it?" I asked.

A man from Poteete's posse stepped forward. "My railroader's watch has one."

I took the watch, then cut off a piece of fuse about a

foot long, placed it on the ground, and lit it. Made a mark in the dirt every five seconds next to the burned spot and had a fair idea of how much I needed to do the job. Got two sticks ready and gave the rest back to Poteete. The company of marshals and prisoners gathered behind the tumbleweed wagons near several smoky fires.

Bix walked me to the edge of the trees at the bottom of the hill. It had got pretty dark by then.

"Once you step out of these trees, Hayden, you'll have to crawl almost a quarter of a mile to the house. Good thing we don't have much moon, but I'd feel better if it'd cloud up a bit."

"Yeah, well, you can't have everything. Bix, when this is over, we're heading for Fort Smith. No more detours." The way I said it made my meaning as clear as a bell rung on an icy morning.

As we talked, most of the marshals filtered through the trees and stationed themselves in a line on either side of us at the base of the hill and waited.

"This might take a while. Don't let this bunch get too anxious and start shooting at things they can't see or identify. I don't want to be carried off this hill with a bullet from Poteete's pistol in me," I said under my breath.

Waited another five minutes. Just as I crawled away from Bix, Harry Tate took up a spot on the other side of a pile of brush near us and lit one of the panatelas he favored. The cigar was about as big around as my little finger and seven inches long. I knew if he put some effort into the enjoyment of his smoke, he could usually waste about an hour. Figured he'd manage to get about halfway through it before I'd reach the cabin. Nothing blocked my way. Hill didn't have enough timber on it to make a wooden nickel. Just a few blades of grass for cover. Guess no one saw me. Got lucky. Couple of clouds came up. Did my best north Kentucky, Shawnee sneak and the bunch inside must have been pretty tired too.

Found out later four of them had denned up in the cabin—Bryce; Fat Jack McNair; his partner, Bug Eye Taylor; and Gooch Bonds.

Marshal Conner carried a warrant for ole Gooch. We wanted him for sure and all the others if we could take them. The one called Bug Eye had one blue eye and a big brown one that kind of bugged out. He'd killed several people, men and women, who mistakenly laughed close to where he happened to be standing. Ugly son of a bitch was real sensitive about that brown eye. Found out later, most men thought him insane. They were more afraid of him for that than for his peculiar appearance.

Well, I fumbled around in the dark for a good little while before I finally came upon the door to the place. Moved over to one side and pitched the first stick of dynamite up against it. Explosion blew the door across the room. Hit Gooch Bonds where he sat at a table in the middle of the cabin. Killed him dead as hell in a preacher's bedroom. Concussion almost knocked me back down the hill. But the smoke and confusion gave me just the chance I needed to roll the second stick across the floor. It stopped under the table. Detonation turned it into a rocket.

Bix said the roof kinda puffed up like someone opening an umbrella. Then the table shot through and sent splinters flying for a hundred feet in every direction. Table had a lantern on it that spilled. Thing lit up like the ball from a Roman candle. Harry almost swallowed his cigar. Said it looked like a comet flying toward them.

Landed on the side of the hill just at the edge of the falling debris.

Hell, thought for sure I'd killed whatever lawless bastards were inside. Went in as soon as I could. Splinters, dirt, and paper still fell like rain. Felt around in the dark and found two of them. Dragged them outside one at a time. Waited for Bix and Poteete to bring the rest of the posse up. Bryce came around just as Bix and Handsome Harry rushed up carrying lanterns and torches.

Bix said, "Hot damn, Hayden. This 'un here's Bryce and that big 'un there's Gooch Bonds. Hell of a job, son!"

Bonds must have weighed nigh on two hundred and fifty pounds. I had a terrible time getting him out of the rubble. Big ole door busted him up something frightful. Poteete and his crew dragged the other two out. They couldn't hear for about an hour and bled from lots of cuts and scratches. Altogether, though, they came through getting blown up in fairly good shape.

Bug Eye Taylor suffered most. Impact of the explosion knocked that big ugly eye of his right out of his head. Johnny found it under their kindling box the next day. Poor one-eyed doofus carried that awful thing around in a little leather pouch till they hung him. He charged people a dime to look at it. Amazing how much money a man can make on a big brown eye.

Next morning, Bryce asked to talk with me. Johnny had him shackled to a rear wheel on the wagon. His broken nose and split scalp had covered his shoulders and neck with crusted blood. A piece of splintered wood, pulled from his right leg, left another large brown pool just above his boot top.

"I'll just be royally damned. You're the child what

brung me to heel?" He shot me an angry, squinty-eyed examination from head to foot. Curled a split lip and spat at my feet.

I kicked it back at him. "That's right. And instead of spitting at me, you ought to be thanking whatever God listens to scum like you that I didn't lob that second stick of dynamite right into your lap. You'd be shaking hands with the devil right now if I could have seen you."

He leaned back and let out a long ragged breath. "Well, young Marshal, I'd been awake for four days and just dozed off. Otherwise, I'da heard you a-coming. Them other dumb bastards couldn'ta heard the M.K.&T. from Kansas City if it'd gone right through the place. Bug Eye and Fat Jack couldn't make a half-wit between 'em. Only one worth more'n a gob of spit was Gooch— and you done kilt him, you son of a bitch."

"It could have all been avoided. Why didn't you just give it up?"

"Give it up? You mean surrender? That's rich. I ain't never surrendered to nobody for nothing. And the first time I get a chance, I'll get out from under this thing and kill you like a cur."

I moved up as close to him as the smells of stale urine, gunpowder, burnt clothing, and sweat would allow and whispered, "Few weeks ago I watched six men all hang at the same time. When Judge Parker sets Maledon loose on you, I'll be in the first row. Just before you soil your britches in front of several thousand decent folk, be sure and look for me."

He swung at me with his free hand. Kicked out with his good leg when I danced away. "I'll kill you, you scar-faced son of a bitch! Then I'll kill your family. Then I'll kill your dog and any cats you own." I walked away, and he kept yelling. "I'll remember you, boy. I won't forget that big rifle or the crease on your face. I'll come looking for you when I get loose."

I strolled over to Bix, Poteete, and some others just as an argument pimpled up.

"Bryce and his bunch are mine and I want 'em!" Poteete yelled. He shook his finger in Bix's face.

Conner grinned and acted like he was talking with a small child. "Sorry, Louis. You didn't catch 'em. Hayden did. They're ours."

"Not on your life, Bix. Me and my men spent three days trying to roust these killers out and we'll take 'em back to Fort Smith."

"I think you might have to take that up with Marshal Tilden, Louis."

"The hell with Marshal Big-Rifle-with-a-Reputation Tilden. I don't give a personal damn what he thinks."

Climbed on Thunder and urged her up between them. The Winchester rested across my arm. "You cornered them, Marshal Poteete, but you didn't go in and get them. I did. They'll stay with Marshal Conner and me. And that's my final word on the matter."

"Your final word on the matter my big, hairy behind." He snatched at my reins.

Bix grabbed him from behind and pulled him back. His chin rested on the taller man's shoulder when he said, "I never knew you for a fool, Louis. I'd let this go if I were you." Poteete glared at me like his head might explode. Big purple veins in his neck jumped and twitched.

I bumped Thunder in the sides and pulled up next to Johnny Peterman, waiting in the wagon. "Get them going, Johnny," I said. "A beautiful woman in Fort Smith needs to see me."

We left Poteete and Bix standing there in the dust and headed our bunch out. What with the ten whiskey runners, Dangerous Dave and his two friends, and the Bryce bunch we led quite a parade.

The crowd made Johnny's job more difficult by the minute. " 'Bout all we need now's a tuba player, someone to pick a banjo, a squeeze box, and a monkey, and we'd have ourselves a real honest-to-God hoot and holler carnival."

Harry almost fell off his horse laughing. He kept saying, "That's it, Johnny. Talk to us. Tell us about it. Maybe we can pass the plate later."

Bix caught up in about half an hour. Pulled up beside Handsome Harry and me. "Poteete get over his fit?" Harry asked.

"Well, not entirely. But he'll probably calm down in a year or two." He smiled at his own joke. "He seemed to think you're out to get yourself a reputation there, Hayden."

"I just did what Judge Parker hired me to do. If a reputation follows, I can't help that."

"Don't pay any attention to Poteete, Hayden," Harry said. "He's a hot headed windbag. You told him the exact way of it all. He and that bunch of never-sweats he calls deputies coulda been up there for a month, and Bryce would still be sittin' in his shack picking his teeth."

"I agree," added Bix. "But Louis expects to hear a great deal more about the rifle-totin' Mr. Tilden in the future." He paused, then said, "Unless someone kills him pretty quick."

"Jesus," Harry mumbled. "That's a sobering thought."

The rest of our trip perambulated along uneventfully. The hard cases, chained to the wagon, seemed to lose a lot of their fire once they saw the great Morgan Bryce brought down. Local criminals like Dangerous Dave and Gooch Bonds were one thing—Bryce was something completely different. New stories about me got told with every step they took from the Bryce hideout to Judge Parker's court.

By the time our prisoners reached that dungeon of a basement jail, my name got spoken in tones reserved for men feared and respected.

Spent most of my days for over a month after that in Judge Parker's court either testifying or waiting to testify. Honest to God, the man could put on a trial faster than any judge I ever saw. But no matter how fast he went, a trial took time, and all us marshals had to be available. Hated that part of the job.

First thing Elizabeth said when I walked into her store was, "Why, Mr. Tilden. I had a dream about you last night. You were standing under my window and talking about the moon and the stars." How can you resist a woman who dreams about you and compares you to Romeo?

Took her out every time she was willing to go. She liked Julia's and several other little restaurants. I remember sitting across the table one night and realizing that I loved the sound of her voice. I had never fallen in love with a woman's voice before. Fell for hers like an anvil dropped in a well. 'Course I really enjoyed squiring her around town, too. Learned from Elizabeth how much pleasure can be had from being seen with the most beautiful woman in town on your arm. Don't let anyone ever tell you any different. There's just nothing like it.

We kept company often enough for her to make sure my sartorial needs got properly looked after. She advised me in the selection of a new suit. Said I'd make a better impression in court if I didn't show up in my trail duds. When she finished, the Colt and badge were the only things that kept a lot of people from mistaking me for a banker or lawyer.

I appreciated what she did for me. Any man would. For the first time in my life grown men stepped aside when I walked down the street. Women blushed and smiled if I tipped my hat in their direction. In the beginning, their reactions embarrassed me a might. But it didn't take long to get used to such respect. Elizabeth always believed those with any kind of reputation commanded a type of esteem and fear that showed itself in such displays of deference. Have to admit, I liked it. When we entered a restaurant or hotel, favorable treatment usually followed.

Fortunately I didn't have to stick around for Morgan Bryce's comeuppance. State found more witnesses willing to appear at his trial than any other before it. Man had managed to make a lot of enemies. Just before Judge Parker put him in the dock, Harry Tate stopped me in the hallway outside the U.S. marshal's office.

He said, "Hayden, you're just the man I've been looking for. I'm taking a party out next week. Want to have you along with us."

I liked the man. Enjoyed his company. Trusted him. So I said, "I'll be glad to go with you, Harry. I've had about as much of sitting around a courthouse as I can stand for a while. Tired of spending my time away from Elizabeth doing nothing but looking for sundown and payday. Don't like the idea of leaving Elizabeth again, but I'm ready for some action."

"Glad to hear it. By the way, I'll be carrying a warrant

for a no-account piece of trash called Killin' Bill Barber.
He used to run with Magruder. If we can find him he
might just know where ole Preacher Bob's holed up.
Pulling out Monday morning. Meet you down at the
ferry."

As I said my good-byes to Elizabeth on the Sunday
before my second raid into the Nations, something wonderful happened. I held her hand, kissed her cheek, and
turned to walk away. She pulled me back and kissed me
with such passion it left no doubt how she felt.

"You must be careful," she whispered in my ear, "and
come back to me safe and well."

"You know why I have to go. If there's even the
slightest chance I might run across Bob Magruder, I have
to take it. And there might be more than a good chance
this time out. Harry's carrying a warrant for a man Magruder used to run with. If we can find him Saginaw Bob
could be nearby. You needn't worry, my dear Elizabeth.
No matter what might await me in the Nations, or any
other trail I have to travel, I'll always come back to you."

"Mr. Tilden, It's been a long afternoon. Could we take a
break? Start again tomorrow morning?" Franklin J. Jr.
dropped his pencil in his lap and massaged his right hand.

"Whatever works for you, son."

"What I want you to do is sit down tonight and make
some notes about things you'd be willing to discuss tomorrow. I'll be back at around ten in the morning, if
that's agreeable?"

"Son, Carlton, Black Jack Pershing, and I aren't going
anywhere. By tomorrow morning I'll have you a whole
raft of things to talk about. Just clear it all with Nurse
Leona Wildbank before you leave. Sure wouldn't do to

get her ticked off at us, would it? Gal's big as something that ought to be rotating on a spit and can dust our feathers like we was poultry ready to be plucked. So don't leave till you talk to her."

He smiled, struggled to his feet, shook my hand, and said, "I guarantee everything will be cleared with the mysterious and powerful Miss Leona." He turned away, stopped, and came back. "Want you to know before I leave, sir, that this has been one of the most interesting afternoons I've ever spent interviewing anyone."

"Glad to hear it, Junior. Look forward to seeing you in the morning."

Few minutes after he left, I woke Carlton up, helped him into his wheelchair, and we went to supper. If you have to live in a home for the aged, Rolling Hills is about as good as it gets. But sometimes the food really gives me the willies. Most of it's some kind of paste like that bottled baby food. Once in a while it'd really be grand to suck on a big ole juicy piece of beefsteak. But every time I mention it to the head nurse, she gets this look on her face like someone who's just been told vampires are real.

Sat at the desk in my room till almost midnight writing down everything I could remember from that first few years with Judge Parker. The special jobs he sent me out on started right after my trip with Harry, Billy Bird, and Travis Teel.

It's awful quiet at midnight in an old folks' home. Shouldn't come as much of a surprise. Places are as close to the grave as you can get without being there. 'Bout the only thing that might break a man's line of thought is those old gomers who sit up in bed every once in a while and start screaming. Fortunately Carlton and me haven't got that far gone yet. 'Course, Carlton's so old I'm not sure he would scream if you set him on fire.

Anyway, it's the perfect time to think about your past, I guess. Only two ways to go once you get to a place like Rolling Hills. You either can't remember anything— or you can't forget. I could remember everything like it happened yesterday.

5

"WORTHLESS SCUM SHOT HIM IN THE BACK"

GOT TO HAND it to Junior, he kept his word. At exactly ten o'clock the next morning, he flopped into the overstuffed chair I moved onto the porch and had waiting for him. One minute later, he started scratching in that pad of his.

"Where's your checkers buddy?" he asked.

"Carlton's not feeling too good this morning, Junior. He has his good days and his bad days. Today's one of the bad ones. When you get to be as old as he is you're lucky to have any kind of a day. Takes a while for some people to realize it, but the older you get, the older you want to get. Carlton might be ninety-two, but he'd sure like to be ninety-three or a hundred and three. Personally I'm going to be surprised if he makes it through the winter this year."

Junior looked uncomfortable. "Sorry to hear that."

"Well, son, it's just life."

"Where's the cat?"

"He'll be around. General Black Jack Pershing's probably older than me and Carlton combined in cat years, and just like all old tomcats he comes and goes any way he likes."

"What've you got for me this morning? Hope you had a chance to make a few notes last night."

"Made notes. Raring to go."

"Yesterday we stopped just as you were about to go out on your second trip to the Nations. As I remember it, Handsome Harry Tate led the party and Killin' Bill might be a waiting in the boonies with Saginaw Bob."

That time out we traveled in the company of an old marshal named Travis Teel. He'd been around from the very beginning of Judge Parker's term.

"Judge hired Travis right after he got off the train back in 'seventy-five," said Harry as Teel shook my hand. Everything about the man was round. Round head. Round belly. Mustache and chin whiskers made the bottom half of his face look like a black circle inside a white one. I wondered if his feet matched the rest of his body. That lack of sharp edges made him appear shorter than his actual five feet and nine inches.

"This one's Billy Bird. Billy will be our jailer this trip." The young marshal looked like a twelve-year-old boy, and in many ways resembled his name. Tall, thin, and long of arm, his gangly appearance disguised a steady, dependable trail mate and a deadly skill with his pistols.

"Not a good idea to get into a quick-draw contest with Billy," Harry bragged. "We've all tried to beat him. No one's managed it yet." The boy smiled, blushed, and kicked at the dirt with his toe.

"Aw, shucks, I ain't that good, Harry. Don't be leading Mr. Tilden along with things that just might not be true." Marshal Bird had one of those personalities that drew you to him and made you feel like you'd known him all your life.

From the ferry, Harry moved our little party north of the area Bix Conner covered on my first trip. A week out of Fort Smith led us past several lakes. They were crystal clear in 'seventy-nine and 'eighty. Surrounded by heavy timber. Sometimes, we even saw Indians in the distance.

"Most likely Creeks," Billy noted. None of them ever approached us.

I wanted to meet a real Indian. The Shawnee had been murdered out and pushed out of Kentucky long before I got born. The possibility of an encounter with living, breathing Plains Indians fascinated me far more than the likelihood of a gun battle with men as bad as those we'd caught on our first raid.

I asked Travis so many questions about the Creeks, he finally said, "They'll keep their distance, 'less'n they want something."

Harry led us along and a bit south of the Canadian River. "Judge Parker's had a boatload of complaints about a bunch of rogue cowboys in this area," he explained.

"Good men gone bad," quipped Billy. "They start from Texas with cattle drives that pass through the Nations along the Shawnee and old Chisholm Trails. They get tired of the backbreaking work, or see a chance to get rich quick by low means, or get into trouble with their trail bosses, or any of a hundred reasons, and they end up out here running with others of the same breed. Ole Killin' Bill used to be one of 'em, but he graduated to bigger and more deadly pursuits when he and Saginaw Bob hooked up together."

Travis lit a cigar that looked like a mud-covered tree root and started talking before he flipped the match away. "These ole boys raid overland mail stations, steal cattle wherever they can, and generally cause trouble with anyone they run up on. Most are nothing more than amateur highwaymen, but some graduate to murder and mayhem of every sort imaginable."

"Hayden," Harry chimed in, "lot of these men are just as bad as gangs like the James bunch, but we don't have enough newspapers or dime novels out here to entertain the public with their exploits. I brought a whole stack of John Does this time in addition to the one for Killin' Bill. Be real surprised if we don't use all of 'em."

We stopped at a couple of the overland stations and found out a new and violent group of cowboys roamed the countryside led by a steely-eyed killer name of Jug Dudley.

Just north of McAlester, Otis Frye, an old stock handler wearing bib overalls, wiped tobacco juice off his chin as he described his encounter with the gang. "They was four of 'em misbegotten Texians," he said. "Caught me and my friend Orval Rabb 'bout five mile out yonder in the sticks. We was a-driving strays back this way, and them yahoos took the stock and then demanded money. Ain't had two nickels I could rub together in so long done forgot what they look like. The one they called Jug shot hell out of Orval and laughed like it were something funny to see a man die like that."

Harry shook his head and said, "Describe Dudley for me and the other marshals."

"Medium tall, scraggly black hair down to his shoulders, chin beard, grayish blue eyes, and an ugly, saw-shaped scar that ran from his right ear all along the jaw to his chin. Beard couldn't grow over it." He pointed at his own face and made a sawing motion along his bony jaw.

"Match anybody you ever heard of before, Harry?" asked Billy Bird.

"Yeah. This feller's been around for a while. He's one of the men Judge Parker described to me before we left Fort Smith. 'Course, didn't know his name then. Think I'll just write him down on this John Doe right now so I don't forget it. If we can find witnesses like Mr. Frye here so easy, this bunch has probably done numerous crimes that haven't come to light yet."

"Did you see which way they headed after the killing of Mr. Rabb?" asked Travis.

"Went south and west. Toward the Muddy Boggy." He raised a trembling arm and pointed a shaky finger in the direction of the dying sun.

Sounded like something awful to me. "Muddy Boggy? What's that?" I asked.

Billy Bird laughed. He snapped his reins over the mule team and turned the wagon south. "An unpleasant garden spot favored by cattle and horse thieves—lots of hidden bluffs and dry washes. Great place to hide stolen stock or just lay low."

The Muddy Boggy turned out to be muddy, but any bog that might have been there had either covered over with ice or was on the way to it. Flakes of snow had begun to fall, and the cold sharpened with a wind that blew steadily from the west.

Harry and Travis found a sheltered bluff near the river and had Billy pull up out of the wind. We attached a tarp to the wagon and stretched it to some bushes on the side of the bluff.

Billy piled scrub limbs and twigs at one end of the shelter. We got a fire going, and pretty soon our rough outpost turned right homey.

"Here's how I see it." Harry scratched at the ground with a piece of broken driftwood. "We'll use our new camp as a base. Billy stays here. The rest of us will scout the bluffs and wooded patches along the river. Each of us will take a different area. If we find anything, we come back to camp immediately. I don't have any doubt the Dudley bunch is around here somewhere, but I think we'd best not face them alone."

Early the next morning, under a sky the color of wet gray slate, we set out on our search. Harry went north along the east bank of the river. Travis Teel walked his horse across a shallow spot and went south on the west side. I struck out south and east traveling in semicircles away from the river. The hardened earth made some of the steep-walled washes treacherous. The hunt proved difficult and dangerous.

Sometime after noon on the third day, I rested Thunder and leaned against a scrubby tree trying to get out of the biting wind. What sounded like shots crackled off to the west. Tried to put a better ear on the situation, but the wind came up. Rattling tree limbs and rustling grass drowned out anything more than a few hundred feet away.

Got back to camp just before dark that evening. Harry

had already come in and was sipping coffee with his dinner. Billy handed me a plate and seemed happy we'd made it back again.

I squatted by the fire and poured myself a cup of Billy's potent up-and-at-'em juice. "Where's Travis?" I asked.

Billy cast an anxious glance in the direction of Travis's trail. "He ain't come in yet."

"Did either of you hear shooting just after noon today?"

Billy shook his head.

"Not me." Harry pitched his remaining coffee on the coals and poured himself a new cup.

"Little after midday thought I heard shots off to the west. Happened real fast. Wind kept me from hearing anything else. I've noticed in the past that Travis always beat me back and managed to be first in line for every meal."

Billy laughed, but quickly glanced down the river several times. "Ole Travis has a fondness for food unlike any man I've ever met. I've seen him take the Mustang Steak House's challenge one time. You know, that place where they say if you can eat one of their biggest steak dinners you don't have to pay."

"I saw him do it." Harry smiled at the memory. "They brought out a piece of beef about the size of a wagon wheel and, what with the bread, taters, and other side dishes, it made a meal big enough for four normal people. Travis ate every bite of it. He said he could eat two of 'em. You wouldn't believe he could do it just by looking at him." His speech slowed as he remembered his friend. "I heard tell he almost starved a couple of times when he was a child. Man is a serious table grazer. Don't miss a meal. Never even been late."

Billy grabbed the coffeepot and doused the fire. We moved the horses to a spot behind the wagon and under the bluff. Dragged up several more logs and closed off the open end of our temporary fortress. Took up positions behind our new fortifications. Slept with our weapons at the ready.

Next morning Billy said, "I don't think a fire is going to hurt anything." He filled us up with biscuits from an iron kettle and lots of strong coffee. Harry and I struck out to look for Travis as soon as the light got good. As usual, Billy stayed with the wagon. He waved at us with his Winchester when we topped the far bank.

Fancied myself something of a tracker, but my skill was that of a greenhorn compared to Handsome Harry Tate. Every bent twig, scuffed rock, or scratch on the hardened surface of the ground pointed him in the direction of Travis's past trips over the previous four days. Late that afternoon, he managed to sort out the numerous trails and seemed certain we followed the path left the day before.

About two hours later, in a tight, steep descent to a sheltered wash that led back to the river, Harry reined his horse to a sharp stop and dismounted. He placed his right index finger to his lips and pulled a shotgun from his saddle bindings.

We picked our way from crevice to crevice. When the wash opened back out onto the slow-moving stream, a long, wide sandbar flowed into the water. Not a hundred feet from us, near the only tree in sight for two hundred yards around, lay Travis Teel's body. Soon as I spotted the corpse I knew Killin' Bill, and Saginaw Bob, would probably have to be put on a back burner for a bit longer.

We sat in the last crevice of the wash for a long time and waited to see if anyone else might be about. Harry whispered, "Whoever did this is probably long gone, but it don't pay to get careless now that we've found him."

Once he got satisfied we could approach the body with some degree of safety, we left our hiding place in a running crouch. I kept guard while he examined Travis.

"Worthless scum shot him in the back when he dismounted over there." Harry pointed to a spot hard by the slow-moving water. "Two men came at him, maybe three. They got him before he had time to react. Probably didn't even know what hit him." He rolled the corpse over. "He went down, and they shot him at least three more times. First shooter must have been in those trees on the bluff behind him. It was a well-planned ambush, Hayden. Guess they spotted him snooping around, set him up, and murdered him."

Harry stumbled to his feet and stared down at his friend. Muscles in his jaws clenched as his face reddened. He took his hat off and stood for several moments rubbing his eyes with the back of his hand.

We carried Travis back to our hiding spot in the wash and continued the examination. Killers had picked him clean. Only thing they left was his long johns. Later, we found his horse almost a mile away. The big palomino must have spooked when the shooting started. Draped Travis over his saddle and covered him with a rain slicker. Then we hurried back to camp as fast as our new load would allow. Not much talking on the way back. Upset can't come close to describing Harry Tate.

Billy rolled their friend in a piece of tarp and tied it with rope. We found a nice spot overlooking the river for the burial. Picked a place far enough above the high-water mark so the grave wouldn't float away with the first gully-washing rain. Then we all scoured the surrounding area for what rocks we could find and covered him with them.

"You got a Bible, Hayden?" Billy asked.

"No, sorry."

"Oh, I understand. It might sound strange, but there's something about this evil place that keeps men like Harry and me from exposin' a good book to its influence. Just hoped you might accidentally have one with you."

I'd barely known Travis Teel, but could see the impact of the man's death on the other two marshals. They lingered over the grave, mopped their faces with bandannas, and kicked at the ground as men often do when confronted with something beyond their understanding or control.

They'd been his friends. Traveled that trail with him before, sweated together in the summer and shivered in the winter. Figured it might be a comfort to them if some words—any words—got read. So I hurried back to camp and got the thick book Elizabeth sold me the day I arrived in Fort Smith.

And as the cold wind sliced its way across the empty land, I read aloud, "From *Julius Caesar,* act two, scene two. 'When beggars die, there are no comets seen; the heavens themselves blaze forth the death of princes. Cowards die many times before their deaths; the valiant never taste of death but once. Of all the wonders that I yet have heard, it seems to me most strange that men should fear; seeing that death, a necessary end, will come when it will come.' "

As we trudged back to camp, Billy Bird pulled at my

sleeve and said, "Always admired Mr. Shakespeare. Them words you picked fit Travis right down to the ground. Mighty glad you were here to read over him."

We talked late into the night about what we would do. Finally Harry said, "Think we should leave the wagon here, take what supplies we can carry, and run these jaybirds to ground. Don't know who we'll be chasing, but, by God, Travis Teel's murder deserves chastisement of the first order."

"I'm ready." Billy jabbed at the embers of our fire with a stick like a man about to explode.

"Hayden, under normal circumstances I'd be the first to make every effort to bring these men in alive. Not because we'd lose money if we don't, but because it's the right thing to do. I've never had a problem letting Judge Parker parcel out any retribution before, but the men who murdered Travis need killing double-quick."

"Amen." Sparks shot into the air as Billy threw his stick into the flames. "The level of arrogance necessary for anyone to think they could get away with backshooting a U.S. marshal makes me mad enough to bite the head off a hammer."

Next morning, Harry picked up the trail where we found Travis. We ran our horses hard to the south and west. By the time Billy made camp that night, Harry estimated we'd covered almost fifty miles.

He pulled the woolly collar of his sheepskin coat up around his neck and snuggled down into his bed. "This bunch was so brazen, they haven't even made any effort to hide their trail."

"They probably thought Travis was out here alone, and that no one would ever know what happened to him. Well, I can't wait to see the surprise on their faces when we bust their worthless asses." Billy snapped his blanket like a whip, then dropped onto it and fell asleep in less than a minute.

It took three more days before the opportunity to bust their worthless asses finally presented itself. By then, we'd run out of the Territories and crossed the Red River into north Texas.

"Aren't we out of our jurisdiction, Harry?" I asked.

"Son, you're a deputy U.S. marshal in possession of a fistful of John Doe warrants. You can go anywhere in the United States, and hell itself if necessary, to serve them. Sadly, we're not in the balmy realm of Hades today. We're in Texas. Them Texian boys think they've made it home safe and sound. That feeling is about to go through a serious reformation."

We tracked that bunch to a used-up carbuncle of a town named Black Oak. Only way that nasty burg managed to hang on to existence rested just inside the doors of two saloons. They dominated the tiny jumble of clapboard buildings along a single street.

"Those saloons have whores working in 'em. Even if those women are uglier than one-eyed, three-legged dogs, men will find them and indulge their pleasure for as long as their money lasts. I'd bet everything we can make in a year that we'll find Dudley and his bunch doing exactly that." Harry smiled and urged his horse toward the saloons.

He left Billy and me on the edge of town beside a broken piece of tree that'd been hit by lightning. The name of the town wandered in a childish scrawl across a board nailed to the blackened stump. We waited there for almost half an hour before he came back.

"They're all in that palace of swill at the end of the

street. If you can call this pig-run a street. I checked their horses, and they're for sure the ones we've followed all the way from the Muddy Boggy." He dismounted and squatted. "Our boys are the only people in town other than the whores and gamblers. Business seems to be pretty bad around here right now. We come back in six months this mud pie won't be nothin' but a bad memory."

"You're certain these are the right men, Harry?" I asked. "There's no doubt in your mind they're the ones who killed Travis?"

"No doubt, Hayden. Their ponies are all tied out front of a place called the Salt Fork Saloon. One of those men shot Travis Teel in the back, and at least two—maybe three—of the others were there and helped finish him off. I don't know about you, but I'm not going to have any problem shooting as many holes as I can in these big-headed brush poppers."

I watched Billy the whole time we talked. He hadn't bothered to question whether we were in the right place or had the right men. He spent the time Harry and I chewed the situation over doing the things necessary for him to face gunfire and survive. Checked the big Colt strapped high on his waist. Then pulled another pistol from his saddlebags, loaded it, and pushed it under his cartridge belt against the small of his back. The shotgun he carried behind his saddle got loaded last. When finished, he leaned against the rump of the palomino with the scattergun propped against his hip.

Studied the face of each man for almost a minute before I finally said, "Well, guess we'd better get at it. Let's go cage as many of these jaybirds as want to stay alive."

Billy jerked his blaster up to the ready. "Now that's exactly what I wanted to hear."

We led our horses into town. Tied them to the hitch rails in front of the first dilapidated building, which declared itself the Red-Eye Saloon. I watched the other marshals as they began to strip off all their rain gear and heavy leather coats.

"Take off anything that might interfere with your gun handling, Hayden," Billy advised. "These boys ain't gonna go peaceably. Least I hope not."

"They're in that place next door." Harry pointed toward the Salt Fork Saloon. He pulled the pistol from his shoulder rig, opened the loading gate, and carefully added a bullet to the empty safety chamber. Then swapped it for his belly gun and did the same.

I levered a round into the .45-70, left the hammer back, and waited for them to finish getting primed. Then we all moved into the street and walked carefully past the six cowponies. Their owners had tied them in front of the only whiskey vendor in town who could say he possessed something that actually resembled a real saloon.

All those stout little animals sported the livery most people would normally associate with Texas cowboys. Three of them had woven horsehair headstalls decorated with hammered silver. Braided rawhide lariats hung beside chaps, and each Denver saddle had a yellow rain slicker tied behind it. Mustangs had been rode hard and left out in the cold. Always figured that if there'd been a stable in town, the cowboys would've boarded their mounts. As it was, their horses had to wait while the urges of men gone bad got satisfied.

Harry stepped through the door first. Billy followed

and went to his left. I moved along the wall on Harry's right.

Three of the cowboys sat at a table across the single room from the door. Two more stood at the bar along the left wall between the three of us and their friends. A sixth man appeared to have passed out on the floor beside a badly abused upright piano in the far right corner.

Billy glided to the end of the bar closest to him and laid the shotgun on it. He moved one step away, reached behind his back with his left hand, and slipped his fingers around the grip of the pistol hidden there. Harry held his cocked gun behind his right leg. I let the Winchester rove from one side of the room to the other.

The laughter and noise that greeted us quickly died away as everyone in the room realized that men wearing badges and loaded for bear were eyeballing them. Couple of rough-looking harlots draped over the cowboys at the table moved away and ran for a door behind the bar. Bartender slid along the wall and disappeared with the women.

In a matter of seconds that dying dram shop became frozen in time. The quiet interrupted only by snorts from the quivering slug sleeping on the floor beside that dilapidated music box.

In a voice that sounded like it came down from Mount Sinai with the tablets, Harry said, "Boys, I'm Deputy U.S. Marshal Harry Tate. The man on your left is Deputy U.S. Marshal Hayden Tilden, and the stringy feller over there is Deputy U.S. Marshal William Tecumseh Bird. We have warrants for your arrests." He turned to his right and slightly sideways toward the cowboys. "You will give up the man who shot Marshal Travis Teel in the back out on the Muddy Boggy in the Nations last week.

We want him right now. You present that man to us, and we'll see that the rest of you get a fair trial in Judge Parker's court on the charge of accessory to murder."

No one moved or said anything for about ten seconds. Then a scar-faced man, who'd been leaning on the bar, stood and moved back toward his friends at the table. "You lawdogs gotta have a lotta hard bark coverin' yore dumb Arkansas asses to come down here and try to arrest Texas boys. Yore badges and warrants ain't worth spit hereabouts. We don't answer to nuthin' 'cept Texas law. So you can fold them warrants five ways and stick 'em where the sun don't shine." He stopped beside the table and pulled his coat away from his pistol.

"I do believe I have the pleasure of addressing Mr. Jug Dudley," said Harry. "I have one warrant especially for you, sir. The others are John Does, but they'll work just fine on your friends."

The man who remained at the bar said nothing, but pulled his coat back to reveal a big Remington tucked in his belt. Two of the three men at the table stood and made all the motions of those prepared to go down shooting. The cowboy left seated seemed reluctant to be a party to what was clearly about to transpire. He placed his hands on the table and clamped his fingers together as though to signify his wish to stay out of the fight.

Cold wind slipped under the door and tiptoed up my spine as sweat ran down my jaw and dripped onto the floor. Dudley hooked his thumbs into his gun belt. The fingers of his right hand tapped a spot a few inches away from the walnut grip of his Colt.

"By Godfrey, boys, did you hear that? I'm known. That means you're known too. We'll be even more famous when we get through squashing these Arkansas dung beetles. Tomorrow, people all over Texas and the Territories will know about the Dudley gang."

The bullet from Billy Bird's pistol ripped through Dudley's skull and snuffed out his life before he even had a chance to blink. He fell backward like a drowning man trying to claw his way to the surface and landed upright in the chair behind him.

Man at the bar tried for his gun, but it barely cleared his cartridge belt when a shot from Billy's hideout punched a hole in his chest as big as the bottom of a whiskey bottle.

Harry's right hand snapped up. Bolts of flame a foot long jumped from the Colt's silver barrel and burned twin caverns in one of the drunks at the table.

Fourth man kicked his chair back and jumped for the door behind the bar. A slug from my Winchester dropped him like a twelve point rack of antlers with the buck still attached.

Blasting inside that cramped cow country oasis nearly deafened me. For fifteen seconds or so, couldn't hear much of anything. The muscles in my arms trembled. Acrid blue-black smoke hung in the air like fog along the banks of the Arkansas early on a warm spring morning. The three of us stood there coiled up and quivering. Spring steel with fangs, waiting for the next move.

The living man left at the table frantically waved his hands like a deranged M.K.&T. brakeman signaling his engineer. Three of our four weapons covered him. His stricken glance darted from one of us to the other.

"Don't shoot me, Marshals. I ain't heeled. I didn't have nothin' to do with the killing of your friend." Tears rolled down his cheeks.

Handsome Harry's words fell on the man colder than

sleet on Travis Teel's grave. "Sir, you will stand and go to Marshal Bird. Do be careful. You've seen how deadly he is. It would be to your benefit to heed what you've just witnessed." He stepped aside and allowed the terrified cowboy to move out of the line of fire. Billy escorted the man outside and placed him in shackles.

Harry and I examined each of the fallen outlaws. The one at the bar had been shot squarely in the heart and died before he hit the floor. A smile lingered on his lips as though he felt certain he'd beat Billy Bird to the draw.

Harry dropped his warrant in Jug Dudley's lap. He leaned over, his face only inches from the dead man's, and sneered, "Consider yourself served, you murderin' gob of spit. After today, nobody will ever know who Jug Dudley was. I'm gonna bury you deep and not put up a marker. By tomorrow afternoon no one but your mother will even know you were ever amongst the living." He grabbed the man by the chin, jerked the head to one side, and slid his finger along the jagged scar. Then he spat on the corpse and stalked away.

Unfortunately the brush popper brought down by my shot wasn't as lucky as his extremely dead friends. My aim had been off by the slightest margin. Bullet ripped a huge hole in his gut, but didn't kill him outright. It took a bit for the numbness of his injury to give way to the pain. When it did, he died long, loud, and pitiful. Tried to make him comfortable, but nothing really helped. He screamed, wept, and cried out for his mother all night long. Death didn't come for him till early the next morning.

The drunk who'd been passed out on the floor slept through the whole dance. Next day, all he could do was shake his head and marvel at what he'd missed.

Black Oak's undertaker had abandoned the place over a year before we got there. Harry enticed two of the local elbow-benders to help with the burial of Dudley and his men. True to his word, he put them in the ground in a patch of woods just outside town. No markers were erected for them. We could have gone back a month later and not been able to find the site.

On the long, cold trip back to the Muddy Boggy and our wagon, I pulled Harry aside and asked, "Why haven't you said anything about Billy's quickness with his pistols?"

"What do you expect me to say?"

"Just that we might have been able to get more of them alive if he'd waited a minute or so longer."

"Hayden, if Billy hadn't done what he did, you and I might both be dead right now. Dudley and the others were only a heartbeat away from being shot by me when Billy jumped in. Best advice I can give you about this job happened back there in Black Oak. Never give a bad man an even chance. If he'll let you do it, take him alive. If not, kill him before he kills you. Know it sounds harsh, but out here you have to do it that way or you'll end up dead as Travis Teel. I'd sure hate to hear Elizabeth read Shakespeare over you."

Well, that outing turned out the way far too many of our ventures into the Nations would in the future. Hell, we'd start out thinking we might find men like Killin' Bill Barber and Saginaw Bob but end up running all over the country because the real truth about law enforcement out in the Nations was that anything could happen and usually did. When the only law west of Fort Smith hung on our chests people seemed to come from under every rock and bush wanting us to check on something for them. More often than not, we would get diverted by criminal activity more dreadful than anything we'd planned on solving.

Anyway, Harry's party managed to pick up enough other miscreants, malefactors, and reprobates to make our trip an economic success. During the quieter moments of that second raid, I took some time to think on the events of the recent past and just how far things had come.

In the short span of six months, I'd gone from being a Kentucky farm boy, on the way to being a Texas farm boy, to a point where many recognized me as one of the most dangerous of Judge Isaac Parker's pack of lawdogs.

Met and squired the lovely Elizabeth Reed around Fort Smith. My finances were such that I had little to worry about for the foreseeable future. And, to tell the truth, no one was more awed or fascinated with the persona of Deputy U.S. Marshal Hayden Tilden than the man himself.

Magruder still ran loose somewhere in the Nations, but sooner or later he'd stumble or someone would give him up. He didn't know it, but death was waiting and its name was Hayden Tilden.

In spite of knowing all that, I couldn't have imagined in my wildest fantasies what was in store for me when we arrived at Judge Parker's courthouse on a cold, nasty day in February of 1879.

6

"He Made the Move with His Eyes"

WE DELIVERED OUR cargo of riffraff late in the afternoon of a Friday. Harry tried to schedule our arrival in the hope of taking the weekend off. I even entertained delusions of spending a good deal of my free time with Elizabeth. But all of us knew we'd have to sit around in the office till calluses began to form on our rumps, while we waited to testify if needed. And, true to form, nothing worked out the way I hoped or expected.

Barely settled myself into a cane-bottomed chair near the potbellied stove in the U.S. marshal's outer office when Judge Parker's private bailiff, George Wilton, visited me. Mr. Wilton was a tall, bald-headed, black gentleman who sported one of those big ole handlebar mustaches. Highly educated. Handsome dresser. Always wore a three-piece suit, tie, and polished boots.

He leaned close and spoke in a low, conspiratorial

tone. "Marshal Tilden, the Judge wishes to speak with you in his private office."

"Do you know why he wants to see me, Mr. Wilton?"

"Yes, sir, I do. But I am not at liberty to say at this time. His Honor heard of your return from the Nations and sent me to find you immediately. He awaits your appearance presently."

Being one of the newest of Parker's men, I wasted no time accompanying Mr. Wilton. When we entered the Judge's private chambers, he stood, shook my hand, and motioned for me to sit.

"Thank you, Mr. Wilton. That'll be all. Please close the door so Marshal Tilden and I can talk in private."

Wilton said, "Yes, Your Honor," and bowed himself out of the room.

Two large windows in the wall behind the Judge's desk hid themselves behind heavy drapes. A single lamp supplied the sparse light available. Strands of smoke from the wick floated toward the ceiling.

The day Judge Parker hired me, nervousness kept me from realizing the size of the room. He had one of those red leather couches decorated with lots of buttons stationed along the wall beside the entry. A low table brimming with copies of the *Fort Smith Elevator* sat in front of it. Glass-fronted cases, six or eight feet tall and stuffed with law books, covered almost every available inch of wall space. The private library gave the room the feel of a place where important decisions got made. That feel was reinforced by numerous framed documents on the wall behind the Judge's desk.

He leaned forward and rested his elbows on the desk. "Before we begin, Marshal Tilden, I must ask you to tender your most faithful promise that anything said in this room today will remain here."

Couldn't imagine what he meant or what he was getting at. We sat there staring at each other for several seconds, before I came to myself and said, "You have my promise, sir."

"Good. Very good." He leaned back in his chair, but maintained a serious and official demeanor. "Harry Tate gave me a full report on your conduct during the unfortunate events surrounding Travis Teel's demise on the Muddy Boggy. I have observed your progress with Marshal Bixley Conner and Handsome Harry with great interest."

"Do the best I can, sir." I fiddled with the rowel on my spur.

"You've surpassed all my most deeply held hopes for you, Hayden. Marshal Everett Lovelady's trust and belief in you has proven well placed."

"Thank you, Judge Parker." Felt uneasy with the situation to begin with. His compliments didn't help much because I still didn't know where he was headed.

A moment of silence hung in the air as if he wanted the gravity of what he was about to say to thoroughly take hold. His piercing stare made me squirm deeper into my chair.

"I have for some time now searched for a special man—a man capable of doing a very particular job. I believe you are that man, Hayden. You're young, new to this business, dedicated, and a quick learner. Traits I feel necessary for what I'm about to propose."

Being somewhat limited in life's experience, I was, of course, flattered by such praise from a man so powerful and famous. "You honor me greatly, Judge Parker."

"You do yourself the honor, young man. The conduct, skill, and willingness to perform that you've demonstrated for other, more experienced men speaks volumes for your future with this court. For those reasons, and because I believe you might well be the only man in my cadre of marshals who can do the job my way, I've asked you here today to take on a special assignment."

That almost rendered me speechless. "What kind of special assignment, Judge?"

"One which requires hard decisions, quick action, and, most especially, unflinching loyalty to me."

By that point my confusion bordered on total. He could see he'd lost me, and immediately said, "Let me approach this proposition by telling you a little story. Get comfortable. This will take a few minutes, but, trust me, there's a reason for it."

Screwed myself farther down into my leather throne just as he started. "Three weeks ago, in Strong, Arkansas, a one-dog town just north of the Louisiana state line, a nefarious killer named Comanche Jack Duer broke out of jail."

"Never heard of the man, Judge. Who is he?"

He slid a stack of wanted posters across the desk. The roughly sketched face of Comanche Jack glared at me from the top page.

"Jack Duer started his slide into lawlessness at an early age. A few weeks past his fourteenth birthday, he killed his stepfather after the man whipped him for not properly feeding the family's flock of chickens. It was first reported that he beat the man to death with a shovel. Truth of the killing proved far worse than the legend."

"Worse?"

"Oh, yes. Documents contained in this file indicate the

stepfather had been a God-fearing man who just happened to have married a lady named Edith Duer and took on the responsibility of a son destined for the gallows." The file folder with Duer's name on it followed the same path as the wanted posters. The size of that stack of documents indicated a long criminal career.

"A single killing must make but a small entry in a pile of paper this big."

"You're very perceptive, Hayden. Before his stepfather's death, Jack Duer fought with everyone in his hometown. Lied, and got caught in those lies. Cheated, and became known for it. Stole, and flaunted the pilfered items in the faces of the owners. Bullied older and younger children, and had been hauled in by the local sheriff for stabbing youngsters unthinking enough to stand up for themselves. According to court-recorded testimony, he set fire to several barns and once killed a cow because, and I quote from the record here, 'I jest couldn't stand the goddamned mooing any longer.' "

"Couldn't stand the mooing?" He smiled wryly at my amazement and continued.

"You can read it all yourself later. Shortly after the cow killing, he took a double-bit axe to the stepfather and chopped the living man into four fairly equal parts. He then shot his mother and set the family home ablaze. Neighbors testified that he laughed like a thing insane as he rode through town setting fire to anything he could put to torch. Then he ran for the Nations and took up with one of the worst gangs of cutthroats you can imagine. Schmoker Pratt and his bunch."

"Schmoker Pratt?" I twisted in the chair as another fat file folder slid across the desk and stopped next to Comanche Jack's.

"Mr. Pratt matriculated at the knee of Bloody Bill Anderson. Duer couldn't have found a more accomplished thief and murderer to fall in with. Schmoker took an immediate liking to the boy and made sure Duer rode at his side on raids into the far reaches of Texas, Nebraska, and Louisiana. Schmoker held a virulent hatred for Indians, especially the Comanche. He liked to conduct what he called Injun hunts after he'd robbed, raped, burned, and pillaged. Seems once his blood got up, he just couldn't quell an obscene appetite for murder until he rubbed out at least one Indian. Jack Duer evidently enjoyed the insanity of the killing immensely. His apprenticeship proved a huge success."

"How long have these two men been at this kind of behavior?"

"Years. More than any of us in the law enforcement business would like to recount. Duer became known as Comanche Jack because of the twenty-four scalps that adorn the back of a beaded leather coat he took from its owner—just before he skinned her alive. Those who've seen the coat, and lived to tell of it, say it gave him the appearance of a grizzly bear riding a horse."

"And he just escaped from jail? How'd he get caught?"

"For reasons I've been unable to discover, Jack stumbled into Strong, Arkansas, afoot and in pretty sorry shape. Local sheriff recognized him. Sheriff had once seen Duer shoot a child to death during the robbery of a bank in north Texas. He made the mistake of throwing Duer in his jail and sending a telegraph bragging that he had the infamous Comanche Jack safely in hand."

"Why do you consider his telegraph a mistake?"

"News of the capture swept through Fort Smith like a springtime twister. People threw Comanche Jack parties.

Celebrated his seizure and prospective appointment with Mr. Maledon and the Gates of Hell. All happened during your last visit to the Nations. No one here had any doubt he would hang. I even had offers from a dozen God-fearing folk to take Mr. Maledon's place on the gallows. Sadly, Schmoker Pratt heard of the capture, too."

"Pratt broke him out?"

"In a manner of speaking. He sent a notorious stomper named Springer McKlugg, and his cousin Rhoney Old-man, to do the job. If I know Schmoker Pratt, he most likely told his henchmen they'd be stripped naked and dragged through cactus if they didn't bring Duer back. So, they kicked the door to the jail down at about two in the morning three weeks ago. Only person with Duer at the time was the unfortunate sheriff. John Creed, the town mayor, telegraphed me that his man lived in the jail and kept a garden behind the building. Oldman and McKlugg dragged the poor wretch outside. Comanche Jack beat him to death with a long-handled hoe."

I tried not to appear dumbfounded by this tale of de-rangement and homicide. No two ways about it, the story appalled me. Covered my feelings about the whole thing with my newly acquired lawdog face. Learned the trick through careful observation of Bix Conner, Handsome Harry Tate, and Travis Teel. They called it "the stare." Copied that and other mannerisms. Used them when they worked to my advantage.

The Judge continued, "I'm told by informants in the Nations that these monuments to human depravity are currently celebrating Jack Duer's recent pardon at a hole in the ground named Kingfisher Creek. It's a jumble of shacks near a stinking little ditch so far down the Canadian it may be completely out of the Nations. I don't care about that. I want these men caught or killed."

Couldn't believe what I'd just heard. "You said 'killed' didn't you, Judge?"

"Caught or killed." He stressed the word *killed*. "Whichever you can accomplish with the least trouble. This is the first in what I feel will be a series of similar assignments, Marshal Tilden. In the past, men with posters out on them have been caught by accident for the most part. I want you to take on the job of finding the worst of the worst, and bringing them back, or killing them on the spot. I don't care which." His voice had a sharp, determined edge about it.

Had to think that one over for almost a minute. "When I arrived here, you told me you wanted them all brought in alive if possible, didn't you, Judge?"

He stood and moved to the window on the left behind his desk. The heavy curtain kept the lighting in the room subdued. He pushed it aside with his finger and stared at the grounds of the former army fortress below.

"Hayden, I want you to become the sword in my mighty right hand in the Nations." He didn't look directly at me. "No one must know of the exact agreement we make here today. No written contract will exist. After this meeting, all instructions will come from Mr. Wilton. He will, by his own means, present detailed background stories, wanted posters, and files pertaining to new assignments at any spot designated by you for that purpose. The information might be presented to you verbally, as it was here, or merely in the written form you have before you. I'll leave those details to Mr. Wilton. When you walk out of this office today, I hope you will have agreed to my offer. If you do not, details of this conversation must never go any farther."

I felt like a man holding a lightning rod in each hand who'd just been hit with a bolt big enough to cook a herd of buffalo in its own grease.

He faced me and said, "I must speak to Mr. Wilton for a moment. Please take that time to consider my offer." He started for the door, but stopped. "By the way, you'll be paid one hundred dollars a month, and whatever you might be able to make through the posted rewards on the men you capture or kill. And, since I recognize how important it is to you, if Saginaw Bob should turn up you will also have my permission to drop whatever you might be doing at that moment to pursue him." Then he disappeared into the outer office and gently pulled the door closed.

Didn't know what to do there for about ten minutes. But, in the end, I decided such chances rarely come around twice, and that passing on the offer would be the rough equivalent of drawing a straight flush and then folding because you lost your nerve.

After an absence of about fifteen minutes, Judge Parker burst back into the room and returned to his chair. "Well, can I count on you, Hayden?"

"Yes, Your Honor, you can."

"Good man. I knew you would make the right decision. The pictures that appear on those posters are the best we have. From what I've told you, it should be easy to spot Comanche Jack. Just look for that horrid coat of his. The others will most likely be nearby when you find him." He pushed a map across the desk to join the other materials.

"I've marked their approximate location in red. You can go alone, or take anyone who's willing to accompany you. My advice is to pick one man, stay out of sight, move at night when possible. Don't draw any more attention to yourself than necessary and go directly to Kingfisher Creek."

"If I have to kill these men, Judge, how can I prove who they were? Bringing a corpse back from such a distance might be nigh onto impossible."

He studied on that for a minute or so then rummaged in a lower drawer of his desk and pulled out a black bag. "Inside you'll find an ink pad and a small roller. Ink the palm of each dead man, and press it to the back of his poster. I'll take your word of its accuracy, and personally make certain that all bounties due you are paid forthwith."

"Well, guess that just about says it all. Have any suggestions on who I might ask to go along?"

"I leave all such details in your hands, Hayden. But I will approve whatever decision you make and see that no questions are asked. Everyone around here has more snakes than they can stomp. No one will even notice what you're doing. Now, go spend the evening with lovely Elizabeth. You can chase after this scum tomorrow."

He shook my hand vigorously and patted me on the back as he ushered me to the door. "Good luck, Hayden. Good hunting. And Hayden, do be careful." I thanked him and the thing was done. Didn't know it then, but the next six years were signed, sealed, and delivered.

Thought a long time on who could help me run Comanche Jack to ground. Liked Bix Conner, Quinten Moon, and Handsome Harry. Respected them because I'd worked with them. They were worthy of any man's trust. But I'd seen Billy Bird at work with his pistols. If two of us got caught in a tight, his blazing speed and deadly accuracy standing by my side would be a great comfort.

Late that afternoon, I pulled him aside and told him as little as I could about my meeting with Judge Parker and my plans for the trip. He smiled like I'd flattered him.

"I'll go with you, Hayden. Proud to." We shook hands on it and agreed to meet the next morning at the ferry.

Elizabeth's disappointment with my hasty departure was obvious. Gave her the bad news in the office of her father's store. Surrounded by accounting ledgers, ink-stained bills, and stacks of coins, she held my hand and looked at the floor. "So soon. So soon," she mumbled.

After dinner, when she kissed me good night, I thought my spurs were going to melt. For about ten seconds she had me thinking of going back to the Judge and squelching the whole thing. 'Course, those thoughts didn't have any serious chance of taking hold. Felt pretty certain the Judge had all but handed me an opportunity to rid the world of Saginaw Bob if I happened on him, and I couldn't let it pass.

Next morning, a new saddle hung on the gate to Thunder's stall. The envelope with my name on it contained a short note that read: *Hayden, I bought this from a drummer last week. It's called the California model and it's much lighter and more comfortable than your old saddle. I hope you like it. Elizabeth.*

Billy bragged about my new seat to the ferryman as we crossed the Arkansas. "You know, Charlie, wish I could find a woman who'd buy me somethin' that nice. Never seen one like that afore. All that fancy toolin' on the skirt, fenders, and stirrup leather really stand out there, Hayden. Better keep an eye on that one. Them Texas waddies spot it, you'll never see it again." He didn't stop admiring it till after we got a day out of Fort Smith.

We were considerable lucky with the weather. Warmed up slightly. Days weren't bad at all and nights were right tolerable. 'Course, I never cared for sleeping on the ground and hadn't got accustomed to it during my camp-outs with Bix and Harry. Guess there's probably lots of folks who think that anyone born and raised on a farm just loves rolling round on the ground any chance they get. Not me. Hated being dirty. Never went barefoot like my childhood friends and disappointed my father by not getting excited about those coon hunts he loved so much.

Billy allowed as how it would be nice to have a dog along. "Big hairy dog can keep you right toasty at night, and, if you teach him right, he'll bite the hand off'n any-body what touches you. Sometimes you don't even have to teach 'em. They'll do it anyway."

"You ever had a dog, Billy?"

"Yep. Great big 'un. Finer animal never drew breath. Called him Snapper. Worthless poltroon named Sluggo Blevins shot 'im. Claimed the dog peed on his foot. 'Bout a week after ole Sluggo killed Snapper, he got into an argument with a short-tempered drunk sittin' next to him in a two-holer behind a saloon named the Gold Rush, down in Texarkana. Feller shot ole Sluggo graveyard dead right in the middle of his business. I thank God nightly for the departure of that sorry piece of human waste." He flashed a toothy grin.

Three days into our westward march down the Cana-dian, I mentioned to Billy that I'd never had much use for handguns. "But I admire the level of skill you showed when you busted Jug Dudley out."

He grinned with pleasure at the compliment. "Some time and attention and you'd be just as good as me. It's an easy trade to latch on to."

"I don't know, Billy. The rifle's served me right well."

"Yeah, but it ain't worth spit in one of them up-close, nose-to-nose dustups. Back there in Black Oak, your big ole rifle caused that poor dumb cowboy some serious sufferin'. Near as we was to 'im, you needed a pistol or a shotgun."

Late that afternoon, he took the Colt I'd bought at Arkansas Post and dismembered the weapon on his saddle blanket. "I'm gonna take any burrs or rough spots down with my Arkansas stone. Then I'll stick a tiny piece of leather behind the main spring down here where it screws to the frame. Makes the hammer easier to thumb back. Old hands call it 'tuning the trigger.' When we get back to Fort Smith we'll get you a brace of well-seasoned pistols. This one'll do in a pinch, and once I get it back together it'll be a bunch easier for you to snap off a round or two."

"Where'd you learn how to 'tune the trigger'?"

"Aw, back in 'seventy-four, 'bout a year after Colt first started sellin' these Peacemaker guns, a feller callin' himself a factory salesman showed up at Reed's. Had a company gunsmith with him. He tuned both my pistols while I watched. I've done the same for several of the other marshals since. You'll be surprised at the difference this'll make in the action."

An hour later, he handed the gun back. "I unloaded it so you can practice your draw. Since you carry the gun across your belly, the move to it's different than mine. Your hand has to start out closer to the weapon. Personally believe a holster should be up high on your hip, the way I wear it. Just makes carryin' the thing while ridin' or pullin' it a whole bunch easier. But every man has to do what's most comfortable."

For the next few days, he made me practice drawing the gun and snapping off rounds as we rode along. I moved my holster to my right hip and tried to get everything arranged exactly the way he had his. Never matched his speed, but after so much practice I came close. He advised me on my grip and how to point and squeeze, rather than try to aim every shot.

"Usually the only time you're gonna fire one of these things is when you're so close to the feller shootin' back you could probably spit on him. In Black Oak we couldn'ta been more'n ten feet from those old boys." He snatched his pistol from its holster, gave it a fancy spin, and dropped it back. "I ain't ever seen a serious pistol fight yet where the opponents were more'n eight or ten feet away from each other. My personal rule is, don't git in a rush, but git 'em out fast and blast away. If you keep your head, and you're worth anything at all as a shot, you can just about bet you'll hit what you're pointin' at."

"Don't think I'll ever be able to match that shot you put in Jug Dudley, Billy. Which leads me to a question I need to ask. Why'd you bust him out the way you did?" We'd stopped on the trail, and he had me shooting at twigs and rocks he placed at various distances.

"He made a move for his gun."

"I could see him too. Didn't see his hand move."

"He made the move with his eyes. First move's always there. Once you've seen it, you'll recognize it from then on. Some ole pistoleros would argue with me 'bout that, but I'm pert sure they're wrong. If I hadn't popped Dudley when I did, he'da killed Handsome Harry—and maybe you." He tugged at my sleeve to correct the direction my pistol was pointed.

The man's affection for his revolvers bordered on obsession. He spent lavish amounts of time fussing with them. When I questioned him about it, he said, "You have to take care of 'em. Clean 'em. I've always felt they're kinda like a woman. Take good care of 'em, and they'll never let you down. I know how you feel about that Winchester, and that's fine, but you can't tote that big sucker with you everywhere. You need something easier to carry, something more personal. When you get to where you feel like you're caressing the grips when you pull a pistol, you'll know what I mean."

Swore to myself I'd become just as accomplished with a handgun as the rifle. No way to deny it, Billy's shot to the brain of Jug Dudley so impressed me with its speed and accuracy I decided I had to become as good—if not better. Figured such skill could only help when Saginaw Bob finally got lined up in my sights.

Five days out I realized Billy hadn't bothered to look at the Judge's map of the Nations. 'Course, I'd told him where we were headed. He seemed unconcerned. "Ever been to Kingfisher Creek, Billy?"

"Oh, yeah, several times. Old hands like Bix and Travis used to call it 'Thieves' Paradise,' but it's as far from 'Paradise' as a pig is from feathers. Harry and me visited the place 'bout six months ago. Good ways out, but it ain't hard to find."

The lush timber just west of the Arkansas gave way to a region of stunted trees and much flattened land. That became even more barren the farther west we went. During the day, the wind never stopped blowing, which prompted Billy to observe, "Think the good Lord created

this place one afternoon when he was pissed about something. Wildest and worst come here when they've sinned
beyond savin'. It's the closest spot to perdition I've ever
been or ever want to see. Keep 'em loaded, and be watchful, Hayden. There are evil men behind every rock out
here."

Our eighth night on the trail, we bedded down without
a fire. 'Bout the time my head hit the saddle, thought I
heard gunshots north of our camp in almost exactly the
spot Judge Parker had marked on his map. Climbed the
highest tree I could find and saw light in the distance.
Kept thinking, tomorrow, we'll catch you tomorrow—or
we'll kill you.

Next day, we staked our horses to scrub bushes under
an outcropping of rock. Snaked our way to the top of a
runty hill overlooking a rough camp almost half a mile
away. Several slapdash buildings dotted a low, greasy
spot next to the creek. Buck and battened walls had aged
to a muddy gray color, and the roofs on some of the
unoccupied ones appeared to have caved in.

"Them shacks seem to have just growed up like weeds,
don't they." Billy squinted through his long glass. "Most
of 'em ain't much more'n lean-tos. Don't know 'bout
you, but it ain't my idea of anything like 'Paradise.' "

Watched that camp all day. Watched and waited. Felt
it best to keep an eye on them and take in as much information as we could before doing anything else. We
were downwind of them. The place smelled mighty bad
even as far away as our hiding spot. By the time we got
back to our horses we'd learned a good deal.

"Well," said Billy, "there are at least six of 'em.
Maybe seven. Comanche Jack's there for sure. I recognized that coat soon's he came outside. Already knew

Springer McKlugg and Rhoney Oldman. They're the two sleeping in that lean-to nearest the creek. Think that great big feller, with the ragged hat sportin' the red plume, was Schmoker Pratt. Him and Jack staked out the biggest of them lean-tos, the one in the middle."

"What about the two others?" I asked.

"Didn't recognize them or that skinny one that kept shufflin' back and forth from shack to shack. But I'd bet my saddle, anyone travelin' with this bunch sure ain't teachin' Sunday school in their spare time."

We decided our chances of nabbing any of the gang away from camp bordered on remote to impossible, and catching them each at separate times was virtually unthinkable.

Billy came up with the best plan. "We'll wait till 'bout three in the morning and try to take 'em by surprise. Go in with shotguns. Lot easier to hit 'em in the dark with one of these nasty short-barreled poppers." He breeched that twelve-gauge of his, pulled each shell out, examined it briefly, and dropped it back. Snapped the gun closed as if he thought the discussion was over.

Figuring out how to arm ourselves was one thing, but it was left for me to bring up the tougher decision. "Billy, do we try and catch them, or do we just kill them?"

He didn't have any more problems with his conscience at Kingfisher Creek than he had at Black Oak. "Any one of those men down there would slit your belly open, pull out your guts, and set them on fire 'fore your living eyes. They ain't carryin' them big ole coffin-gripped bowie knives for nothin'. Our posters say alive or dead. Accordin' to you, the Judge said caught or killed. Money's the same either way. It's as clear as I need to see it. I say we kill 'em. Personally like this kind dead, else they might do for us on the trail back. From what we saw this morning, they'll all be so drunk tonight they'll never know what hit 'em."

After seeing my own family murdered, killing three of the men responsible, and shooting that cowboy in Black Oak, I didn't have much trouble going along with Billy on the thing.

Been thinking about what I'd do ever since we crossed the Arkansas. Judge Parker made it pretty clear to me that he didn't care one way or the other. Far as I was concerned, Duer, Pratt, McKlugg, Oldman, and anyone else at Kingfisher Creek would never get another chance to chop up living people with a double-bit axe if we put an end to them right then and there.

'Bout three the next morning, we crept into camp. They didn't have any dogs, and no one stood guard. Full moon made everything pretty easy to see. Whole place smelled of bad whiskey, dead animals, and outhouse leavings.

Billy whispered, "Anyone this nasty don't deserve to live. Sons of bitches shouldn't be breathin' the same air as decent folks."

We just waltzed in like Saturday night at a barn dance. Went straight to the shack where we'd seen Commanche Jack and Schmoker Pratt that afternoon. Billy slipped inside. I stood guard. Knew any gunfire would rouse the others.

For about ten or fifteen seconds didn't hear anything. Then, two deafening blasts lit the inside of that mud-roofed shack like Fourth of July whizbangs. I knelt beside the doorway in a shadow cast by the crumbling roof. Pulled the shotgun tight to my shoulder.

Three or four murky figures stumbled into the darkness

jerking at their pants. One of 'em said, "Come on, boys, that there shootin' sounded like it were right here in camp."

One of his friends had a plan. "Best check on Jack and Schmoker."

In the dark, those boys limped toward me mumbling, cussing, and waving their guns. Waited till they were so close I couldn't miss—maybe twenty, twenty-five feet away. Closed my eyes for about a second. Kept me from going blind from the muzzle flash. Opened up on them with both barrels. Twelve-gauge sprayed a pattern of buckshot that cut through them like weeds under a scythe. Blast stopped all movement in the open space in front of the lean-to. For a while it was so quiet you could hear crickets shushing each other.

"Everything safe with you, Hayden?" Billy stepped out of the lean-to, breeched his shotgun, and dropped new shells into the chamber.

"Fine, just fine, Billy."

He snapped the gun closed and started for the men I'd blasted. "Looks like you sent these ole boys to the devil's doorstep." He pushed at the bodies with the barrel of his shotgun and rolled one over with his foot. "Hope you nasty sons-a-bitches enjoy your new home in Hades. Say hello to Satan for me."

We dragged the men he'd killed from the shack to the spot where my three dead ones lay. Billy searched each man, but their ragged clothing contained no money and little else of any value. He'd just finished on the last one when we heard noise near the stock pen. Before we could get there, the sound of a horse running hard for the Canadian sailed back to us from the dark.

Billy cocked his ear toward the retreating thump of the

hoofbeats. "Must be the sixth one. That skinny one I didn't recognize. From the sound of it, he's travelin' light. Stupid jug-head's goin' straight back the direction we came. He'll be easy to catch. I'd be willing to bet we have him by tomorrow night."

Two hours later the sun came up, and we identified the bodies of Schmoker Pratt, Comanche Jack Duer, Springer McKlugg, Rohney Oldman, and a well-known rapist and killer called Stinky Jack Kegley. Anyone who'd ever been within ten feet of the man knew how he got his nickname.

Slathered ink on the hand of each corpse and pressed it to the back of his poster the way Judge Parker told me. Below every inky picture I wrote, *This is the hand of* and then the man's name.

Billy scratched his chin and watched in silence, until I'd pressed the inked palm of each man to his poster. "New one on me, Hayden. Never seen or heard of such a thing."

"The Judge told me how to do it. It's all we need to prove our claim when we get back to Fort Smith."

Soon as I got those men identified, Billy scrounged up every piece of rope he could find in the camp and hung the bodies from several trees along the river. Above the head of each man he tacked a copy of his poster. Schmoker Pratt got strung up last. In bold letters on the back of his poster Billy wrote, SHOT AND HANGED— MURDERER, THIEF, CHILD KILLER.

I argued for burying them, but gave in when he said, "This'll be a warnin' to those like 'em. Good many of their kind stop here one time or another. Word'll get around. The bad 'uns will find out who did this too. Just hearin' the name Hayden Tilden in about six months is gonna make some of them ole boys mess their pants like bad kids eatin' green apples."

Soon as Pratt got swinging pretty good, we opened the corral and turned their horses out. Wanted to take the animals and sell them, but knew they'd slow us down on our run for the one who got away.

Then, we rode like devils all day long. Let Billy run the trail. He went at the job like a banshee on a horse. Early the next afternoon, we spotted our rider through my long glass. He'd slowed to a walk.

Billy squirmed in his saddle and held the glass to his eye for a long time. "You know, Hayden, we work it just right, we'll be able to catch or kill the last of Schmoker's bunch 'fore dark. World'll be a safer place when they've all been sent to a festerin' perdition."

So we made one more sprint toward our unsuspecting prey just about the time he tried a new dash for freedom. Rider was around three hundred yards away, running across a nice flat spot that gave me a good target. Called Billy to a stop and jumped off Thunder with the Winchester in my hand. Flipped the rear sight up and adjusted the peep to what looked like the right distance. Squinted through the hole and squeezed off my shot.

Report from the rifle raced behind the bullet and just about the time it got to the outlaw he turned and looked back at us as his horse stumbled and fell. Rider went headfirst into a clump of thick brush.

Billy took his hat off and slapped it against his leg. "I do declare that was the most amazin' rifle shot I've ever seen." He sat in the saddle, stared, and shook his head in disbelief.

"Don't be making too much out of it, Billy. Shot at the man, not the horse."

Didn't have any trouble finding the horse. Rider took a bit more effort, but we finally spotted him still tangled up in the briars and bushes. We dragged him, scratched and bleeding from numerous cuts, out of the brambles. His hat fell off when Billy shoved him to the ground.

"Whoa, now. What've we got here?" Billy stumbled back like a man who'd put his bucket down a well and come up with a skunk.

The girl pushed thick black hair out of her eyes. A sugar-loaf sombrero had hidden the ebony cascade that now flowed down her back.

Billy jerked his hat off and stood shaking his head. "Don't know what I expected, but, my God, she sure ain't it."

The girl crawfished along the ground until a sizable rock got in her way. She pulled herself up on it and sat with her face in her hands. "Could I have some water? I haven't had a drink since yesterday." She sounded done in. Her voice had no strength. Its raspy quality made her hard to understand.

I gave her one of my canteens. She pulled down more than half of it in one gulp, and then spent the rest washing her face. Billy brought some whiskey and rags from his war bag, and pretty soon I realized that our stray just might be quite a looker under all that dirt and blood.

He kept dousing pieces of cloth with the liquor then handing them to her. Didn't take long before most of her cuts were clean.

"Can you tell us your name, miss?" he asked.

"Talbot. My name's Missy Talbot."

Didn't particularly want to ask the next question, but had too. "Why were you in the company of such worthless men as Schmoker Pratt, Comanche Jack, and the like?"

"Who are you, sir, and why did you shoot my horse?" Some metal crept back into her voice. She sat up straight and gave me a hard look. Her eyes gleamed like case-hardened steel. Pale blue. She never blinked.

"Deputy U.S. Marshals Hayden Tilden and Billy Bird at your service, Miss Talbot." We both nodded and touched the brims of our hats. "You left a bunch of bad men back there. I'm sorry, but I must ask you again, how did you come to be in their company?"

Her shoulders sagged. Then the story started—slow and painful at first, faster as she went. "Think it was three weeks ago. Maybe longer, maybe not." She shook her head, ran her fingers through the inky colored hair. Pulled at the twigs and briars in it. "The man I worked for, me, and two of his other girls, were traveling south along the trail from Dodge City. Herby, that's the man I worked for, liked to winter in Dallas. Had a good season in Dodge, and got started a bit late this year." She bent over with her elbows on her knees and stared at the ground. Didn't speak for several seconds. Then she sat up and stared directly into my eyes. "Herby was trying to get us across the Canadian River when this huge, nasty man with a red plume in his hat flagged us down." Her eyes went vacant and her voice became more distant. "He killed them all. It happened so fast I couldn't believe it. Would've killed me too, but his gun misfired. He said it was a sign and he didn't like to go against signs. So, he stole what he wanted from my dead friends, then took me back to that pigsty on the creek. We were alone for the first day or so. Then the others came. They took turns going at me. I actually thought it would never end. Even planned to kill myself. They were such animals. Last night something woke everyone up. I heard shots. Seemed like they all vanished. So I stole a horse—and ran."

Her flat tone carried almost no emotion, but she kept clenching and unclenching her fists. And as I watched, a single huge tear formed in her left eye and rolled down her cheek. That drop of water was a messenger who came as a warning of something horrible to follow. When it touched her lips, she began to sob. Her head fell, and she cradled it in her hands again. Her body shook, and the horrors of her capture escaped in torrents of tears.

Billy recoiled like a puppy that had just discovered a porcupine. His understanding of women appeared non-existent and of crying women, he knew even less.

"Do somethin', Hayden. Do somethin'." He made little ushering motions at the girl and bobbed his head in her direction.

I put my hand on her shoulder, leaned down, and whispered in her ear. "They're all dead, Miss Talbot. Billy and I killed them all. They'll never hurt you or anyone else again."

She leaned heavily against me and clutched at my arm till she hung from my shoulders. I sat on the ground with the sobbing girl attached to me until she wept herself to sleep. Billy covered her with a blanket. Later that night, as he snored away, I sat with my back to the fire and bit my fingers as tears streamed down my own cheeks.

The girl's experience sounded so like that of my mother and sister that when the full impact of what confronted me finally came, I found it almost too much to bear. In an effort to keep from stepping over the boundaries of my own sanity, I found comfort in the knowledge that I might not have been able to save Rachael or my mother, but at least I had saved Missy Talbot.

When I finally fell asleep, I dreamed of my home in Kentucky. My family gathered for supper. The table had been moved outside beneath a tree in the front yard, because of the summer heat. I sat across from my mother, who smiled at me and said, "I see you've made a new friend. You must take care of her. I want you to promise me that you'll always look after Missy. Will you promise me that, Hayden?"

"Yes, Mother, I promise."

"I'm so pleased, son." She reached across the table and touched my fingers. I awoke, and found Missy Talbot sitting beside me, clutching my hand.

"Am I right here? You've just said that you became Judge Parker's secret bounty hunter. His own personal assassin?"

Over our heads, the ceiling fan lazily pushed air around, but the rising heat of the day required something more forceful to really help cool us down. I pulled my private set of Brown's Funeral Home fans from the stock I kept in the magazine rack beside my chair and pitched one into the boy's lap.

"Use that, Junior. Have to get it going pretty good as the day goes on. Big magnolia tree there behind you will get mighty fragrant pretty soon. Sometimes the odor is almost overpowering."

"You didn't answer my question, Mr. Tilden. When you and Billy shot Duer, Pratt, et al., hadn't you become Judge Parker's bounty killer?"

Let that one hang there over the table for a minute before I answered. "Yes. But don't act all surprised and stunned on me here, Junior. Told you from the start that I performed a special job for Judge Parker. Duer and Pratt just happened to be the first of a long list of snakes I took pleasure in stomping for him."

"You took pleasure in killing people?" He said that like he wanted to hock up a gob of something and spit it out on the table.

"Duer and his bunch weren't people. They were the closest thing to animals you can be and still wear boots and walk upright. Between the five of those men, Billy Bird and I estimated they'd slaughtered something in the neighborhood of fifty people. Some of those folks died in ways too awful to describe. But just for the record, I'll tell you about a couple of their better efforts." Took a big sip from my glass before going on.

"Not long after those two joined forces in the Territories, they broke into the ranch house of a man named Duckworth out in the Creek Nation. They nearly beat him and his wife senseless, but stopped so he could watch the whole gang take turns going at his wife for two days running. Then they shot her and cut off her head while he watched. Just for giggles, they set him on fire and laughed while he burned. We know all this because one of Pratt's bunch, a murdering slug named Jimbo Kitchens, got caught not long after that little party and confessed to the whole thing like he was proud of it. I read his sworn statement in the package the Judge gave me on the gang. Kitchens should've hung, but tried to escape and got accidentally shot thirteen times in the process. That's just one of the numberless reasons I would have helped Billy kill them whether he actually wanted me to or not."

Junior swallowed hard. "Jesus," he mumbled under his breath.

"Don't get all soft and mushy brained on me here, boy. The worst people living in North America found their way to the Nations. No other place like it ever existed in the history of this country. Personally rubbed out a bunch of them evil skunks and won't be made to feel guilty about it by the snot-nosed likes of you. Duer, Pratt, and that bunch should've been drawn and quartered, set on fire, hung, and shot—best I could do was shoot a few of them a time or two. They were just as dead. Thank God."

His eyes blinked so fast, thought he'd take off and fly around the porch. "Okay. Look, I don't want to get into a bare-knuckled debate with you about capital punishment."

He got this puzzled look on his face when I started laughing at him. "Good thing, Junior. Might be eighty-eight years old, but I'd still give you a pretty good fight and just might put a black-'n'-blue butt-kicking on you. If it came to pistols and knives you wouldn't stand any more chance than a grasshopper in a tornado." Slapped my knee and laughed out loud.

"You don't have a gun on you now . . . do you?"

"Oh, absolutely not, son. Well . . . maybe just a little one."

He shook his head and said, "Lord almighty, old man, you are full of surprises, aren't you? Do the nurses know about that?

"Well, no, Junior. Never had any need to shoot a nurse—at least not yet. However, Leona Wildbank has tempted me every once in a while."

7

"YOU CAN'T SAY NO"

I PUT MISSY Talbot in a room near mine at the Hotel Pines. For the first few days after our return from the Nations, didn't see the raven-haired girl at all. I fell into the routine of court appearances and listening to the testimony and horror stories of the other marshals. Checked on her every day, but she refused to open the door when I knocked and would often mumble excuses through the tiny crack she allowed when we spoke.

Then one afternoon about three or four weeks after our arrival in town, I pushed open the frosted glass door of the hotel and almost ran over her in the vestibule. Her black hair swung freely down her back and her face glowed in a way I never expected possible. She wore a new cream-colored dress that had a stand-up lace collar whose frilly top tickled her chin and a hat that matched her dress with white gauze that came down over her eyes. She looked every inch the well-bred, sophisticated lady.

"I just couldn't bear to have you see me until I was presentable," she whispered as she pressed herself against me at the stair landing. The deep voice and southern-fried accent dripped of swampy bayous, cotton fields, and white-columned homes. For some reason I hadn't noticed that sound during our return from the Nations.

The cuts and scratches on her face had all but vanished. Any fine lines left were disguised with the skilled use of a pearl-handled fan. Scrubbed and cleaned, she smelled wonderful. I recognized her perfume as that used exclusively by some of Elizabeth's more prominent and wealthy female friends.

My lack of worldly experience with women did not change when my quickly made relationship with Elizabeth manifested itself. She kept me on the straight and narrow and also eliminated any reason for visits to the saloons and houses where women who practiced the same trade as Missy worked. That didn't mean I wasn't aware of them and where they could be found. Every man who lived on the edge of the wildness knew where to find whores.

"I had to look my best for you." She reached for my hand and took it in hers. "I'd like to take you to dinner, Marshal Tilden. Think that's the least I can do for the man responsible for my deliverance from that vile beast Schmoker Pratt."

"You don't have to do that, Missy."

She smiled as I glanced nervously around the hotel lobby. My face flushed and my ears burned from the rush of blood that colored them.

"Why, Mr. Tilden, I do believe you're blushin'. You've never been taken to dinner before by an appreciative female, have you? Well, there's always a first time, and tonight's the night." She firmly grasped my elbow and guided me through the door and onto the boardwalk.

Figured the best method to deal with the situation was the unvarnished truth. "Missy, I've been seeing someone ever since my arrival in town. I don't think it would be proper for me to mislead you about such things." She squeezed the muscle of my arm as she escorted me down the boardwalk.

"Ah, yes, Miss Elizabeth Reed, I believe. The lovely blond whose father owns the dry goods store across the street." She waved in the direction of Reed's Mercantile as though it was a nuisance insect. "You needn't worry, Hayden. I'm not out to steal you away from your lady. I know my place. But that shouldn't keep us from being friends. You saved my life. I owe you more than I can ever repay. A meal won't hurt anything. Besides, Miss Reed will understand. I know you'll tell her, and if you don't, someone else will. It's just an innocent dinner between a famous marshal and the woman whose life he saved." Her voice dripped of magnolia trees and mint juleps. She squeezed my arm again, fluttered her eyelashes, and smiled.

Turned out to be a marvelous dinner. She'd already made the arrangements at one of Fort Smith's finest restaurants. Place named Le Coeur Rouge. Frenchy feller named Paul LeMat owned it. On the way to New Orleans, he fell off a riverboat after someone hit him in the head and robbed him. Washed up in Arkansas. Despite the primitive condition of the place, he decided to stay. My sweet Lord, but that man could cook.

His restaurant had eight tables covered with white linen. Each decorated with a glass vase that held a single red rose. Always wondered where he got those roses. He served good wine, fine food, and exceptional cigars. Altogether, Le Coeur Rouge smelled better than any eating joint I've been in since. There's just something about French pastry that stays with you once you've got a whiff of the real stuff.

Found the beautiful Missy Talbot charming, gifted with a quick wit, and when she laughed everyone around her smiled. Men turned bright red if she paid them any attention. About halfway through the meal, I realized it wouldn't take much to be attracted to her in a way I didn't want . . . and had given no thought to until that moment.

On the way back from the Nations, she'd slept next to me on the ground. Allowed it because I felt sorry for the shattered girl. Now, there seemed to be nothing left of the broken creature who had clung to me like she was drowning in the horrors of Kingfisher Creek. What sat across the table that night was an astonishingly confident woman who focused all her attention on no one else in the room but me. Any man who can say he wouldn't be flattered by such attention is a liar, and I'll tell him that to his face.

Over the after-dinner wine, she said, "I arrived in Dallas, Texas, barefoot and starving. My father left me in a wagon and went out to hunt for food. He never came back. To this day, I still don't know what happened to him. After Mother's death, friends had encouraged our move from New Orleans to Texas. They called it 'the Promised Land.' " Every time she spoke I got this image of sagging bayou trees draped with Spanish moss.

She twirled her wineglass around between her fingers and called for the waiter to refill it. "I'd just passed my fourteenth birthday at the time and, within a week, was taken under the wing of a kindly man who promised me everything I could ever want—oldest story in the book. Herby Fallon had worked his trade long enough to know he had something special in me. I got treated accordingly."

Her perfume, mixed with the wine and another fragrance I couldn't identify, excited me in the most unexpected way. I sat, stared into her eyes, and wondered what she had in mind for dessert.

"Herby always saw to it that his girls were educated, clean, and well-dressed. He took us to different towns around the country at various times of the year. We visited Kansas City, Memphis, or New Orleans and, occasionally, one of the large cow towns in Kansas. No matter where we went, Herby always tried to get us back to Dallas before hard cold and winter set in. He loved Dallas winters. That obsession with warm weather brought him to the banks of the Canadian—and his death—at a time of the year when we would normally have been in Texas for a month."

I wondered, but didn't question, how she'd come by enough money to afford this obviously expensive evening. The meal, wine, and after-dinner drinks had cost a great deal. But there was never any mention of a check.

When the last ashes from my cigar were crushed out, she said, "I think it's time to go now."

The waiter bowed as he pulled her chair back. "It is always a great pleasure to serve you, Miss Talbot." He clicked his heels together, bowed again, then kissed the back of her hand.

"I have been to Fort Smith once or twice." She took my arm again and smiled as we left our table. Every man in that room watched as she swayed her way out onto the boardwalk.

I stood aside when she opened the door to her room. "Please come in, Hayden. I have something special in mind to finish off our evening."

I hesitated. Elizabeth might understand dinner. Not this. But the temptation proved too much for me. She was beautiful, and I was young and weak. Stood there for so long, she offered the invitation again.

"I promise not to bite." She took my hand and pulled me inside. "At least . . . not too hard."

Almost every place a garment could hang in that room was decorated with something lovely and feminine. She led me to a chair beside the only table and poured me a glass of wine from a bottle that waited in a silver bucket. Her glass touched mine, and she slid into my lap as she sipped the deep red liquid.

"What's about to happen is as much for me . . . as it is for you. I need you tonight, Hayden. You can't say no." She leaned forward and kissed me. When our lips parted she said, "We can continue the story of my life some other time."

"But, Missy, I—I . . ."

"Don't speak," she whispered. Then, she kissed me inside out. My toes almost chewed a hole in the soles of my boots.

I made something a bit more than a half-hearted effort at resistance, but the wonder of that evening and the spell cast by Missy Talbot's beauty made it impossible to push her away. We clung to each other, immersed in the raw need of the moment. I fell into her bed and watched, unbelieving, as my clothing flew toward the ceiling then dropped to the floor in a heap.

"Missy, I knew girls back in Kentucky, but, in spite of all the things that have occurred recently, we're about to enter an area where I have no experience." Didn't know for sure if it was the thing to say or not. And in the end it didn't really matter. Once she got me going in the right direction, my excitement—and her skill—led me into an encounter I never expected and gypsy palm readers couldn't have foretold.

She pulled my head down on her breast and whispered, "I know you wanted this to happen on your wedding night in the arms of the lovely Miss Reed. But here it is, Hayden. Close your eyes and enjoy it."

I jumped headfirst into a fiery web of passion spun by that black-haired gal. She made love like sunrise would be the end of us.

About ten minutes into the heat and fire of her, she hissed, "No other man will ever see me like this." When we finished, she slept curled around me as though her mission in life was to protect me from the future.

The next morning, we took breakfast in her room. While we ate, she detected the confusion of my mind. "I don't love you the way your Miss Reed does, Hayden, but I do love you. Make no mistake of it. You and I are forever linked in a way others will never be able to understand. For the rest of your life, I will always be somewhere nearby, and I will be there for whatever you might need."

"Missy, I don't know what to say."

"You needn't say anything." She paused, and went into deep thought for a moment before continuing. "As you've probably detected, I have no concerns when it comes to money. I found out early on where Herby kept his, and how to get it if anything ever happened to him.

What he had is now mine. I got it all, and I don't think anyone even knows yet that he's dead."

"Are you trying to tell me something here, Missy?"

She stared at me for a moment. "I plan to settle in Dallas. There's a hotel down on Houston Street I've always admired. I think I'll buy it. I've always liked room service, and there's no better way to get it that I can think of than to be the owner of a good hotel."

"What about your life before we met?"

A frown brought hard creases to the edges of her lips. "I don't plan to ever go back to the life I led before we met, but I can't yet deny the past." She stood, went to the window, and peeked at the street below. Light poured through her transparent gown. "I'm leaving for Texas in the morning. You can reach me at . . . let me see . . . yes, the Empress. I'll call it the Empress Hotel. I'll be back this way as soon as I can, but for now I have business that needs my attention."

Blood thundered through my eardrums. I couldn't believe it had all happened to begin with, and now it was over. I felt like a man trying to ride two horses at the same time that gets thrown and kicked to pieces.

"I know this is all very sudden, but it can't wait. I have to go now. You could come with me, but I would never ask such a thing of you because I know you wouldn't do it." She took my hand and kissed the palm. No one had ever kissed me in such an intimate manner. It brought me to tears. "At least we have one more night," she whispered in my ear. "The stage doesn't leave till tomorrow."

The next morning, I stood in the street and watched her coach dissolve into a cloud of gritty Arkansas dust. As suddenly as she'd appeared in my life, she vanished.

Nothing left but the faint smell of her perfume on the front of my shirt.

Next time I saw Elizabeth, she misinterpreted the change she detected in me. "I understand," she said. "It's just the Nations. Although you came here with a ready-made reputation, Hayden Tilden, nothing could prepare a man for the realities of that devilish place." My guilty feelings for what had happened kept me from making any effort to change her mistaken belief.

A week to the day after Missy left town, Handsome Harry pulled up a chair beside me in the U.S. marshal's outer office. "Hayden, I just heard that Saginaw Bob and his most recent gang of disciples robbed a bank in Texarkana yesterday."

"Yesterday? Who told you?"

"Got a telegraph message from local law down there. He said Bob managed to murder a bank teller, and two blundering gobs of spit with him trampled a child to death as they fled the scene of the crime."

"No one tried to stop them?"

"Posse of farmers and storekeepers chased 'em into the Choctaw Nation. They gave it up when Bob and his bunch ambushed them over near the Kiamichi Mountains and killed an Arkansas deputy sheriff."

"Good Lord, Harry. Three more dead?"

"There'll a lot more than three by the time we're able to put a stop to the Preacher. That slippery, ground-huggin' snake's been around a long time. I suspect he'll kill again before we can do anything."

I jumped out of my chair and jerked the office door open. "Not if I can stop 'im."

Judge Parker gave me a fistful of John Does. Billy and I were on the trail the next day. We took a tumbleweed wagon and a jailer named Ellis McPherson with us. I pushed 'em hard and managed to get to the Jacks Fork River in little over a week. We poked around in every crevice and ravine we could find. Even spent three days on Pine Mountain—nothing out there, absolutely nothing.

When the weather started to go bad, Ellis said, "We best lay up at the first stock station we can find. This here stuff is gonna get a lot worse before it clears up."

Two days later we pulled up in a rotten hole in the ground that had a sign over the stockman's shed that read, ANTLERS—HOME OF THE BIGGUNS.

Ellis stopped the wagon. "I wanna get out of this stuff, but I gotta tell you boys that I don't care for the look of this place at all." He had a good point.

"Looks a lot like Kingfisher Creek, don't it, Hayden?" Billy laughed, but I could tell it wasn't really a joke. "Even so, we need to get our animals sheltered and get inside ourselves. This stuff is changing to ice fast. My butt's gonna be froze to my saddle pretty soon."

"He's right, Hayden." Ellis broke ice off his hat brim. "I don't mind the cold so much myself, but these horses gotta get out of it and right soon."

Billy and I followed the wagon as it rolled up to the largest of the so-called houses. Several smaller shacks and sheds surrounded it. We rode past all of them and stopped just outside the door with the sign over it. As Ellis tied the reins to his hand break, a volley of gunshots exploded from the windows and doors.

Billy and I jumped off our horses. Pulled rifles and shotguns as we went down. Landed behind the water trough. The horses pulling the tumbleweed bolted. Then, a second volley splattered mud, ice, and wood splinters all around us.

We lay on our backs looking at our toes. Billy grinned and punched me with his elbow. "Can you believe we were less than twenty feet away, and they just burned up almost a dozen rounds and didn't even hit us, a horse, or the wagon?" He rolled over on his side and yelled, "Ellis, you alive?"

"Yeah, I'm alive. I'm under the porch. So don't shoot me when you start blastin' these dumb clod kickers. But hurry up and do somethin'. They's big ole dogs under here. The sons-a-bitches ain't real friendly. They's a blue tick hound next to me has the biggest teeth I done ever seen on a dog!"

Billy chuckled. "Hayden, if we had a stick of dynamite you could pull that Morgan Bryce trick again. We'd jus' blow 'em outta there."

"Billy, I can't believe they fired on a party of marshals. They have to know who we are. Everyone in the Nations recognizes these wagons."

"Well, ole hoss, it's mighty obvious you ain't been at this long enough. I've had people shoot at me when I've been in the company of fifty deputies." Another round of gunfire sent ice balls flying all around us.

"Sweet Jesus, Billy. We can't just lay here forever."

"Nope. You're right about that. 'Course, these boys might just be drunk on some kinda homemade skull-buster and don't have any idea what they're doin'. But we're not gonna find out layin' here on our backs."

He jumped to his feet with one of those sawed-offs in each hand. I almost passed out. "Billy, what the—?" He took three steps toward the porch and fired one barrel from each of the guns at the front door. Buckshot ripped it to shreds. The other two barrels opened the windows on either side of the splintered entry.

Tall and thin like he was, nobody would believe he could've pulled such a stunt. I didn't believe it, and I saw it. The discarded shotguns bounced off the frozen ground as he leaped to the right side of the open doorway with a pistol in each hand.

He motioned me around the corner of the rough plank building. "You cesspool-dwellin' pieces of human dung had better come outside with your hands in the air, right now. If I have to come in there, I intend to kill everything living."

"That's it, Billy. Talk to 'em. I thought they'd done killed me. I want 'em all dead," Ellis yelled from under the porch. "If you leave any of 'em alive, bring 'em out here, and I'll beat their worthless asses to death with one of these dogs."

Rounded the corner of the back wall in time to find the legs and behind of a big-bellied fat boy danglin' from the only window. He'd jammed that ample gut in so tight he couldn't get loose.

Ran back to the front. Ellis sat in a rockin' chair on the porch. "Billy's inside," he said. Dirt covered him head to foot, and pieces of straw stuck out of his shirt and breeches. He pulled makings from his vest pocket and started rolling a smoke.

Stepped over the shattered door. A dead man leaked blood underneath it. Looked like he'd been peeping through one of the cracks when Billy blasted it.

"Hayden, come over here and help me get this big stupid jackass out of the window."

Man hanging in the window had a bloody gash on top of his head, but didn't appear much troubled by it. Billy wiped off his pistol with a bandanna and sighted down the barrel to make sure the monstrous tub of gut's skull hadn't bent it.

Fat man rubbed his head with the back of his bloody hand. "Damn you, you badge-totin' bastard, that hurt!"

"Yeah, well, it'da hurt a lot worse if'n I'd shot you with it." Billy looked at me and grinned. "Grab that arm and let's see if we can get his considerable carcass outta this crack he's done got stuck in."

Well, we worked like field hands for almost ten minutes and didn't have any luck till Ellis went 'round back and pushed while we pulled. That finally broke him loose. Ellis slapped him in shackles and made him sit out on the steps in the icy rain. Dragged his friend's body outside and dropped it beside him.

Ellis kicked the big man on the leg. "What was his name, Tubby?"

"Smith. Gander Smith."

"And you? What's your name?" Billy kicked him from behind.

"Spenser Donahoue." He stole glances at the corpse, but refused to give it a real good look.

Billy grabbed the man by the ears and pulled his head around. "Look at your friend there, Spenser. He's dead, dead, dead, and you're one lucky sucker you dropped your pistol when you tried to climb out of that window or you'd be layin' right there beside him."

Donahoue stared at the shot-riddled body of Gander Smith and started to blubber like a baby. Then he confessed to everything from original sin to the murder of President Lincoln. After about ten minutes of screaming and crying, he pissed himself.

"Aw, Jesus." Ellis jumped away from his captive.

"Good Lord, man. Don't you have any self ree-spect at all?"

I got tired of all the bawling and whimpering and started to walk off. But just as I turned away, something caught my ear. "What'd you just say?" Grabbed the neck of his jacket and jerked him back onto the porch.

He dropped to his knees and pleaded like a man about to be executed. "I didn't run over that little gal in Arkansas. Gander done that, and you kilt him deader'n Andy-by-God-Jackson. It warn't me. I swear it. Gander done it! Gander wuz the one!"

"Where's Saginaw Bob Magruder?" Veins in my neck popped out like rope twisted for a noose.

"What? Who? What'cha mean? I doan know no Saginaw Bob. I ain't never he-erd of no Saginaw Bob." It was almost pitiful to hear a grown man whimper that way.

Several of the stockmen who lived in the surrounding cabins came out about then. They milled around the wagon and gaped at Gander Smith's shot-peppered body.

A tall feller who heard Donahoue yelled, "The fat dung slug is lyin'. That there Saginaw Bob was with 'em when they come. But he left early yesterday mornin'. We 'uns was happy to see him go. He kilt our foreman and head stockman 'thin ten minutes of arrivin'. He carried a big Bible with a pistol inside it. Man read the book at 'em when he shot 'em. Most evil thang I ever witnessed."

Whatever Donahoue saw when I turned back to him strangled off all the whimpering he had been doing. Stood in front of him with the Winchester at waist level and put the muzzle against his temple. Billy leaned against the wall right next to me, and later said he barely heard me speak.

"You've got ten seconds, maggot. I want to know where Magruder went. If I don't know by the time I say ten, there won't be anything left of your head but the bone that holds it to your shoulders." Levered a shell up and started counting. Got to eight, and Spenser Donahoue—thief, murderer, rapist, and child killer—messed his sizable britches.

Took my hat off and held it in front of my face to knock down the pile of brains I figured would splatter the porch. "Nine."

"He's gone to Texas!" he screamed. "Snuck off on us. Left us here with nothin'. Took all the money and left us here. Gone to Texas, I swear it." Tears rolled down his cheeks, and the smell from his pants spread.

Lowered the muzzle and let it rest on his shoulder. "If I find out you've lied to me, you worthless pile of dog dung, I'll decorate trees with your guts. If Judge Parker hasn't hung you first."

Billy put his hand on my shoulder and pulled me away from the outlaw. "Always wondered what them dime novel writers meant when they said, 'The man's voice sounded like spit sizzlin' on a hot stove.' I know exactly what it sounds like now."

Jumped off the porch and started running toward Thunder. Billy ran behind me and screamed, "Where you goin'?" Come on, Hayden, where you goin'?"

"You heard him. I have to go to Texas," I yelled over my shoulder.

He caught me, grabbed my arms, and twirled me around. "Listen to me, Hayden. We can't go anywhere right now. Weather's too bad. I've been out here longer than you, and I'm tellin' you, we've got to hunker down here for a while. Ellis was dead-on right. This stuff's gonna get a lot worse before it gets better. Anyone caught out in it just might die."

Tried to pull away from him. He held tight. "I'd watch your back if you wanted to carry that big ole Winchester right into Satan's private vestibule, and you know it. But I can't let you go out in this stuff. You'll die, and Bob'll get away. We'll catch him someday, Hayden. I promise. Today just ain't the day."

Reality settled in. Sagged against my saddle. He eased his grip. Icy rain fell like bullets. Thunder jerked and stamped at the discomfort. "You understand, don't you, Billy? I can't let that man live if there's a chance I can send him where he belongs. But you're right. Weather is probably going to get much worse. I can feel it. By the time it passes we'll probably just have to go back to Fort Smith and wait for spring before we do any more wagon work. Thieves and killers are just like us. They'll either have to go south or den up till the grass greens up again." Grabbed the reins and led Thunder to one of the shelters beside the head stockman's house. Felt awful because I'd missed Magruder again.

We took over one of the smaller empty shacks and set ourselves up for a long stay. For the next three weeks, we played poker, talked, told lies, and tried to stay warm. Thought I knew weather, but Billy had been more accurate than I could've imagined. Freezing rain stuck to everything in sight. Ground got so slick it was almost impossible to go outside. Trip to the outhouse became a dreaded occurrence. Well water froze. Put rocks in the bucket and dropped it straight down but couldn't manage to bust a hole in the stuff. Had to break hanging ice off the roof and cook it on the stove for drinking water. Couldn't even think about taking a bath. Ellis got pretty ripe. 'Course, he didn't bathe much to begin with. But, some of the dogs got to where they just loved the man.

When it finally warmed up and everything thawed a bit, we dragged ourselves back to civilization. Arrived in Fort Smith with only Spenser Donahoue in custody. Felt bad enough about pulling Billy and Ellis along on that wild goose chase I paid them each fifty dollars out of my own pocket. It was the least I could do.

During the cold frozen weeks until spring, my love for Elizabeth grew. When we weren't together, I found myself thinking of her. Almost without fail, those thoughts would lead directly to memories of the time I spent with Missy Talbot. Tried to put her out of my mind, but didn't have much luck at it. I was drawn to each of them for different reasons and sensed a profound guilt because of those feelings. My mother had taught me to love one woman above all others, and I'd begun to see how difficult such a thing could be. If Elizabeth knew about Missy, she never mentioned it.

Eventually I began to think in terms of marriage and the possibility of a family. I'd never given much thought to such a thing in the past, but there it stood directly in front of me in all its blond-haired, blue-eyed beauty. Couldn't bring myself to deny that I much preferred Elizabeth's company to the barrenness of my room at the Pines. And, besides, Missy had made it abundantly clear before she left that our "friendship" would remain just that as far as she was concerned.

Then, spring popped out on us. The dogwoods blossomed, and the job took me back to the Nations for weeks at a time. My thoughts of love and marriage had to be put on a back burner.

During one of those raids, we captured another introducing rascal named Dunlap Wing. As I led him from the wagon to the courthouse, he started mouthing off to some of the other prisoners. "Well, you boys can talk big all you want, but none of you is anywhere near the man my friend Bob Magruder is. If'n you mess with Dunlap Wing, you mess with Saginaw Bob. Such actions could be deadly for the doer."

Grabbed that human blowfly by the collar and shoved him into a side room off the hall that led to the old cell-block. Slammed the door shut and pulled one of the new ivory-handled Colts Billy had found for me. "I don't have time to talk this over, Wing. Tell me where you last saw Bob Magruder. If I don't have that information in the next ten seconds, there'll be a small item in tomorrow's *Fort Smith Elevator* about how a petty whiskey runner named Dunlap Wing got himself shot six times while trying to escape from the custody of Marshal Hayden Tilden, hero of the Plains." Cocked the pistol and pushed it into his right ear.

"Christ on a crutch! You don't have to get violent with me, Mr. Tilden. I'll tell you anything you want to know." He shrank into a quivering heap on the floor. "Saw Bob in Dallas 'bout three or four weeks 'fore you caught me. That means 'bout a month or so ago, he was there. I swear it! That's all I know!"

"Where in Dallas? Where was he staying?"

Wing struggled to his feet. "Bob likes them young whores, you know. They's a pair of twins in particular he really likes in Dallas. Names is Hunter, Sally and Susan, I think. Anyways, they plies their trade at a house called Gertie's over near the Trinity River. You go to Gertie's, and you'll be real close to Bob."

"You'd better be telling me the truth, Wing. If not, I'll

come back and see to it that you're in misery up to your armpits."

"It's all the truth. Honest to God. But I'd appreciate it if you wouldn't tell Magruder that it wuz me what ratted him out. That's just in case he kills you afterward, you understand. 'Cause if he found out about this little talk we done had here, my life wouldn't be worth a pile of petrified prairie dog fritters."

Bix Conner passed just as I pulled Wing from our meeting. "Bix, would you move this man inside? Have something I need to take care of."

"Sure thing, Hayden."

Wrote Judge Parker a quick note, swung by the stable, saddled Thunder, and rented another horse. Stopped at Reed's long enough to kiss Elizabeth good-bye, then rode as fast and as long as my body and two horses allowed.

Ten days or so later, stepped off Thunder's back and stood in front of the Empress Hotel. Missy Talbot, owner and operator, ran from the building—and jumped into my exhausted arms.

8

"My Visit Today Doesn't Require You to Undress"

SHE KISSED ME on the cheek and stepped away from the bed the next morning. "You know, Missy, guess I could just try to fool myself and say it's because I'm still tired and hungry. Or maybe the memory can't compare to the reality. But I do believe you're one of the most beautiful women I've ever seen."

"Why, Marshal Tilden, you silver-tongued devil. You know exactly what a southern girl loves to hear, don't you?" She smiled and disappeared from the room to return a few minutes later carrying our breakfast on a lacquered tray.

She bathed me. Made me feel like the only man alive. Her attentions were such, that for brief moments during that first day, I almost forgot why that bone-jarring trip brought me to her.

On my second night in her bed, I dreamed again of the horrors of Arkansas Post. The dream still came to me often. It always ended when I found what the Magruder gang left of my mother. At that point, I'd jerk myself back into consciousness and sit, shaking violently, on the edge of my bed. The nightmare seldom bothered me during my hunts in the Nations. But when I relaxed, the terror of that day always weaseled its way back into my thoughts.

At breakfast the next morning I said, "Missy, I'd like you to show me around Dallas. Maybe we can take a buggy ride. There's one place in particular I want to visit. Believe it's called Gertie's."

She exploded. "Gertie's? Why would you want to go anywhere near that nasty dump?" Her syrupy Louisiana accent got more pronounced with her anger.

"The only reason I'm here is because of that 'nasty' dump and two girls named Hunter."

She sat with her butter knife in her hand like she intended to use it to remove a valuable part of my body. "Sally and Susan Hunter? Those twin whores? Why do you want to see them?" Then she slapped butter on her biscuit so hard it crumbled into pieces.

"The man who butchered my family visited them recently. I have to talk to them. If he's still in town, he'll either go back to Judge Parker for trial or die where he stands. But if he's already gone, I want to know where and how long ago." Pulled on the leather coat Elizabeth sold me, and buckled my pistol belt around my waist.

She didn't move from her chair. Her voice could've cut glass. "Clarise! Clarise, come in here."

A beautiful black girl who couldn't have been more than fifteen or sixteen floated into the room and did a curtsy behind her employer. "Yes, Miss Talbot."

Missy locked eyes with me and never looked away.

"Tell Samson to bring the carriage around front. Mr. Tilden would like to take in some fresh air."

The fiery mistress of the Empress Hotel owned the finest open coach in Dallas. Its highly polished brass fittings and black paint sparkled in the morning sunlight.

A Negro man, every inch of six and a half feet tall, met us at the front door and helped Missy into her seat. He wore a glistening white shirt, black tie, red swallow-tailed coat and stovepipe hat. His right hand slid under my arm and almost lifted me off the ground and into my place next to his employer. "Let me cover your legs with this blanket, sir. It's a bit chilly this mornin'." He smiled and smoothed the wrap over our legs before climbing into his seat.

Missy gave directions and Samson took us on a tour. She impressed me with her knowledge of the history of each building.

A short distance from the Empress she said, "That big red thing is the courthouse. The old brick one was torn down in 'seventy-one, and they built that hideous thing. Just can't imagine what the city fathers were thinking." She stared at the building as we circled it and mumbled, "I just loved the old one."

Businesses in the center of town looked solid. Many gave the appearance of bricked permanence and a great deal of money.

Missy pointed out a group of workers clearing a plot of land. "Unfortunately, I can't show you our most prominent concern. The distillery burned recently and is only now being rebuilt."

Naturally, the ride impressed me. I'd never been to a town of such size. "Most people believe that when they

take the next census, Dallas will have a population of
more than ten thousand," she bragged.

She even tried to extend the trip by stopping at a dry
goods store, where she bought me a suit of clothes. "The
Sanger brothers own this wonderful store. If you can't
find what you want at Sanger Brothers, you don't need
it," she said. Samson held the door, and she swept past
like a queen.

She smiled as I paraded in front of the mirror. "Why,
Marshal Tilden, how dapper you look. I could easily mistake you for an eastern-educated lawyer or banker."

From Sanger Brothers, we went directly to the Trinity
River district where Gertie's was located. "We're right
on the edge of Deep Ellum," Missy whispered, "but we
don't want to go there. It's dangerous day or night."

A dirt road led us through a neighborhood of large
houses. Samson reined us to a stop at a corner across
from a neat building that gave the appearance of an old
southern mansion somewhere in the cotton kingdom of
the Mississippi delta.

Missy pushed the blanket off her legs and twisted in
the seat as she pointed toward the doorway. "Just past
the vestibule, on your right, will be a bar. There are tables
for poker in a large room on the left. It's traditionally
used as a waiting area for the patrons who wish to socialize before, and after, their visits with the girls."

She'd just finished speaking when a door that led onto
the balcony over the front of the house opened. A tall
and very young-looking girl with flaming red hair
stepped outside. She snuggled deeper into a dark blue
robe, hugged her arms close against the nippy wind, and
turned slightly as an exact duplicate appeared by her side.
They stood with their heads back, breathing in the cool

winter air. For a moment I heard laughter. Then they disappeared.

"Those were the Hunter twins—every man's wildest dreams in the flesh. There's nothing—and no one—they won't do. So long as the price is right." She squeezed my arm and locked me in her gaze. "They don't work alone. They have an assistant who looks over them. His name is Carter Caine. He's not a man to be trifled with. Quite possibly you'll never see him. But rest assured, he's always nearby. Not much over five feet tall, he's strong as a bull and can carve a man up like a trussed turkey. I'm told he carries a pair of razor-sharp bowie knives, and, in close quarters, is more deadly than any gunman—a very dangerous man, Hayden, and completely devoted to those girls. They pay him handsomely to insure their safety. No matter how private a man might think his dalliances with the Hunter girls are, you can rest assured Carter Caine watches." She told me all that in the manner of a woman telling a close friend how to bake an apple pie.

I stepped down from the rig and pushed the door shut. "Missy, the man I'm here for is called Saginaw Bob Magruder. Felt no need to tell you his name till now, because I never expected his trail to lead me here."

"I've heard the name, but haven't met the man," she said. "Be careful of Gertrude Yarbrough, Hayden: she's a sneaky old hag and can be just as dangerous as Carter Caine. Also, should you come upon any of the Dallas constabulary—avoid any contact with them. They've been on a rip ever since Ben Long tried to run all the riffraff out of town back in 'seventy-three. They can be a difficult bunch to deal with. Samson and I'll wait here. Just in case you need us."

The Negro driver tipped his hat and smiled. "If'n you require assistance, sir, jest call out. Samson'll be there double-quick."

I could feel Missy's eyes on my back as I crossed the street. Stopped at the heavy red door to Gertie's house and adjusted my pistol belt. Looked back at the carriage as I turned the knob. Missy leaned forward, hid her mouth with her hand, and said something to Samson.

Walked into that place at a quiet time of the day. Business wouldn't get perking for about another three hours or so. Everything looked exactly the way Missy had described it, except that it wasn't the nasty dump she'd claimed—quite the contrary. Floors were clean, the Persian rugs new, and the furniture highly polished.

Took a stool at the bar. No piano or other music. No loud talk or laughter like you'd expect in a saloon. A soapy pine or cedar smell hung in the air and almost covered up the odors of tobacco and liquor.

A woman, dressed in something black that sparkled like fireworks, lumbered in from the poker room and pointed her enormous bulk in my direction. A glass of whiskey, delivered by a surly-looking bartender, went untouched near my right hand. She stopped in front of me and blocked off my view of the room. Given her size, I figured it possible for her to blot out most of the light coming from outside.

"Good day to you, young sir. I'm Gertie Yarbrough. This here is my place. I don't think I've had the pleasure of makin' yore acquaintance." More like a man's than a woman's, her voice sounded like a crosscut saw going through a piece of rough-cut pine.

Removed my hat and nodded. "Deputy U.S. Marshal Hayden Tilden of Fort Smith. I'm an officer of the court of Judge Isaac Parker and am here on official business, Miss Gertie."

She took the hand I offered and shook it. The heavily painted face twisted itself into a smile, but I could tell she was leery of any stranger carrying a badge—good manners or otherwise.

"Well, I hope we can be of some help to you, Mr. Tilden. If I might ask, exactly what be your business?" She tilted her head and looked at me like she'd found a bug in her food.

"I have a warrant for the arrest of a man called Saginaw Bob Magruder. Informants tell me he was last seen here in the company of two girls named Hunter. I'd like to speak with them, if possible, or if you know the whereabouts of Saginaw Bob, you can direct me to him."

The woman began making eye signals at the bartender behind me. Unbuttoned my coat. Exposed the heavy badge attached to my new vest and the matched pair of pistols at my waist.

Her eyes narrowed and made more signals at the barman. I turned slightly on the stool. The move made it possible to watch both of them. Placed my right hand on the butt of the pistol on my hip and dangled my left against the one resting across my belly.

I hadn't cared for the sullen look of the barman since I first took a seat. I pointed to a spot farthest from me and said, "Mister, I'd like you to go to the end of the counter, place your hands where I can see them, and don't move."

When he'd taken the spot at the opposite end of his highly polished bar, I turned my full attention on the gigantic mound of powder and paint that jiggled a few feet away. She might have been old, but she was as big

as a skinned mule and probably armed to the teeth under
all those black sparkles.

"Make no mistake about this, Miss Gertie, I'm as serious as smallpox when I tell you that if anyone, including you, tries to hinder my search for Magruder, I won't
hesitate to defend myself."

She backed away when she realized her bulk and the
implied threat of violence from her liquor-pouring body-
guard weren't having the desired effect. "I've supplied
men with whatever they've wanted for over thirty years,
Marshal Tilden. Always prided myself on bein' able to
read a man by his eyes. I see death in yours, sir. You
have a way of makin' a person feel like beef hangin' on
a hook."

"Is Saginaw Bob Magruder in this house, Miss Gertie?
Before you answer, be aware that I don't respond well
to liars." Did a deferential little bow in an effort to try
and smooth that jab over a bit. Didn't want to make her
mad if I could keep from it. But, she wasn't having any
of it.

"Fine manners ain't gonna make me like you any better, Marshal."

"Well, then, I'll put it another way, old woman. Answer the question."

She flinched like I'd slapped her. "No. He ain't here,"
she snapped. "You were correct, though. He visited here
till 'bout a week past. He likes them Hunter girls and
pays top dollar for their affections. Likes to have 'em
exclusive, if you know what I mean. Calls every year at
about the same time and stays for a month—sometimes
two. His visits became more frequent when the Hunter
girls came to work here. He's gone now. I don't know
where."

"I'd like to speak with the Hunter girls. Assure you I'll be brief, and will pay for their time if necessary. I'd like your permission, but will speak to them without it." Smiled and did my little bow again.

"Foller me," she said as though irritated beyond describing, then turned slowly like a prairie schooner with a broken wheel and led me to the stairway. Made her ponderous way to a door at the end of the hall on the second floor. She knocked lightly, pushed the door open, leaned inside, and said something I couldn't hear. She stepped aside as I entered and pulled the door closed behind me as she left.

The room covered most of the entire front of the house. It was decorated in the most opulent fashion and had a bed on either side. Matching love seats and mirrors flanked the beds. A bar stood in the middle of the room and sitting on the bed on my right the girls posed fetchingly. They were 'bout as close to naked as you could get, making sure I realized that their hair was truly red. Each had draped a gauzy nightgown over her shoulders and arranged the garment in the most alluring fashion.

With hat in hand, I strode to within a few feet of them. "I'm a deputy U.S. marshal, ladies, and have some questions I need to ask."

"Do you have a name, Marshal?" asked the girl draped over the right side of the bed.

"Yes," echoed her duplicate. "Do you have a name?"

"Hayden Tilden at your service, ladies." Danced from foot to foot in my discomfort. They smiled and winked at one another. "I—I'd be much more comfortable if you'd clothe yourselves, ladies. M-My visit today doesn't require you to undress." My face must've been redder than a Confederate battle flag. They giggled, pulled the gowns closed, and moved to the bar. I sat on one of the stools. The sisters stood across from me and took turns filling my glass with water as I questioned them.

"Bob left last week," replied one redhead.

"Yes, he left last week," said the double.

"Why on earth do you want Bob?"

"He's such a nice man."

"We always look forward to his visits. He's so well behaved and spends so much money."

"So much money," giggled her twin.

I tried to nail them in their places with my most intense lawman stare. Quickly told the story of my family's butchery at Arkansas Post and his gang's most recent mischief in Texarkana.

"I'm here to arrest Magruder and take him back to Judge Parker for trial. If he should choose not to go along with my plans, I'll kill him."

Their behavior changed dramatically. They held one another and seemed genuinely distressed by the things I'd just revealed about one of their favorite gentleman friends.

"My goodness," said one girl.

"My goodness," chimed the other.

"When he visited us," sniffed the first girl, "we all slept in the same bed."

"Yes, the same bed."

"I just can't believe he's done such horrible things, Marshal Tilden."

"Such horrible things."

"Ladies, do you know where he is, and if not, do you know where he went?"

"When Bob left here last week, he said he had business in Kansas, one of those nasty cow towns. But I don't remember which one. Do you remember where he said he was going, Sally?"

"No, Susan. I can't recall for sure. One of those busy, dirty ole places where trail drives end."

"Dodge. He went to Dodge," said someone behind me.

I turned slowly toward the deep, musical sound. A short, stoutly built man dressed in a suit, brilliant white shirt, red silk tie, and polished boots stood in the corner of the room nearest the window. He seemed to have appeared out of nowhere. Almost like he'd grown up through a crack in the floor. His hair was greased to his head, and he'd waxed his mustache to long points. Carter Caine looked like a man who wouldn't hesitate to do bodily harm at the least provocation.

He silently strolled to the middle of the room like it belonged to him, not the girls. Took the stool next to me and poured himself a glass of whiskey.

"Magruder wanted to be there when the herds begin to arrive, and he needed a little extra time to establish himself before the rush really hit. He plans to prey on unsuspecting cowboys, when he can. Steal cattle, when he can. Do whatever he wants, when he can." He smiled, tipped the glass in my direction, and threw the contents down his throat. "I've known about Bob for years, but he knew better than to cause problems for the girls when he visited. He understood I wouldn't take rude behavior well." The redhead closest to him refilled the glass.

"Mister Caine, I presume." I held out my hand.

He stared at it for a moment then smiled and grasped it so tightly I thought my knuckles might crack like pecan shells.

"Mr. Tilden, Bob behaved when he visited with us, and I didn't tell the girls about his past. Such things are

my problem. He paid well for his pleasures, and I have
no quarrel with him in that respect, but I knew him capable of the darkest kinds of evil, if only a few of the
stories I've heard are true. Didn't sleep well when he
came to town. If he doesn't come again, I won't be dis-
pleased." He grinned and twisted one end of his mustache.

"Can you tell me anything else, sir?"

"Only that he carried considerable cash, which he intended to invest in a year's worth of poker playing. I'm
certain he'll supplement that with numerous other nefarious schemes." He sat his glass on the bar and leaned
slightly toward me. "If you truly want Saginaw Bob,
you'll have to go to Dodge. My advice is to take your
time. He'll still be there when you arrive."

I'd heard all I needed to hear. Picked up my hat and
bowed toward the Hunter girls, then to their guardian. "I
appreciate the information, Mr. Caine."

As I stood he said, "Mr. Tilden, I do what I do because
I can't abide a man who would harm a woman. I'd not
heard of your family's misfortune. I knew Benny, Azel,
and Cecil had been rubbed out in Arkansas, but never
heard how or why. If Bob gets back this way I'll take
him for you and hold him till you can come for him.
Crimes such as the one you described here today should
never go unpunished. But if I were you, sir, I'd be sure
no jailer ever got Magruder. He'd probably escape, and
the hangman would never see him. Kill him. If you don't,
he'll likely kill you."

Shook his hand again. "Thanks for the advice, Mr.
Caine. I'll keep it close to heart."

"Good luck, young man," he said as I pulled the door
closed behind me.

Started down the stairs and almost walked right up the shins of a Dallas police officer. He guided me back into the bar, where two more waited at a table near the window. One of the men motioned me to the only empty chair. My guide stopped at a spot by the door and blocked off any exit. The barman had resumed his favorite post. I felt he'd stationed himself near whatever weapon he kept there.

I quickly stepped to the end of the glossy counter opposite the site where the bartender stood. The policemen looked surprised and uncomfortable. I'd placed an obstacle between all of them and me.

"I'd prefer to stand if you don't mind, Officer." Smiled when I said it, but pulled my jacket back.

Man who'd offered me the seat twisted in his chair and looked at his friends as if to say, "Well, we didn't expect this." But what came out was, "Miss Gertie tells us you've spent your time here today intimidatin' and threatenin' people. Our job's to protect the citizens of our fair city, and we don't take kindly to strangers comin' here and conductin' themselves in such a manner. We think it'd be best if you came down to the city jail so we can clear this up without any ruckus bein' raised."

Didn't like the sound of that proposition at all. "Unfortunately I have other plans, gentlemen, and can't go with you just now."

His chair squealed as he pushed away from the table and stood. "I don't think you understand. You don't have any choice in this matter. You'll go with us one way or another." He made a signal with the big stick in his right hand. His friend jumped to his feet.

"We can settle this right here, Officer. I'm Deputy U.S. Marshal Hayden Tilden. This is a warrant for Saginaw

Bob Magruder, a murderer, rapist, and thief. He visited in this house as recently as one week ago and had been here for over a month when he finally decided to leave. I came here to find him and return him to the federal court in Fort Smith if I could, or kill him if I had to. Your friend, Miss Gertie, tried to hide his visit and motioned for this man to move behind me, for reasons I can only guess at. Those are the facts of this day's activities, and I'll tell you again—I'm not going anywhere with you." Pulled my coat completely away from my pistols. They couldn't have missed seeing the badge on my vest.

"Look, you Arkansas clodhopper, we could care less who you *say* you are. Any trail tramp can flash a badge around. You're goin' with us." They lined up, side by side, and slapped the sticks against their palms.

I spoke so low they had to lean forward to hear. "Don't press this matter any further, sir. I can guess at what you have in mind for me. Maybe some jailhouse persuasion with those clubs until someone gets around to admitting that my papers are genuine. I've explained who I am and my reasons for being here. You're not getting anything else. Now, none of you boys is prepared for the kind of gunplay you're looking at. So let's all just calm down and go our separate ways."

For several seconds the three maintained their swaggering attitude. Then the reality of what they'd confronted began to settle in. Cracks started to appear in the front they'd put up.

My black-haired angel swept into the place and rescued me. "Why, Hayden, you terrible man. You said you'd only be gone a few minutes. I feel like I've been waiting for hours and hours." She glided around Dallas's finest and attached herself to my arm. "Come with me, dear man, we have a dinner to attend. You remember I told you we were invited to the opera. The mayor will be very disappointed if Judge Parker's most famous marshal doesn't make it to his party tonight. I'm sure you gentlemen will excuse us, won't you?"

"Miss Talbot, do you know this man?" asked the burly, tight-lipped policeman.

"Why, Officer Brinson, this is the most famous U.S. marshal in the whole of Judge Parker's cadre in Fort Smith. This, gentlemen, is Hayden Tilden." She bowed slightly in my direction, took me by the elbow, and guided me toward the door.

As we passed the bottom of the stairway, Carter Caine appeared for the second time. He stepped between the policemen who followed us and said, "Gentlemen, I see you've made the acquaintance of my good friend Mr. Tilden."

Samson muscled into the middle of everything and shielded us till we got to the carriage. I'd barely seated myself when he cracked his whip over the matched team and urged them into a quick trot away from Gertie's.

Missy hugged my arm to her and said, "You must learn to be more diplomatic, dear man." Ten minutes later, we were back at the Empress and in Missy's bed.

Early the next morning, sat for almost an hour and watched her sleep. Quietly packed, saddled Thunder, and hit the trail to Dodge before she woke.

I left a note on her pillow. *Missy, you've bewitched me again. But Elizabeth has my heart and soon I think we'll be married. You knew it before I could admit it to myself. Be safe. I know we'll meet again. Hayden.*

9

"THAT UGLY FELLOW THERE'S MY BROTHER BAT"

TWO WEEKS LATER, I'd pushed deep into the Nations and was looking for a place to put up for the night when I found a sod house. I'd avoided the stock stations, Indian settlements, and numerous ranches dotting that well-worn path. Wanted to arrive in Dodge, find Bob, and do my business before he knew what hit him.

The howling drew me to the place. A low, pitiful moan that crept into my bones and pulled me toward it. First started hearing the sound long before I got close enough to spot where it came from. When I finally hit the ridgeline of a hill, I could see the spot clearly and pulled my long glass for a better look.

Shack had a corral attached to one end. Chickens pecked and clucked around the front yard. The dog lay in the doorway. Every minute or so, it'd lift its huge head and send up another painful cry. Took me a minute before I realized that the two mounds in the yard weren't piled rocks or boulders. They were dead horses.

I hauled the Winchester out as I climbed down. Tied my mounts to the nearest bush and carefully made my way from rock to rock. Stopped about a hundred feet from the doorway to the mud dwelling.

Dog must've caught my scent. It stood, bristled all over, and began to bark. I took several pieces of jerky from my coat pocket and threw one at the beast. Hunger overcame him pretty quick. He kind of snuck up on the meat at first, snatched it up, and ran back to the doorway. When he finished with that piece, I threw another. Repeated the process over and over. Drew him further from the house each time. Finally had the animal taking the twisted meat from my hand. Its dirty yellow coat was streaked with grayish brown and its head was twice the size of any dog I'd ever seen. Looked like he weighed every ounce of a hundred and fifty pounds.

About half an hour after I started, felt like I'd gained enough of the animal's confidence to get past the spot he guarded. Held a piece of the meat and led him back to the doorway. I could smell what lay inside before I got there.

Some horrible things hid in that house. Entire family of five hideously slaughtered. Looked like the man of the house had gone down first—single gunshot between the eyes, fired at very close range. Heavy black powder burns around the hole in his head. He'd died just inside the open doorway and fell like he'd been killed while he stood there talking to someone. I knew Magruder had been there as surely as if he'd left a sign painted on the wall. Why else would a man open his door and wait to be killed in such a fashion? The Bible fooled him as surely as it fooled my father.

Once the man went down and the door opened, the other killers flew in and massacred the rest of his family. Almost stepped on the dog as I stumbled from the place with my bandanna over my face. He'd gone back to his spot and took up his howling. Didn't know those people, but I cried for all of them anyway. It's hard not to feel for folks done in with a double-bit axe—especially the kids.

Dead man appeared to have been white. The woman and children looked Indian. Couldn't tell which tribe. Kind of figured on Cherokee, but at the time I was a far cry from being an expert. The father had probably been one of those fellows who married an Indian woman so he could live on the land.

Didn't have time to bury them. Besides, I couldn't have broken that ground with dynamite. So I dragged the bodies from the house and lined them up under the wooden roof that covered the end of the corral. Not enough wood for miles around to build a real house. So they'd used everything that could be scratched up to erect the shelter for the horses and protect them from the weather.

Took me several minutes to find a can of lamp oil. Gathered as much scrubby brush and kindling as I could and piled it on the bodies until it was almost a foot high. Knocked the props out from under the roof with the rancher's sledge. It dropped on the mound of brush and covered the bodies completely. Doused the whole thing with oil and fired it up. Dog and I went back to the hill and watched it all burn. He howled like a lost soul in perdition until the fire rubbed out any trace of familiar scent and there was nothing left but a pile of coals.

Couldn't bring myself to stay, and when I left the dog

followed. Camped about ten miles further up the trail that night. At first he lay at my feet, but looked so pitiful that when I motioned for the hairy brute to come to me it wagged all over and seemed happy with its newfound friend. Before I fell asleep, wondered how the animal had managed to get away from the killers and stay alive.

Named him Caesar after my favorite play from Shakespeare's writings. Took him a few days before he reacted to the name, but eventually when I called, he came running.

It didn't take long to notice a streak of frontier independence in Caesar. He'd disappear all day, but once I'd made camp and got a fire started, he'd always come back and sleep next to me.

Two days out of Dodge, I ran into a pair of drunken cowboys on their way back to Texas. I'd stopped for a rest during the middle of the day and sat on the stump of a piece of broken timber, when the cow punchers came stumbling up leading their horses.

"Just be damned. Looka here, Tige. Whaddaya thank we done found?"

"Doan know, Drew. Ain't never seen nothin' that ugly afore."

I tried to be nice. "How you boys doin'?"

Their saddlebags bulged with whiskey bottles, and the liquor'd burned up enough of their brains to make them stupid. "Don't be worrin' yerseff 'bout how we be doin', mister."

"You tell 'im, Tige." The one called Drew stumbled over a rock and almost dropped his bottle.

"Look, boys, I don't want any trouble today. Why don't you just move along?"

" 'Djew hear that, Drew? Thish'ere horse apple says we need to jist move along."

"You gotta lotta nerve there, horse apple. You're out here in the boonies all by yer lonesome. Could be right hard on yer health to go and smart off to folk yew doan even know. Me'n Tige jist might not take kindly to not bein' showed the proper ree-speckt."

"Da's right, horse apple. Tall skinny boy lak you could get yer butt kicked, you doan watch yer manners."

I'd just decided to shoot Tige in the foot when Caesar popped up and put an unexpected end to the squabble. He ambled up behind the cowboy and bit him square in the behind. Latched on like a Mississippi snapping turtle. The screech that drunk wrangler let out almost scared his friend Drew to death.

They both started running. Drew fell down twice before he got out of sight. Caesar held on for a bit. Tige looked like a man trying to drag a big hairy boat around behind him. When the dog seemed satisfied he'd got his point across, he dropped the squealing brush popper like a rag doll, strolled over, and flopped down at my feet.

It all happened so fast I couldn't do anything but sit there with my mouth open and stare at him for about a minute. The wounded waddie held his damaged goods in one hand and tried to gather the reins of his spooky horse with the other.

Got the Winchester and sat back down. Tige finally managed to get mounted again and turned like he was going to charge us, but gave it up and ran when he spotted the rifle propped against my right leg. I handed my new partner a piece of the dried meat I'd been eating. He grunted and snapped it down in one swallow.

•   •   •

Caesar and I forded the Arkansas in the same spot where millions of long-horned cattle and tens of thousands of Texas cowboys had crossed before us. Like most people, I'd heard stories about Dodge, even as far away as Kentucky. It passed all understanding that there I was, riding into the most famous town in the West. As we strolled in, I noticed a rough sign that proclaimed, THE CARRYING OF FIREARMS IS STRICTLY PROHIBITED. MARSHAL JIM MASTERSON. Some enterprising type had added another sign below urging the reader to "try Prickty Ash Bitters."

Tied my horses in front of the marshal's office. Snowflakes swirled on a wind that blew them against my cheeks as I stepped up to the door. Two deputies sat at a desk next to the barred entrance of the jail cells. I pulled the heavy outer door closed and fell into one of the empty chairs beside the potbellied stove.

The man closest to me spoke first. "Can we be of some service, mister?"

"You can point me toward Marshal Masterson. I'm here on official business and need to speak to him directly."

The one behind the desk perked up and asked sullenly, "Might we inquire as to what kind of 'official' business you have with Marshal Masterson?"

Pulled out my warrant and held it up so the men could see that it was an official document of the Western Court of Arkansas. "I'm Deputy U.S. Marshal Hayden Tilden. This is a warrant for the arrest of an infamous killer I've followed from Arkansas to the Nations, and Dallas to here. I wish to discuss this matter with your Marshal Masterson and would appreciate it if you could direct me to him." Pushed the paper back under my leather coat and waited as the two looked at each other and silently decided whether or not to accommodate me.

The friendlier of the two stood and pulled his coat from a peg on the wall next to the entrance. "Name's Jeff Farmin, Marshal." He shook my hand and smiled. "Follow me. I'll walk you over to Jim. He's at his brother George's place with some friends. They take dinner over there most nights. I'm certain he'll want to meet you."

In no longer than the time we talked, the snow had begun to really come down. "Mr. Farmin, can you recommend a livery? My animals need tending."

He turned to a group of loafers sitting on a bench under the jail's window. "Amos, take this gentleman's horses down the street and see they get cared for."

A bent, ragged man who looked like he might have been there when the good Lord created horses, rose slowly and took the reins and the dollar I offered. Farmin smiled. "Don't worry, he'll take good care of them. He's always nearby for errands such as this."

The street swarmed with people, animals, wagons, light, and noise. Every saloon and dance hall had windows that allowed the passerby to gaze at the wonders available inside. Deputy Farmin led me through the door of a place called Varieties and across the gleaming floor to a group of tables at the far end of the bar.

He stopped in the most remote corner of the room and stooped to whisper in the ear of a nicely dressed man who was hacking at an enormous chunk of beefsteak. Seated with the marshal were three other men preoccupied with the same problem. He glanced up from his meal, smiled, nodded at me, and pointed to the only empty chair left at the table.

"Your reputation has preceded you, sir." He smiled again and chewed at the meat, then laid his fork aside and picked at his teeth. "I'm Jim Masterson. That ugly fellow there's my brother Bat. That one over there is Wyatt Earp. The one sitting beside you is brother George. George runs this establishment and employs the best cook in Kansas. Don't know what the man does to steak, but by God they're the best I've ever tasted!"

Tried not to look completely thunderstruck. There I sat at a table with three of the most famous lawmen in Kansas—maybe the entire country. Every deputy in Judge Parker's company of marshals told tales of their deadly skill with the pistol and knife.

The Masterson boys could have been a matched set carved from a single piece of wood. About the same height, they wore well-tailored suits and shaved themselves close, except for big mustaches. Wyatt Earp looked like he belonged to the family. His features were similar to those of his friends, and he barbered himself in the exact same manner. All of them had a substantial, relaxed, peaceful air about them.

Thing that surprised me most was how young they all appeared. Near as I figured it, none of them could have been much older than me. Guess the shock of it showed.

Bat put his fork aside, dabbed at his lips with a sparkling napkin, and said, "Do you feel well, Mr. Tilden? Could we get you something?"

"No, thank you, sir. I'm quite all right. Just tired on account of my recent trip from Dallas—rode long and hard to get here. Almost wore out two fine horses in the process."

Jim sipped at a steaming cup of coffee. "We have a mutual friend, Mr. Tilden. Bat and I've known Everett Lovelady of Pine Bluff for some years. He wired me when you rubbed out Azel Stroud. Bat tried to accomplish the same thing at least twice."

Bat laughed. "Yes, but I had a good deal less luck than you, sir. I personally put at least two good ones in that scurvy dog. Wish I could have seen the skirmish that sent him to the devil. Smiled for two days after I heard Azel had joined Satan in the fiery pit. Probably still be grinning if I could've only seen you tear his ticket."

Wyatt tapped a nervous finger against his cup. "Good Lord. You're the man who blew up Morgan Bryce not long ago. Lord almighty, hoss, you keep at it and every bad man in the West will know your name."

Brother George looked into the corner behind me and almost jumped out of his chair. "What in hell is that?"

I turned around just in time to see Caesar bite at one of his massive feet like he had a flea the size of a dinner plate. "Oh, I apologize, Mr. Masterson. That's Caesar. He and I recently became good friends and traveling companions. Didn't realize he'd followed me inside. I can assure you he won't trouble anyone, as long as they don't bother me. However, should anyone accost me, can't even imagine what might happen." He still didn't seem comfortable. "I can put him outside, if you prefer."

"Oh, that won't be necessary, Marshal Tilden. We've had a lot worse than Caesar on the floor in my place. Just leave him there. I'll send for a plate of scraps. Looks like he could use some fresh meat." He motioned to a man standing behind him, who nodded and went directly to the kitchen.

Jim pushed his plate away. "Understand you're here on business, Mr. Tilden." He pulled a long thin cigar from his vest pocket and nipped the end before lighting it.

"I came for Saginaw Bob Magruder."

Bat leaned his chair back. "Another bad one, real bad. But none of us have ever seen the man. 'Course we've heard about his offenses against the law and humanity at large, but no one here's met up with the infamous Mr. Magruder."

"Well, much to my regret, I've met the man and hope to find him here in Dodge. Want to take him back to Fort Smith for trial if he has a mind to go. I believe, however, he would resist. If such proves the case, I'll show no mercy." They all had to lean forward and strain to hear me over the noise inside Varieties and the town in general.

"Dodge is a busy place," offered Wyatt. "We can help you if you like or just move aside and let you do as you see fit. Whatever you decide, be aware that finding anyone not wearing a sign in this anthill might prove difficult."

Thought that over for a minute and said, "I wouldn't impose on your hospitality, gentlemen. I can recognize Magruder and will find him. Just wanted you to be aware of my intentions in this matter, so there'll be no confusion if anything wayward occurs."

Bat brought his chair back down to the floor. "Everett Lovelady made us aware of Magruder's crimes against your family, sir. Rest assured we understand your feelings and will support you in any manner you require. As sheriff of Ford County, I'll help any way I can."

"I appreciate the kind words, Mr. Masterson, and will call on you if the need arises." My voice had lost all its power. Thought I was going to go to sleep in my chair.

George dropped his knife onto the table. "I have a room in back away from the bar and noise. You'll find it most comfortable, Mr. Tilden." He motioned to his man again. "Show the marshal to number eight, Dave. See he gets anything he needs."

It took all the strength I had left to stand and follow Masterson's man. He led me through one door and down a long hallway. He opened the room and placed the key on a table beside the bed. Offered a tip, but he silently held his hand up in rejection, smiled, and closed the door. Caesar jumped up on the chest at the foot of the bed and dropped off to sleep instantly. Fell into that bed wearing all my clothes and quickly followed him.

Next morning, snow about a foot deep covered the ground. Locals told me at breakfast that such dustings weren't unusual for that time of year, and they'd even seen some terrible blizzards in the middle of May. I counted myself lucky to have managed to make town before the icy weather made its appearance.

I made notes on the locations of all the most popular and widely used saloons. My friends in Fort Smith reviewed places like the Gold Room, Long Branch, Lady Gay, and Main Street on a fairly regular basis.

Most of the largest and better-known palaces of cards and women squatted along Front Street. But the alleyways and side streets also sported a heavy population of less-frequented establishments. Dodge boasted more such places than any town in the West. Even in the middle of the day, and with a foot of snow on the ground, the traffic of people and animals could amaze a traveling revivalist.

Deputy Farmin accompanied me during the first few days. He loved talking about his town. "Cattle trade draws gamblers, whiskey peddlers, whores, pimps, gunmen, killers, and thieves. Poor dumb-ass cowboys are easy pickin's. Not quite as easy as them poor stupid goobers still tryin' to make a livin' huntin' buffalo, but close."

"What about the soldiers from Fort Dodge?"

"Aw, they're almost as easy to bamboozle as the cow punchers, but they're here year-round and tend to have a better understandin' of the resident bunch of toughs competin' for their time and money."

It took some effort, but I got myself pretty familiar with the bartenders and swampers in those establishments where Saginaw Bob might turn up. Tried to avoid revealing my reasons for the inquiries and showed my badge only when necessary.

About a week into my search Farmin and I sat at a table in the Lady Gay when several rambunctious types decided it would be great fun to hurrah the town before leaving. They'd barely got out the door when they started to fire their pistols in the air at anything in general and nothing in particular.

Farmin flopped down under the table and pulled me with him. "By Godfrey, the party's startin' early tonight, Hayden." He laughed and pressed himself closer to the floor when bullets whizzed through the air.

Lawmen, bartenders, gamblers, boozers, and anyone else in his right mind ran for cover. But a drunk called Skunk Mulloy, whose name was more than descriptive, failed to see the urgency of the situation. He bravely guarded his place at the bar and derided everyone under a table.

"Bunch of liddle girls. The whole damned herd of yah oughta be wearin' dresses. Good God, ain't met a Texian yet could hit his own bee-hind with a set of deer antlers and twenty jabs."

Farmin and I followed the Masterson brothers into the

street and watched as they joined Wyatt in a glory-be-to-
God free-for-all of shouting, shooting, and commotion. I
stayed out of the fracas. Figured they had all the fire-
power they needed.

During the course of all the confusion, someone in the
crowd of lawmen actually managed to hit one of the flee-
ing riders. Must have been thirty shots fired. Maybe
more. Some even came from windows of hotels facing
the street.

Farmin laughed and stomped slush off his boots.
"They just wanted to contribute to the general hullabaloo.
Them cowboys get back to Texas, they'll tell all their
friends what a great time a weary wrangler can have in
Dodge."

Wounded man got extremely lucky. Wasn't hit bad,
but he lost blood freely from a sizable hole in his right
buttock. Bunch of the drunks packed snow in his pants
to slow the bleeding. A horse doctor named Gentry, with
a nose the size and color of an apple, dug the bullet out
of the wounded man's behind. He sewed up the incision
while bystanders poured more liquor into the screaming
man's mouth.

When things calmed down, Farmin and I went back to
our table. The other marshals joined us. "Why's there so
much shooting and fighting in a town where so many
famous lawmen walk the streets?" I didn't ask anyone in
particular, but Jim answered.

"We try to keep a tight rope on these fuzz-tailed fellers
if we can, but we don't want it too tight. Not good for
business, you know." He smiled and winked as cigar
smoke curled around his neck.

Earp thumped more ashes on the floor and eyeballed
every man who passed. "You saw the sign posted at the

edge of town about carrying guns. It's effective to a point. Most of these boys will turn in their hip pistols, but a lot of them carry something hidden on their persons. I took an old buffalo hunter into custody one night that had six pistols, two bowie knives and a matched set of derringers under all that stinking leather he wore. Just never know what you're gonna get. Best policy's to approach every man like he's armed, even if it appears he's as nekkid as a newborn babe."

Bat pushed his glass around in a wet circle on the table. "Brother Ed thought he had Jack Wagner disarmed last winter, but the murderin' scoundrel came up with another pistol and killed Ed. Wyatt's right, you never know." All the other lawmen at the table nodded and quickly became lost in memories of a brother and friend felled by a killer's bullet.

Next day, I stopped by the jail. Farmin let me peek in on that poor butt-shot feller. Deputy laughed and said, "Yeah, he woke up this morning afflicted at both ends. Couldn't make up his mind which one vexed him the most."

Wounded cowboy just moaned and tried to roll over to his good side, but the extra hole in his behind kept that from happening. Felt sorry for him, but if you start shooting at men like Earp and the Mastersons such things can occur.

Almost a month went by and I didn't see hide or hair of Magruder. I'd kept in touch with Elizabeth and the Judge all along. Guess he got concerned enough to send Handsome Harry out to check on me. Anyway, after ole Handsome arrived things perked up mighty quick.

10

"Ain't Never Kilt No Marshal"

HARRY TATE HAD a way with people. Especially bartenders. I stuck close to the man. Listened to everything he said to them. But no matter how I approached the problem in the beginning, I never could get folks to open up the way he did. He would start talking about their wives, kids, and dogs, then before they knew it they'd let something slip that ordinarily couldn't be pulled out of them with a pair of horseshoe tongs.

He'd managed to sneak away from me one night and the next morning came charging into our room, grinning like a cat with a belly full of mice. "Think I'm onto something." He grinned and lit himself a smoke.

"What, Harry? What'd you find out?"

"Not sure, just yet. But tonight, we're gonna meet a feller name of Champagne Jack Fletcher over at this bar I found just off Front Street. Think he might have something for you, Hayden."

Digger Scruggs Bar and Gaming House occupied a space about three times the size of my room in George Masterson's place. The long narrow space consisted of nothing more than a plank bar on the left and four poker tables along the right next to the window. Several oil lamps hanging on the walls supplied some light, but not much.

Harry stood with his hand on the bat-wing door. He studied every shadow then stepped inside. I followed him to the corner table, farthest from the entrance. A bland-looking middle-aged man, wearing a threadbare suit and stovepipe hat, pushed a chair toward Harry with his foot. Looked at me like I might be the biggest pain he'd ever had in his nether regions and let me get my own seat. 'Course, he sat up straight and got to talking real fast when Caesar strolled in, flopped down next to my chair, and gave him a serious looking over.

"What is that? Is that ugly thing a dog? That your dog?"

"When he wants to be."

"What the hell does that mean?"

"Well, he goes and does as he pleases. 'Course, he don't like it much if people touch me. Can't imagine why. Couple of weeks ago, he bit a Texian's behind clean off when the feller threatened me. If I was you I'd keep my voice down." I winked at Harry and watched the gambler squirm. He shuffled some cards around on the table, but kept one eye on Caesar.

"Come on, Jack. You told me last night you might have some information 'bout Saginaw Bob Magruder. Hayden here's the man who needs to hear it, so get to talkin'." Harry leaned over and nailed the man with his gaze.

"Him and his bunch tried to get me to throw in with 'em. Gave it some thought at first, but found out pretty quick I didn't want no part of their plans."

I reached down and scratched Caesar's ears. "What kind of plans?"

He dropped his cards on the table and started talking fast and low. "Him and them apes he's ridin' with worked this here table for about a month. They'd get the suckers loaded then cheat 'em at cards. If Bob couldn't separate the poor bastards from their money at the table, couple of outside men'd catch 'em in an alley and get it that way. They've already killed at least three I know of—and maybe more. Bad folks, Marshal. I've met some scary ones in my time. Saginaw Bob's bunch is the worst I've ever run across."

"How many?" I asked.

"Three. That's all I ever met. 'Course, there coulda been more I never seen, but three for sure. Bob called 'em his disciples."

Harry shook his head and pulled out a scrap of paper and a nubby piece of pencil. "Tell me their names."

"Look, Harry, I'll tell you all I know, but you've gotta promise me it won't go any farther than right here. That bunch finds out I talked to you, my life won't be worth a sack full of buffalo chips."

By that point, we'd all three leaned in on the table and were talking so no one else could hear us. Caesar grunted, rolled over, and went to sleep.

"When Magruder got to town, he had two men with him. Nate Stover and Josh Strieb. Stover's a big, hairy, dumb ox with fists the size of rusty anvils. Bare-handed, he can crack a man's skull like a peanut shell. He's about as smart as a water dipper and deep as a Kansas riverbed

in August. Never goes anywhere without his partner, Josh
Strieb. Strieb lets Stover handle any violence unless
there's gunplay. If shootin's necessary, Strieb's a dangerous man. Carries a set of them Smith and Wesson .44s
and can get off twelve shots faster'n any man I ever seen.
Don't have to be accurate, if'n you can spray that much
lead and don't care what you hit."

"You ever heard of these men, Harry?"

"Yeah, both of them. I thought Stover got himself
killed a while back. Separate, each man's dangerous, together they're a hell-made union I don't even want to
think about. Last I heard they'd killed twenty-seven people between them."

I felt like I'd been struck by lightning. "Bet they're
the ones who murdered those poor folks I found out in
the Nations."

"You talkin' 'bout a family livin' in a sod house out
in the Cherokee Nation?" Fletcher threw down a shot of
whiskey and refilled his glass. His hand shook.

"Yes."

"They bragged 'bout that killing the whole time they
wuz here. Bet I heard that story fifty times."

Harry pulled at Fletcher's sleeve. "You said he had
three men. Did you know the third one?"

"Valentine Gibson—smart and very dangerous. Them
others killers feared the man, if you can imagine such a
thing. Even Bob. Think he'd rode with Bob a time or
two before. Anyways, while Bob gambled, one of the
others would watch. If Magruder won, so much the better—if'n he lost or if a particular player at the table took
more'n Bob, the lookout informed the two outside men.
Then, they all followed the poor wretch and robbed him

of his winnings, and in at least one instance I know of, his life."

I couldn't believe they operated in such a casual manner and got away with it. "No one caught on to them?"

"Hell, no! Poor dumb cow pushers what got robbed never saw who took their pokes. Magruder sat right here playin' cards, while his men did all the dirty work. Besides, they never used any kind of reason to the thing. Some nights, they didn't bother anyone. Then they'd grab 'em three . . . four nights in a row. They're unpredictable. How would anyone have ever caught on?"

"How'd you find out about what they were doing?" I asked.

"I wuz broke. Needed money. Magruder staked me, and I sat in on the games for 'bout a week. Threw everything I could his way. He let me win two or three times a night just to keep up the right image. He kept sayin' that this time he was gonna retire. Wanted to go back home to his family in New York. Needed a big stake for that. Conquerin' hero come back home thing, you know?"

Harry pushed his paper and pencil back into the pocket of his coat. "You said three."

"What?"

"You said they'd killed three people."

Fletcher bent over and shielded his mouth like he was afraid the words would hurt. "Few nights ago something happened out at the cabin. But I ain't sure what. Wasn't there. All I know is that Nate slipped up last night and said his back hurt from havin' to drag a bunch of rocks up to cover two bodies. Don't know how he could even tell his back hurt. Man had the worst case of the grippe

I ever seen. All of 'em except Bob had it. Hope the sick bastards didn't give it to me."

I couldn't wait for him to get around to the point any longer. "Where are they?"

"The cabin's 'bout five mile outside town. But they're all gone right now. Heard 'em say something 'bout movin' some horses over to Spearville. Think they'll be back tomorrow or the next day. I could take you out there in the morning. You could set up and grab 'em when they get back."

I pushed my chair away from the table. "No, we'll go tonight."

Harry looked surprised. Champagne Jack blinked several times and threw down another shot. "Tonight. I ain't goin' out in this stuff tonight. Tomorrow morning's good enough, ain't it, Harry?"

Harry ignored the man's pleading eyes, but took up his cause. "Hayden, he might be right. I've seen snow-storms like this turn into blizzards so fast I couldn't believe it. Got caught in one of 'em back in 'seventy-three. My horse froze."

I twisted in the chair and bent so close they could feel my breath. "We'll go tonight, and that's my final word on the matter."

Turned out a bit more than five miles. Champagne Jack bellyached every foot of it. Eventually had to loan him my extra coat. Snow let up about half an hour after we left town. Clouds parted, and a moon big as a dinner plate lit everything up like daylight. The shack was easy to find. When we got there, smoke was curling from the chimney and a lamp burned inside. We hid our horses in a clump of trees about a hundred yards away. Harry crawled up on a high knoll with his glass while the gambler and I waited below.

He slapped his arms against his chest and stamped his feet. "We gonna have to stand around out here in the snow all night long. I'm freezin' to death."

My patience with the man had about reached its limit. "Jack, that coat you're wearing cost me thirty dollars, and it's the warmest thing I own. You won't freeze to death, so shut up till Harry gets back."

We didn't have to wait long. Harry came stumbling through the foot deep layer of snow less than five minutes later. "Well, there's somebody down there. They've got makeshift curtains on the windows, but I could see 'em moving around against the light from inside. Don't know how many, though. Counted seven horses in the corral, but that don't mean much. They could be stolen. Hasn't been any movement around the place lately. Moon makes this layer of white look like icing on a cake. No prints going in or out."

We stood there staring at each other. He didn't say another word till I limbered up my shotgun. "I know there's no way to talk you outta this, Hayden. But we need to ponder what we're gonna do some before we go stormin' in."

"I don't think so, Harry. No one down there expects us. We'll surprise them and won't even have to fire a shot. I'll go in first. You come in behind me. Bob and his boys find themselves staring down the barrels of these big scatterguns, they'll throw in their hands pretty quick."

I could tell he still didn't like the idea, but he went along with it anyway. We left Jack with the horses.

Just as we walked away Harry turned to him and said, "Don't even think about runnin', Jack. You move from this spot before we get inside and I'll find you, even if I have to follow you to sunset and half a day further."

We walked right up to that door bold as whores in church. Stood back and together ran against it. I covered the room, and Harry watched my back. A greasy man, wrapped in a blanket, sat so close to the fireplace it's a wonder he didn't flare out like a lucifer. He threw up his hands and tried to stand, but couldn't. For a minute, I thought I'd walked into the inside of a buffalo. Felt like he had a whole tree burning. Harry ran from corner to corner, but couldn't find anyone else.

"I ain't goth nothin' worth havin'. They's some paper money in thath boot yonder." He blew his nose on a piece of nasty cloth. Sounded like a winded mule slobbering. "Mebee five dollars. 'S all I've goth. Yew can take that if'n yo're the kinda low lithe scum'd rob a poor thick man."

"We're U.S. marshals, you stupid bag of puss. Where's your pistol?" Harry jerked the man up by the front of his long johns, shook the blanket out, snatched up a belly gun and pushed him back into his chair.

"U.S. marshals? I ain't done nothin'. Whath yew breakin' in on me like thith fer? Ain't done nothin', I'm tellin' yuh." The grippe had his head so plugged up I could barely understand him.

"Where's Saginaw Bob Magruder?" He'd been looking at Harry, but the edge on my voice jerked his head in my direction, like he'd been whipsawed.

"Well, he ain'th here."

"I can see that. Where is he?"

Champagne Jack stumbled in and went straight to the fire. He unbuttoned the coat I'd loaned him and fanned it back and forth, to get more of the heat next to his body.

"You know this little weasel, Jack?" Harry turned him away from the fire with the barrel of his shotgun.

"Yeah, I know him. Name's Hollis Doyle. He takes care of the cattle and horses Bob and the boys steal."

Doyle went into a coughing, sneezing fit that sprayed liquid for three feet before he finally said, "Damn yew, Jack. Yew leadth these lawdogs hereth? Bob findsth out yew brung 'em, he'll render yew out fer squzz."

I stepped over to the hacking ferret and put the muzzle of my shotgun in his right ear. "I want to know where Saginaw Bob went, and I want to know now."

He got real still. "Yew ain'th gonna shooth me."

Harry snickered. "Don't bet your life on that, Hollis. If Bob Magruder had done to me what he did to Hayden there, you'd already be dead."

All of a sudden he got religion. "Waith now. Waith justh a minute. Don't be getthin' trigger happy, Marshal. I'll tell yew whath yew want to know. Jes' take thath thing outta my ear."

I stepped back, but left the barrel resting on his shoulder.

"They'th went over to Spearville with some horses yetherday. Bob wanthed to get rid of 'em 'fore the weather goth so bad we couldn'th move 'em. 'Speck they'll be bacth . . . day ather tomorrow."

I couldn't believe my luck. So close, and he had slipped away again. "Harry, sometimes I do believe the man has a guardian angel. Yesterday. If we had just known yesterday."

Harry had moved over to the table in the center of the room. He scratched at a spot on the surface of the rough wood, then bent down and dug up a clump of dark mud from the floor. "What's this, Hollis?"

The weasel refused to look up. "Whath? I doan seeh nothin'."

Harry stood and held his soiled fingers out. "Blood, Hollis. I think this spot under the table's blood. What happened here?"

Doyle got all jumpy and started squirming around in his chair. "I didn'th have nothin'th to do with that. Nothin', absolutely nothing."

"Nothin'?" Harry moved closer to Doyle. "What was the nothin' you didn't have anything to do with, Hollis?"

Jack danced from foot to foot. He stripped my leather coat off and opened his vest and shirt. The sweltering heat caused water to drip from his nose. "Bob did it," he blurted out.

Hollis jumped out of his chair. "Shut yer stupid mouth, Jack. I'll tell Bob 'bout this, and he'll use the skin off'n yer cods fer a coin purse." Then he fell back into the chair like he might not ever get up again.

"You wanna go to jail for what Bob did, Hollis? Tell the marshals what happened here the other night. Nate let it slip that two men got killed here. You wanna hang in Bob's place?"

Hollis glanced from face to face like a trapped animal. "I wasn'th here when ith happened. I'd gone out to feed the stock. They was thirty horses here. My sweet Lord, marshals, it wasth all I could do to keep up with 'em."

Harry pulled a chair across the room and sat down. "So, neither one of you saw what happened, but you both know about it. Get on with it, Hollis. I can't wait to hear this story."

Hollis sagged like a sack of feed with a slit in the side. "Three or four nightsth ago Nate and Josh came stumblin' in after a day of drinkin'. Two fellers who no one knew came back with 'em." He sneezed and noisily blew his nose again. "They sat around drinkin' and carryin' on so late, I took my sthuff outside and put up under the lean-to where I could be close to the stock. Early next mornin', them two strangers pulled gunsth on Nate, Josh, and Val. Said they's gonna rob everybody. Can yew believe it? Dumb bastards thunk they could go an' rob three fellers ath bad ath them boys. Anyhow, I guess they'da done it, but jest 'bout then Bob opened the door and blasted hell out of both of 'em. Shootin' woke me up. Time I got to the door them fellers had started to bleed out right there under the table. I think Bob hit one of 'em four times. He's the one what leaked on the table."

Harry lit a cigar not much bigger than a handmade with a twig from the roaring fire. "And I guess none of you other churchgoing, upright citizens fired a single shot."

"Well, Val mighta got in five or six. They was tho much gunsmoke in the air, I couldn't tell. When I came in, Bob and Val were in a screamin' match. Bob called all of 'em dumber than Arkansas jackassesth for bringin' them others out here. Val said if Bob didn't watch his mouth, he'd end up deader'n Custer. Things kinda went downhill from there. Started to run off, but figured if Valentine Gibson killed Saginaw Bob Magruder I wanthed to be around to see it. Coulda tole my story to the newspapers and got famous. But it didn'th work out. I think they's both so bad, they's 'fraid of each other."

I felt like a man who'd just been told that he'd lost everything in the world that meant anything to him—for the second or third time. Harry saw how Doyle's story affected me and immediately tried to get my mind moving in another direction.

He stood and thumped the piece of cigarillo into the flaming fireplace. "We'll take these two back to Dodge and let Deputy Marshal Farmin lock 'em up. Then, we can come back tomorrow and lay a trap for the others."

"What're you talkin' about?" Champagne Jack's vocal lack of pleasure with Harry's plans bordered on belligerence. "You ain't lockin' me up. I helped you find this place and gave you enough information to get me killed. You lock me up and them ole boys'll know exactly where to find me."

"Sorry, Jack." Harry started for the door. "But you're gonna have to spend some time in the pokey."

"Yew boysth can do whatever yew want, but yew ain't lockin' me up." Hollis rubbed his raw nose on the sleeve of his long johns.

Harry's fuse ran completely out. He twirled and cocked both barrels of his shotgun. "Get out of that chair, Hollis, and get dressed."

Ole Hollis turned whiter than the stuff on the ground outside. "Thsure, Marshal. Thsure. Just calm down."

He stumbled out of the chair. It took almost five minutes for him to pull on his ragged clothes and worn-out boots.

We started for the door, and Harry stopped so abruptly I ran into him. He turned and pulled Champagne Jack up beside him. "Give me your hat, Jack."

"What? What you want with my hat?"

"Just give it to me." Fletcher handed the well-worn stovepipe over, and Harry took off his own Beaver and stuck it on the gambler's head. "Hayden, put yours on Hollis."

The little man started backing away from the door. "What yew doin'? This ain't right. Why yew wanth histh hat on me? Yew cain't do this to us. We ain't gonna let yew do thish."

Harry poked at Hollis with his shotgun. "We? When did you two become a couple, Hollis? Put it on him, Hayden. I think there's something strange goin' on here."

I figured Harry had his reasons, so I grabbed the greasy varmint and pushed the hat down on his head. "Now, you two go out first. Hayden and I'll follow."

Doyle took to shaking so I thought he was going to collapse. Champagne Jack looked like he might have a stroke. The words came slobbering out of his mouth. "What you gettin' at here, Harry? Why're you doin' this?"

"Well, just step outside and walk over to that clump of brush where we tied the horses, and we'll all see." He jerked the door open, grabbed Jack by the neck, and pushed him outside. Doyle started squealing like a stuck pig. I latched onto his collar and shouldered him out behind his partner.

Harry dropped to the floor and yelled, "Get down, Hayden!"

I'd barely managed to hit the dirt, when a hail of bullets riddled the doorway, windows, and everything around us. During the second or two between volleys, Harry rolled over to the table, pulled the lamp down, and snuffed the flame. "Get to a corner. It's gonna get a lot worse."

For the next few minutes, that shack got so many new holes punched in it I got to thinking it was going to look like a flour sifter when the shooting stopped. We curled in the corners and stayed as low as we could. Eventually, things quieted down.

"Don't move till I do," Harry whispered. "Cock your weapon and follow my lead."

Several minutes passed before I heard the crunching of snow as the bushwhackers moved toward the cabin. Harry waited so long I'd begun to think they would be inside before we did anything. Then someone outside yelped like a branding iron had been stuck to the bottoms of his feet.

Harry tapped the butt of his shotgun against his belt buckle and said, "Now." We rolled to the doorway and fired. Four barrels of twelve-gauge buckshot peppered everything in front of that door. I heard at least two people scream, then the running and yelling started. We reloaded and waited for the noise to die down.

"Let's stay put till—" Harry didn't get a chance to finish. We heard horses crashing through the brush not far from where we'd hidden our mounts. "I think we can go out now, Hayden."

Champagne Jack and Hollis Doyle had barely made it out the door, when they got cut to ribbons. Harry retrieved his hat and pitched mine to me. Twenty feet from their bodies another fellow squirmed around on the ground holding his guts. He kept blubbering, "Oh, God, oh, God!"

Harry grabbed him by the collar and dragged him back to the cabin. We picked him up and put him in the only bed. He screamed and cried the whole time. I relit the lamp and Harry sat on the edge of the bed, poked around at the wounds, and shook his head. Good-looking kid, long blond hair, gray eyes. Couldn't have been more than sixteen or seventeen. Dressed in a handsome leather jacket decorated with silver conchos. Gun belt and boots matched the jacket. He carried a pair of those Richards' conversion Colts with stag grips. Beautiful pistols. Right one was still holstered. Later we found the other on the ground near the bloody spot in the snow where he first fell.

Once the boy bled down enough, he stopped yelping. He held his gory hand up and stared at it like it wasn't attached to his arm.

"It don't look good, son," Harry said. "Think you caught a whole barrel of shot all by yourself. Why don't you tell us your name, and where your pards are headed?"

Kid kept staring at his hand. I pushed his arm back down onto his belly. "What's your name?"

Frothy red liquid and spittle formed around his lips. I pulled the jacket back and found several more holes higher up on his left side. "Whitey." He wheezed and air gurgled from the wounds in his chest. "Whitey Hawkins."

"Where'd your friends go, Whitey?" Harry sounded tired.

Watery eyes wandered around in his head before he finally gurgled, "Bob said this'd be so easy. We'd just kill you boys . . . and head for the Canadian. No one'd ever find us." He coughed, and more blood came up. I wiped his mouth with my bandanna. "Sounded good tuh me. Ain't never kilt no marshal afore. Couple of them tinhorn town laws . . . but never a marshal." He smiled. "Figured I'd have a right smart reputation . . . if'n I could brag 'bout killin' two U.S. marshals." His eyes rolled up in his head for a second. I thought he had left, but then he came back. "Bob seen that feller with the big rifle at Digger's place—askin' questions. Paid Jack a hundred dollars to cook up a lie—about us bein' out here. He'n

Hollis can put on quite an act—cain't they? We followed you dumb Arkansas clod-kickers all the way out here." He coughed again, and almost sat upright, then fell back into the rough bed. "That sorry Magruder'll tell any kinda lie you can imagine to get a body to do what he wants. Hard to believe he's really a preacher. Sure would like to see that church down in Texas where he preaches." He held his hand against the tip of his nose and struggled to speak. "Just like . . . to see my hand again. Mighty cold in here, don't you think? Ain't gonna make it—am I, Marshal?"

"No, son. You ain't gonna make it." Harry pulled a threadbare blanket up to Whitey's waist and tenderly tucked it around his legs like a mother putting her child to sleep. The boy's arm dropped like a felled tree, and he stopped moving. A single jagged breath oozed out, and his eyes popped open in surprise.

Harry sat and stared at that kid for the longest time. "Hate seein' a man this young die so awful. I know he'd have killed us both, given the chance, but that don't make the way he passed any easier to take."

I pointed to the door with my shotgun. "We've got to go get the rest of them."

Harry glanced along the line I'd indicated. His shoulders slumped, and he ran his hand over his face. "They'll be real easy to track till the snow starts to melt." Just as he said that, Caesar peeked in. He ambled over, sat down at my feet, and dropped a chunk of bloody rag on the floor.

"What is it, Hayden?"

I rolled the material around with the toe of my boot. "It looks like the seat of somebody's pants. That must have been the yelping we heard just before we blasted them. He's gone and done another trick like the one he did on those two cowboys we met south of the Arkansas."

We stood there staring at the creature as his tail swept a smooth spot on the dirt floor. Harry bent down and carefully patted him on the head. "You think he could trail Magruder's bunch?"

"Don't know. Never tried to get him to run track before."

Harry rummaged around in the pile of discarded clothing and other goods littering the floor and held pieces of it under the animal's nose. The dog got more and more agitated with every shirt or pair of pants. Then, Harry came up with a shirt like a preacher or gambler might wear. Caesar went crazy. Dog grabbed the garment, ripped it to pieces, then pissed on it.

Harry kept scratching around and found another one that looked almost the same. He rolled it into a ball. "Let's get these fellers to Dodge. We can get some rest, then tomorrow we'll see if the dog will run the track. If he does, it'll make things a lot easier."

We made it back to the cabin early the next morning. I rubbed Caesar's muzzle with the garment Harry had saved. Didn't even have to urge him into the chase. He started running and it took everything we could do to keep up. The hairy devil turned out to be a lot more than a simple trail mate, and the longer we ran behind him, the more I believed he'd lead us right to Magruder.

Eight days into the chase we'd made it out of the snow cover and topped a hill near the North Canadian, back in the Nations. We were all about give out. Caesar had run himself footsore, but when we stopped, he got agitated.

Harry handed me his long glass. "There's smoke coming from that clump of trees. Only a sliver, but if you look hard you can see it. We can leave the horses under the overhang cut into the bluff yonder and catch them by surprise."

While we checked our weapons he whispered, "These boys won't go down easy, Hayden. I'd bet my horse, they fight like cornered wildcats. Best we adopt the Billy Bird method. Shoot first—and sort it all out later. Give me about ten minutes while I circle around on the other side, then we'll catch the sons of bitches in the middle." He started toward the stand of trees. I looked for Caesar, but couldn't find him.

As I snapped the cover of my watch closed and started in the direction of the camp, saw motion out of the corner of my left eye. Caesar was creeping through the trees toward our quarry like a panther stalking game. Acted like he knew exactly how we wanted to take those boys. Snaked my way into the trees.

Before I'd managed to move in very far, heard Handsome Harry call out, "Come on in, Hayden. Come on in."

I stepped into a grassy clearing. A shallow stream made its way silently through the camp and eventually into the Canadian. Staked horses stamped and snorted a short distance from a fire that'd burned itself down to a barely smoking pile of ash. Harry stood beside a log on the other side of the creek. A strange and elderly figure sat on the fallen tree. On the ground a gagged man, wrapped in rope, struggled to be free. Caesar made a grunting sound of recognition deep in his chest, bounded past me, and jumped the creek into the open arms of the old man.

The scene I walked up on shocked me right down to my boot soles. Two of the bandits had died in the most horrible fashion. A skillfully applied knife had sliced through their throats. They had jumped from their bedrolls and stumbled about the camp slinging huge gouts of blood in every direction. Dark shiny pools of the sticky liquid decorated the ground. Drops, specks, and flakes of the stuff could be seen on bushes, trees, and rocks. Figured the largest of the corpses had to be Nate Stover, and the other one his friend Josh Strieb. My imagination couldn't fathom how such a thing had been accomplished. I waded the stream and stopped in front of the old man, who grinned from ear to ear and rubbed Caesar's head roughly.

When he spoke, the words came out slowly, broken by his effort to remember the exact terms he needed. "Yes, I know you. You sent Peter Waxon and his family to the other side—on a raft of fire." He waved toward heaven like he knew the place well. "Saw you do it. The dog followed, when you left. A good dog this one. The Waxon children loved him. He loved them. Dog cried much. His grief was great. You saved him from it. Such sorrow can kill people. I've seen it. Sometimes animals give up too. I was happy when he went with you." The old man put his head against the dog's neck. A single tear rolled down his leathery cheek and disappeared in the heavy fur.

"How . . . How . . . How could you know such things?" I looked to Harry for an answer, but he just shrugged and shook his head.

"You could not see me. I became invisible—like the Father, the Son, and the Holy Ghost. I found the Waxons before you. Heard you arrive, then became the air, the smoke, the wind, the grass." He waved at the heavens again, that time with both arms. "You tempted the dog with meat. You wept at what you found in Waxon's house. Grown men should weep at such a thing. I liked your fiery burial. Waxon would have approved. His ancestors made the last trip the same way, I think."

He threw the blanket off his skinny legs, stood, and stretched. His bony spine snapped into place like segments of a chain pulled tight. He was dressed in a loose homespun shirt, leather britches, vest, and moccasins. A knotted blue and white bandanna circled his head and kept a cape of gray hair out of his eyes. His thick belt held a Colt pistol, and an enormous knife, similar to a bowie, hung in a scabbard on his left side. Highly polished silver decorated the belt and matched the studs on the legs of his britches. Heavy bracelets protected each arm, and a clump of animal fur, attached to the knot in his bandanna, held several feathers that swung across his back as he walked. For some moments he stood at the stream's edge and stared at the two dead men as if to make sure they hadn't moved.

The rhythm and pattern of his speech never changed. He seemed in no hurry. "Followed you to Dodge. Found these men. Watched. Long time. Wanted to kill them. White people would've hung me. No matter my reason. Thought to kill them in their cabin. They slept little. Drank much. Missed the Dark Man. The one who dressed in black. He will not die as quick as these. His death will be long and hard. I look forward to his screams." He turned, made his way back to the log and his blanket. "Saved this one for you. He'll tell where the Dark Man went. We will find him. Have no fear. His time grows short. Many souls call for his death."

Harry made motions at me like I should question the stranger. When I didn't say anything, he took over. "What's your name? Where are you from?"

"Daniel Westbrook was my white name. Long ago, long ago." He answered absentmindedly into the air like we'd disappeared. "My family came west back in 'forty-four. Going to O-ray-gon. Papa said paradise on earth. Indians attacked my people not far out of Independence. Fourteen years old. They carried me away. Lived with the Cheyenne for a time. Others stole me from them—hard life for a time. Had to become one of them. Ended up with some Cherokee folk in the Territories. Over the years moved back and forth in both worlds. The Waxon family fed me when I passed. Gave me a place to sleep. Their children pleased an old man who'd lost his. Mrs. Waxon read the Bible. She learned at Indian school. Woman had a fine voice." He pointed to the bodies in the grass. "Those men paid for her death with their lives. This one—and the Dark Man—will pay, too." He pulled his blanket tighter about his shoulders. "My Indian brothers call me Daniel Old Bear."

"You killed these men? No one helped you?" Decrepit as he appeared, I couldn't believe he'd managed it alone.

He almost laughed. "They slept. I became invisible. Hid in the smoke from their fire. They could not see me. Could not hear me. They drank. Snored so loud they could not have heard buffalo stampede. Woke them with my friend Death. He walked beside me and took them away. He had followed them since they left the Waxons. You came here prepared to do the same. I did it for you." He smiled, reached down, and jerked the gag away from the mouth of his captive. "Now—we will talk with this one."

The whites of the killer's eyes narrowed, and he spat at Old Bear. "Gimme my pistols. I'll kill you and these other two at the same time."

The old man smiled and leaned closer to his captive. "I have always admired bravery. Even from a child killer. We will see how brave you really are." He turned to a bag lying beside him on the log and pulled a biscuit tin from it. Holes punched in the top of the box formed the shape of a five-pointed star. "My friend here came from Texas. Traded a good knife for him. Bet he's hungry. No chance to catch a fat mouse lately."

He popped open the tin and dumped the biggest spider I'd ever seen on the man's chest. That killer's eyes got so big I thought they were going to land on the ground right next to my boots. Handsome Harry jumped almost ten feet and pulled his pistols so fast his hands were nothing but a blur.

With both guns cocked and ready to fire, he snapped, "Well, by Godfrey. I'd heard of 'em, but that one's the first I ever saw close up."

I still couldn't believe it. Never saw anything like it in Kentucky. The thing slowly raised two hairy legs and almost stood up on its back ones as Old Bear held his hand in front of it. Black and big as a potato, it followed the hand like a dancer led by a skilled partner.

I pointed and shook my finger at the thing. "It's a spider, right?"

Harry holstered his pistols. "Yeah, but a very special kind. Mexican tarantula."

The word had a powerful effect on Old Bear's prisoner. "Ta-ran-tula? Tarantula? I don't care what you call it. Just git it off me!"

"What's your name, child killer?" Old Bear waved his hand back and forth in front of the huge creature. "Long as he can see my hand, he won't move. Tell me your name."

"Valentine Gibson, for cryin' out loud. Now get that thing off me!"

"Not yet. Need to know more. Where is the Dark Man? One you call Preacher."

"Went to Hays. I swear it. Paid us to watch these lawdogs and kill 'em when they came out of the cabin. Ain't seen him since two days 'fore we laid for 'em." Old Bear dropped his hand, and the beast took a hesitant step toward Gibson's face. "Oh, Jesus! I told you what you wanted. Please, oh, God, please." The hand came up; the spider stopped and waved at the old man again.

"Mexican who traded him to me called him *el picador*—the biter. Last time he came out of his tin house, nipped a man on his nose. 'Bout a week later, nose started to rot. Then fell off."

Gibson's eyes darted from one of us to the other. "Oh, God. Don't let that thing bite my nose off. Honest to God, I'll tell it all. Just get 'im off me."

Old Bear leaned over and almost whispered, "Where after Hays?"

"What? Whaddaya mean?"

"Where did the Dark Man go, after Hays?"

"Not sure. Said something 'bout visitin' friends here in the Nations. But I don't know who or when he plans on comin' back." Big drops of sweat rolled into Gibson's eyes. He tried to blink them away, but he wasn't having any luck at it. I could tell he didn't want to move much for fear that hairy critter would jump right on his face.

"Who killed the Waxons?"

"Magruder killed the man when he opened the door. Nate and Josh did the woman and kids."

The hand came down again, and the spider took another step. Gibson made a sound like a horse being choked to death with a piece of barbed wire.

"You killed no one. Such a nice fellow."

"Oh-h-h, I've kilt my share, but never an unarmed man or defenseless woman and kids. I didn't know what Magruder was gonna do. Nate and Josh just went crazy. Started in on those folks with an axe. Awful—just awful. Oh, please, God, stop 'im. Marshals, don't let that thing bite my nose."

The gunfighter was near hysterical. Old Bear raised his hand; the bug stopped again. Gibson had to have been staring almost directly into the creature's eyes. It sat, kind of humped up, only a few inches from his chin.

Soon as he'd said Hays, I lost interest in much else he yelped. Knew I'd missed my opportunity at Magruder again, because there wasn't a coon-dog's chance Harry and I would be chasing out to points past Dodge. We needed to get back to Fort Smith.

Old Bear looked up. "You want to ask any questions before *el picador* goes back in his house?" Harry shook his head.

The old man let the creature climb onto the back of his hand. Gibson tried to shrink away as the wrinkled fist and its rider passed a few inches from his face. The box lid snapped shut and, faster than pigs after a pumpkin, the leathery hand reappeared holding that big knife over Gibson's throat so tight beads of blood sweated off the blade.

Harry jumped toward them. "Hold up there, friend! You can't kill him."

The old man held the knife tightly against Gibson's throat. "Why not? He's told all he knows. Or all he wants us to know. We have no need of him. He should join those others. There in the bloody weeds."

Got down in a squat, so the two of us were on the

same level. "I know you want to kill him. I want to kill him. Harry wants to kill him, too. But we can't. He has to go back to Fort Smith. Might be worth a lot of money, for all we know. If there's posters on him, or any of those I printed up in Kansas, at least this trip won't be a total waste."

Old Bear looked me in the eye. Then smiled. "For you, Tilden. Because I saw you weep for the Waxons—I'll let him live. For you."

The blade gently slid across Gibson's throat and left a tiny line of blood trickling into his collar. "Just a little something to remind you of our talk," said the old man as he stood and moved to the far end of the log.

After I inked their hands, we buried Nate Stover and Josh Strieb right where they fell. Old Bear took buttons, pocket watches, knives, and tobacco pouches from the bodies. He hung them from the crooked crosses we put over their graves. I thought about reading from Shakespeare, but decided such a gesture would be wasted. Men like those didn't deserve to go to the next world on the wings of great and uplifting words.

We each took a horse to lead and started for Fort Smith. Old Bear turned out to be a godsend. He kept us away from any contact with other men in the area and got us back home in record time.

Almost nine months had passed since my family had been murdered. I was tired to the bone and needed a serious rest. Couldn't wait to see Elizabeth and decided the time had come for us to get married. I'd seen too much of the brutal and wicked in men, and, even though I tried to push it down, I hid a growing concern that something wayward might happen on the hunt that would keep me from ever seeing her again. When I stepped down off Thunder in front of the Hotel Pines in late April of 1879, I'd decided I wanted her as close to me as possible from then on.

11

"IT BE FULL OF GOLD COIN"

WAS BACK IN Fort Smith about a month, when I sprang the big question on Elizabeth. Took me that long to build up enough nerve. Fortunately the Judge didn't have anything pressing for me at the time and, true to his word, no one questioned my idleness.

She made us a picnic lunch that day. We rode out past the cemetery and threw a blanket on the ground on a bluff overlooking the Arkansas. May had popped out all cottonwood blooms and azaleas. And honestly, if I closed my eyes right now, God could send me back there in a heartbeat as sure as geese have flat feet. Sometimes in my dreams, I can still smell those azaleas—and Elizabeth's perfume.

She folded her red-checked napkin and laid it across her lap. "What are you thinking, Hayden? I'm very concerned. Ever since you and Harry got back from Dodge, your mind has been somewhere else."

"You're right. I've had some important things to think about."

"I've seen this happen to other marshals. After they've been in the Nations for a while, they change. I'd hoped it wouldn't happen to you. But I know how awful some of the things you have to see can be. Last week Bixley Conner made it back to town with that horrible man who had his way with the poor Johnson girl, then killed her before he threw the body in the Poteau River." She placed her hand on mine. "If you need to talk about it, you know I'm willing to listen."

Her blue eyes misted up, and I thought she might cry. For some reason, it had never really come down on me how deeply she cared. That afternoon by the river those blue eyes told me everything.

"It's not what you think, Elizabeth. I've been trying to work up enough nerve to ask you if, uh . . . well . . . if you'd like to . . . well . . . you know. But I'd probably have to speak to your father first."

She smiled and drew circles on the back of my hand with her finger. "Why, Marshal Tilden. Are you asking for my hand in marriage?"

For about thirty seconds, I couldn't say anything. She had me hypnotized. Felt like one of those carnival chickens that get charmed and can't move. My whole body tingled from the soles of my feet to those fine hairs on the back of my hand where her finger twirled. Then, her hand came up and caressed the back of my neck. Everything in my head exploded. My heart melted right down into my boots.

"Elizabeth, I've been pondering the first time we met. Remember when you dressed me in my western outfit and sold me that book of Shakespeare? Think I knew then. Every time we've been together since that day, I've wanted to say it, but couldn't." Held her hand and stared at the tiny blue veins. "I love you, Elizabeth, and want us to spend the rest of our lives together. Know it won't be a buggy ride. This job doesn't make being married easy for the women who have to wait for their men to come back from the Nations."

Paused for a while to kind of let what I'd said settle in. She smiled, pulled my hand to her face, and kissed it. "I knew you were the one the minute you stepped across the threshold of Papa's store, Hayden." She rocked backward and laughed. Deep, musical, and, like her, beautiful. As though chastising a child she shook her finger at me and said, "I'm so glad you didn't take two or three years to get around to this."

Soon as the question passed my lips and she accepted, I lost control of the world as I knew it. The thing started out slowly, but like a locomotive with a drunken engineer, the passing of every day added to the speed and size of the upcoming event. The original discussion I remember involved a small civil ceremony. But from that tiny acorn, a huge oak of matrimonial sacrament grew.

About a week after the picnic, Judge Parker stopped me in the hall and said, "Hayden, I'd consider it an honor if you and Elizabeth would have the service in my home. It might not be the largest or finest residence in Fort Smith, but it's big enough to accommodate the crowd I know will want to attend."

I told Elizabeth, and she couldn't have been more thrilled. "My goodness, Hayden. I'm so pleased the Parkers want us to get married in their home. I think that would be just grand."

Honest to God, Handsome Harry started acting like he

was my mother. He pigeonholed every deputy he could find and twisted so many arms it's a wonder any of them could pull a pistol. He couldn't have been any prouder of himself when he told me, "Every man in the field is gonna make a special effort to come out of the wilds and be here for the nuptials, Hayden. If they don't show, they'd better have a good excuse. You know, like being gut-shot or having a horse fall on them."

I asked Old Bear, who'd taken on the mantle of adoptive father, and a spot in the corner of my room at the Pines, if he'd seen many weddings. He puffed at his pipe and closed his eyes.

"Been married myself three times—two Indian, one white. Man should pay for his wife. Most desirable Indian girls bring many ponies. White women are far too independent for me. Most times use poor judgment when they pick husbands. One who married me perfect example." He stood and put his hand on my shoulder. "Good to be married, Hayden. Young man needs a woman around. Elizabeth will be good for you."

So, on a sun-drenched morning almost exactly one month from the day she accepted my proposal, Handsome Harry Tate, Billy Bird, and Daniel Old Bear stood beside me and watched as the most beautiful bride anyone in Fort Smith ever saw walked down the aisle of Judge Parker's parlor and took my hand. She wore a dress so white it made me want to shield my eyes, but I didn't. She stepped across the threshold on her father's arm and her luminous face caused every man there to gawk openmouthed in disbelief. Lawmen, hardened by seeing the most awful side of their fellow man, stood in the back of the room in their dust-covered boots and wiped tears of envy from their eyes. Wives, mothers, and grandmothers remembered their time at the altar and wept for all the years that had slipped away since.

When Judge Parker finally said, "I now pronounce you man and wife. You may kiss the bride, Hayden," his living room exploded in a flurry of thrown hats and laughing encouragement. After the reception, we climbed into a buggy Elizabeth's father had bought for us and raced from the crowd to spend our first night as a couple in a cabin miles from town. A hundred people ran behind, throwing rice and cheering. We spent a week out there in the woods. I think it was the happiest week of my life.

The day I got back, Mr. Wilton waited for me in the foyer of the Pines. He shook my hand, offered his congratulations, pulled me to a corner, and said in a low voice, "Judge Parker has a special project for you, sir. Time is of the essence. We have little information to help guide you. All we know for sure is that something dreadful happened at the Minco Springs stage station. A survivor made it to town yesterday and told a story so wild, Judge Parker and I found it hard to believe. I've already spoken with your friends Harry Tate and Billy Bird. They have everything ready for an immediate departure." He placed his hand on my shoulder and squeezed. "Be aware that our informant identified Saginaw Bob Magruder." Just hearing the name made me weak in the knees.

"One of the men tortured and killed was Captain Roland Gatewood. The Judge considered him a valued friend."

My surprise at Magruder's reappearance almost kept me from speaking. "Mr. Wilton, sir, inform the Judge that if there's any way under heaven, I'll find Magruder and bring him in—or kill him. Whichever the sorry bastard chooses."

The handsomely dressed bailiff clasped my hand again. "Good luck, Mr. Tilden. Do take care. The Judge would be crushed if anything wayward happened to his favorite marshal." He smiled, placed a sealed envelope in my hand, then turned and left me to read alone.

The note reinforced what Mr. Wilton had already told me. But it also included a telling sentence near the end of the text: *Additionally, Hayden, I have supplied you with an executable warrant of death for one Saginaw Bob Magruder to be enforced at your convenience.*

My previous departures from Elizabeth had been difficult. That one almost broke both of us. But she held up well, and put on a face I knew she'd prepared just for the occasion. Hated that it came so quickly on the heels of our wedding, but I would have left in the middle of the ceremony for a chance at Magruder—and she knew it. Less than half an hour after I kissed her good-bye, Harry, Billy, and I tore through the Nations as if all the yellow-toothed demons of the netherworld were snapping at our heels. We were trailed, at a comfortable distance, by an old man and a huge yellow dog.

Billy led the way. He had more experience in the western Territories than Harry or me. We deferred to his judgment. Time we reached Minco Springs, the mischief committed there was almost two weeks old. By then, I'd come to the conclusion Magruder's trail would probably be as cold as a Montana winter.

The rugged stage stop sat on a grassless piece of land about five miles south of the Canadian, right on the border between the Chickasaw and Comanche Nations. As we rode in, Billy said, "I knew the men who worked here. Fine fellers, all four of 'em."

A lanky white man came out on the weather-beaten

porch as we rode up. His face lit up in a big toothless smile. He ran to Billy, grabbed his hand, and shook it like he feared we'd all disappear if he didn't hold on.

"Mighty glad to see you, Billy. You other marshals, too. We had some bad doing's out here." His raspy voice sounded like he spoke from the bottom of a half-filled rain barrel.

Billy placed his arm around the shoulders of his friend. "Boys, this is Percy Billings. Percy, the young feller there is Hayden Tilden. The ugly one wearing the beaver hat's Harry Tate." I swear the man almost cried. He put both hands on Billy's shoulders and, for a minute, I thought sure he'd collapse.

"You men tie your animals and come on inside. I'll tell you all about it."

We sat down at a rough, oblong table and Percy poured us up a steaming tin of the strongest coffee I'd ever put in my mouth. "Momma taught me to make it like that when I was a nubbin back in Kisatchie, Louisiana. It'll put hair on you in places God never intended.. But don't get any of it on your clothes. Been known to eat holes in bat-wing chaps." He laughed at his own joke and slid onto the bench next to his friend.

Billy swallowed hard, gritted his teeth, and set his cup on the table. "Zale Avery made it to Fort Smith."

The ragged hostler's head bobbed. "Glad to hear it." The man's hand shook as he tried to raise the cup to his lips again.

Harry lit one of his cigars. He always did that during our question-and-answer sessions. It seemed to help him think at what he liked to call "investigating."

Between puffs he said, "What happened here, Percy? Zale told the chief marshal some wild stories."

Percy's head dipped again, and he started out talking to the top of the table. " 'Bout two weeks ago these men rode up and asked if they could water their animals. Dog Face Freddy, the half-wit, tole 'um to go 'head and take all they needed. Joe Sweat, our station manager, didn't care for the look of 'um, and tole me he didn't understand why men'd come to us fer water when they's a creek runs right 'hind this place and a river just a few miles up the trail."

Harry blew smoke across the table. "Joe Sweat didn't like the situation from the start?"

"No, sir. They all climbed down anyway and 'fore we knew it, they's guns ever'where. Ain't ever seen that many guns 'pear on men so quick. The one they called Bob dressed like a preacher and pulled a pistol out'n a Bible."

He scratched at a spot on top of the table. "They didn't shoot nobody right off. They's just after whatever they could get from outta the four of us, at first. But after they found Joe Sweat's stash of corn squeezin's and got good and ripped, they started beatin' on Dog Face Freddy. One they called Zack Farmer seemed to take uncommon pleasure in torturin' that pitiful wretch."

I'd kept quiet till then. "You know Farmer, Harry?"

"Yep, smiles all the time. Likes to cut folks up with a butcher knife."

Billings shook all over. "He cut Freddy's ear off, Harry. Ain't ever heard such screamin' since the time my youngest brother grabbed a red-hot horseshoe off'n Pa's anvil." He chuckled half-heartedly at the childhood memory then stared at the door like Zack Farmer stood on the other side sharpening his bloody knife.

Billy tried to calm him. "You're safe now, Percy. We won't let anything happen to you."

Poor man took another swallow from his cup and started again. "Well, Freddy flopped around the room here a slangin' blood all over ever'body. The one they called Albrect wanted to get in on the party. He whipped out a pistol and shot Freddy in the foot to stop 'im runnin' 'round the room."

Harry puffed on his cigar and scratched a name in his book. "Crouch Albrect? Did you hear the name Crouch?"

"Yeah. That's him. Albrect hit Joe 'crost the face with his pistol. That's when Freddy started babblin' 'bout the gold."

All three of us said, "Gold?"

Percy scratched his head. "Me and Joe was the only ones supposed to know 'bout that shipment fer sure."

"What gold you talking about, Percy?" Billy put his hand on the man's arm and squeezed.

"You know. That twice a year payout for all the Indian agents here in the Nations. Soon's Freddy squealed 'gold,' Zack Farmer grabbed Joe Sweat by the throat. Scared Joe so bad he told 'em all 'bout how the army coach would come in next day, and how it be full of gold coin for the agents. Magruder'd been watching all of it up till then, but he got in Joe's face and said, 'If you've lied to us just remember this.' Then he whirled 'round and shot Dog Face Freddy square in the right eye faster'n God could get here. Then, they drug ole Freddy outside and went after that liquor for a couple more hours."

Billy kept things moving when he said, "Zale said Magruder preached for you."

"He kept callin' them boys his deacons. 'Round midnight, he jumped up on this here table and started to preach. Ain't ever knowed any man what could preach like that one. Crouch got to screamin' that demons from perdition'd entered his body and was a-gnawin' on his brain. By mornin' they was the drunkest, craziest bunch I'd ever seen—all 'cept for that Vander. He kept to the corner and smoked. Don't think he ever even blinked."

Percy tried to pour himself another cup of coffee, but his hand shook so much Billy had to take the pot and do it for him.

Harry leaned back and dropped his pencil on the table. "Vander Lamorette. He's a bad one. When push comes to shove, you don't want to be in front of that man's guns when he pulls 'em."

Poor ole Percy looked like a man on a runaway horse. The longer he went, the faster he talked. "When we heard the stage a-comin', Magruder made us all shuffle around outside like we's workin'. Coach rolled up, and a cloud of dust came a-swoopin' in behind like a shroud. Captain of the U.S. Army stepped down and had to eat dirt when a wall of pistol fire knocked the driver off the box and killed his shotgun guard. 'Fore that soldier even had time to think, Magruder 'uz on top of 'im and had a gun barrel shoved so deep in his ear it bled."

Billy thumped his finger against the side of his cup. "Them other outlaws just standin' 'round, or were they busy too?"

"They jumped up in the coach and dragged the express boxes out. Lamorette blasted the locks off. Threw the lids back—naught inside but a pile of lead washers. Zack and Crouch screeched like devils straight out of a nightmare. Both of 'em jumped on that captain so fast, Magruder had to fight 'em hisself to keep the man alive." His hands shook so bad he had trouble setting the cup back on the table.

Billy said, "Calm down, Percy. Just tell it the way it happened."

"Well, Magruder started a-screamin' 'bout the money. Told the soldier he'd turn him over to Zack and Crouch if'n he didn't come clean."

I pushed my cup to the center of the table. "Did the captain ever say anything, Percy?"

"Said they warn't no money. All them crazy sons of bitches started yelling. Then the captain said somethin' 'bout that there coach bein' a decoy. That the money'd already passed through, or might come later. If'n he figured on better treatment, though, he wuz wrong."

Billy shook his head again. "Go on, Percy. What happened next?"

"Magruder had 'em bring Joe over. Sat him down on the stoop beside the captain. Tole him to watch what happens when people lie 'bout things he wanted to know. Crooked his finger at that Zack and tole him to show the U.S.-by-God-Army just how serious they wuz."

Harry muttered, "Sweet Jesus."

"Zack jumped over and stuck his butcher knife in Joe's leg. God almighty, he screamed loud. Soldier snapped. Started yellin' 'bout how the army sent out three coaches, and that no one ever knowed for sure which one carried the real gold. Albrect hopped up on the porch and kicked Joe in the back. Then they stomped the hell out of him as he tried to crawl back onto the porch. Zack snatched him up by the hair and cut his throat. Blood spurted all over the captain's boots. Last straw, I guess. That soldier's hand darted down in his boot and popped back out with one of them Colt derringers. He was so close to Farmer when he fired, the muzzle couldn't have been more'n a few inches from the man's nose. Shot punched a hole just above Zack's right eye. Blew his floppin' body into a bloody heap right at Lamorette's feet."

For a minute or so, the poor agitated wretch couldn't speak. His fingernails plowed furrows in the tabletop, and he scraped the floor with his boot heels like he might jump out of the chair and start screaming. Finally, he took a deep breath and told us a story the likes of which no one should ever have to hear.

"Magruder said, 'Tie this blue bellied bastard to that gate like he's on a cross.' Them others drug the soldier to the corral and hung him up on the top rail just like Jesus. They made Zale and me bring this here table and a chair outside. Magruder sat down, dumped a saddlebag of cat-ridges on the table, and loaded his pistols. Then he shot the man in both knees, faster'n you could blow out an oil lamp. Sweet Jesus, the screamin'. Fer the next hour or so, he shot that poor soldier to bits—one little painful piece at a time. My God, but it were an awful thing to see and hear."

"How come he didn't kill you and Zale?"

"Don't know for sure, Billy. When Magruder got tired of shootin' they just hightailed it all of a sudden. Left us sittin' out there on the steps with bodies scattered all over the place. We hid in the weeds and briars till the afternoon run came through. Harvey Boston drove the stage. Man's harder than the barrel on a fifty caliber Sharps. Honest to God, boys, when he seen that poor soldier, he almost heaved his spurs up."

Sometimes a man can remember too much of a bad thing. Percy pushed away from the table, stumbled to the door, and lifted the latch. He turned and said, "I done talked 'bout as much as I usually do in a month or two." Then he ducked outside and left us there with the horror

of it all lying on the table like Captain Roland Gatewood's bullet-riddled body had appeared out of thin air.
For almost five minutes, no one said anything.

So I pointed out the obvious. "Harry, we need to get
him back in here as quick as we can, and see if he re-
members anything that might help us start in the right
direction. Maybe one of the killers said something about
where they were headed."

My words still hung in the air, when Old Bear pushed
the door open. Caesar snapped and growled behind him
as he walked to the table and said, "Look. Dog found.
Under the porch." He dropped the Bible on the table and
grinned. "The Dark Man's luck." He caressed the black
leather cover like it was a living thing. "Now we have
it. His time is running out. When we catch him, I take
his heart. Hide it in place even his God can't find."

I flipped the book open. It fell neatly into two parts—
the left side smaller than its mate. All the pages on the
right had been cut in the shape of the pistol hiding there.
I couldn't believe it. The weapon that killed my father
peeked from the edges of a page that started with Judges,
chapter six, verse five. Billy read it aloud. " 'For they
came up with their cattle, and their tents, and they came
as grasshoppers for multitude; for both they and their
camels were without number; and they entered into the
land to destroy it.' "

Old Bear locked me in his gaze. "Hayden. The Dark
Man goes to Fort Smith. Two days back our trails crossed
north of Wewoka. Seminole lands. Didn't know who they
were, then. They probably made west for a time then
doubled back trying to throw us off. We got lucky."

Harry pulled his knife and scraped at the heel of his
boot. "Why on earth would they go to Fort Smith? If

you're running from the law, why go where all of it lives?"

"I know why." Percy stood in the open doorway. "When he wuz a-preachin', Magruder tole as how he was gonna find the marshal he'd seen in Dodge that carried the big Winchester huntin' rifle. Said he wuz gonna make that man pay for doggin' his trail. Send him to a scorchin' hell, or worse. You boys know someone like that?" Even Caesar turned toward me like he understood the question.

For a few seconds, everything in the room went out of focus. An ugly knot formed in my stomach. Thought I might just end up on the floor on my hands and knees. Then, the scar across my nose stared to burn, and the need for vengeance broke out of me like a branded bobcat. I jumped off the bench and bolted for the door. Harry and Billy chased me outside.

Harry grabbed my arm. "No, Hayden, listen. It'll be dark in a couple of hours. Let's wait till morning."

"You can come later if you want, Harry. I'm going to Fort Smith. Who knows what Magruder might do when he gets there?"

Billy muscled his way between us. "If he's looking for you, what could he do?"

"I can't even hazard a guess, Billy. But I do know the man is unpredictable. The quicker we get back to town the better. Old Bear can take us to the spot where we crossed Magruder's trail and if it leads toward Fort Smith we'll run that way as fast as these horses will take us."

"Hayden, the horses are tired. We're tired. I still think we should put it off till morning." Harry kicked dirt clods around. He stared at the ground like he understood my anger and felt embarrassed because his advice didn't sit well with me.

Old Bear mounted his horse, turned north, and kicked into a run. The dog yelped and fell in behind him. Billy jumped into his saddle, pulled up beside Harry, and said, "Come on, Harry. We can sleep some other time. Those men need killing. I, for one, want to be there when Satan invites 'em into his parlor." His horse spun around in a tight circle, and they fogged out behind the old man's pinto. Harry watched as Billy disappeared. Then he turned his palms up, shrugged, climbed on that big yellow animal of his, and hoofed it after the others before I could say anything else.

Just after sunup a week or so later, about ten miles north of Okmulgee, we found a sight almost as awful as any I ever saw. His name was Dick Little. He and Billy had known each other for years. Billy broke down and cried. Only time I ever saw that happen to him.

Harry squinted through the lens at the smoldering wagon in a tight canyon just below us. Billy grabbed Harry's long glass for a better look. Old Bear raced away from the fire and headed back toward us. I heard Caesar howling off in the distance.

"That's Dick Little's wagon." Billy sounded like a man who couldn't believe his own eyes.

"Who's Dick Little?" I'd never heard the name till then.

Billy's agitation was contagious and quickly spread to the rest of us. He handed the glass back to Harry and turned to me. "He's a traveling blacksmith. I'll tell you all about him later."

It took Old Bear about a minute to negotiate the steep banks of the ravine. He pulled up between us. "Bad, very bad, Tilden. Magruder passed maybe six, eight hours ago."

"Is Dick still alive?" Billy's agitation bubbled out. He could barely stand to hold his horse back.

"Alive. When I left. Maybe gone now. No need to see him, Billy."

Billy whipped his horse down the crumbling banks and galloped toward his fallen friend. We followed but at a considerably slower pace. I knew from what Old Bear said that our presence wouldn't help.

But Harry wanted to talk to the man, if he could. "You have to get information where you can, Hayden. Even dying people can help. Besides, if he names his killers it's same as if we saw 'em do it."

Honest, I'd never been witness to anything like what waited for us. Someone had shot the poor man, then set him and the rig on fire. Don't know how he'd managed to live, much less hang on for hours after it happened. Had to have been the toughest man I've seen in my whole life. His clothes had cooked to his skin and still smoked. He cried and moaned. We couldn't touch him. Billy was the only one who could get close enough to hear the raspy, whispered story he told. Me, Harry, and Old Bear moved away and listened as Billy put his ear next to the burned-off lips and repeated everything he heard.

"Magruder and Albrect came into his camp early this mornin'." He waited and listened. "Big black horse had thrown a shoe. They'd been walking several hours." Another pause. We had to wait between every agonizing breath. "Dick put on a new one. Magruder spotted his big ole Bible. Always sat on the wagon seat. Offered to buy it. Said the book would bring his luck back. Dick said no. Magruder shot him. No warning. Twice. Set the wagon on fire. Crouch Albrect poured lamp oil on Dick and torched him." For a long time Billy just listened. Then he stood and staggered away. Tears streamed down his cheeks.

Later, when we'd stacked the last rock on Dick Little's grave, Billy said under his breath, "We've got to hurry now, Hayden. Last thing Dick told me was how he heard Magruder say he'd get you, or anyone close to you, when he arrives in Fort Smith. He still don't know your name, but he will as soon as he gets to town. People there will be proud to tell him 'bout the famous Marshal Hayden Tilden—and his beautiful new bride, Elizabeth."

Her name went through me like a slug from a buffalo gun. Old Bear vanished. Gone so fast dust still hung in the air like the image of a ghost. I ran to Thunder. Billy and Harry didn't catch up with me till almost an hour later.

Two days later, when we all came fogging up to the west bank of the Arkansas, we found Bix Conner waiting near the ferry landing. Looked like he had twenty horses and a ton of supplies with him. Didn't surprise any of us. Figured he'd just got up a posse for someone we didn't know about.

I stepped down beside him and all I heard him say was, "They took Elizabeth, Hayden."

Swear on my mother's grave, if God himself had walked up and slapped me in the face, the impact couldn't have been any greater. Leaned against Thunder and had to hold on to my saddle to keep from falling. The faces of men I trusted seemed to detach and float around me like moons in a black sky.

Bix rested his hand on my shoulder. "All these horses are for us. I've got two for each man—more than enough to run them evil sons of bitches to ground. They're headed south along the old Butterfield mail route. We ran their track about ten miles 'fore we came back to get better organized. Knew you'd be showin' up soon, so I got everything put together as quick as I could." He pulled at my sleeve and whispered, "I don't know exactly what he meant by it, but the Judge said for me to tell you to execute the last order you got any way you see fit."

Billy had already started moving his saddle over to a new mount. "Well, if there's just the four of 'em, they don't stand a snowball's chance of survivin' this little fracas. You're gonna have to beat me to Magruder, Hayden. After what he done to Dick Little, I made up my mind that bringin' him back ain't worth the trouble. Knowin' 'bout Elizabeth just makes his trip to the next life all the more certain."

I finally found my voice and asked Bix, "What happened? Couldn't anyone stop it?"

"Magruder and three others marched into Reed's bold as brass. Shot old Mr. Reed dead while he was pourin' cornmeal in a sack for Mrs. Hull, the Methodist preacher's wife. They knew what they wanted. Didn't even stop long enough to steal so much as a horseshoe nail. Snatched Elizabeth from behind the counter and scorched the countryside gettin' away."

Harry loosened his saddle cinch. "You said four, Bix. We only knew about three. Magruder, Albrect, and Vander Lamorette."

"Don't know 'bout Albrect or Lamorette. Folks what seen the thing recognized one of 'em as Tollman Pike."

My brain swam in my head like coffee grounds in a

stirred pot. "Who the hell's Tollman Pike? Where'd he come from?"

Bix pulled my saddle off Thunder and threw it on the back of a long legged gray stallion he called Booger. "Tollman Pike and his two brothers've been a problem 'round these parts for as long as I've been chasin' men for Judge Parker."

Billy led his freshly saddled mount over. "Yeah, Remo, Jackson, and Tollman. Tollman's the oldest and the worst of the whole bunch. Bass Reeves put an end to Remo's horse stealin' last year. He's in prison up in Detroit. Heard rumors someone caught Jackson over in the Cherokee Outlet and chopped his head off 'bout two months ago. Don't know if it's true or not."

Bix grinned. "Might not be true, but nobody's seen him lately. We can all hope the blade was dull, if it actually happened."

Harry lit one of his cigars. "Tollman's the worst of the three of 'em, alright. Been on a killin' rip ever since he's big enough to pick up a pistol. Some say, he dropped his first man when he's just nine years old. Count's gone as high as thirty according to the stories I've heard. Personally, I don't believe 'em all, but he just might be more evil than Magruder. If such a thing's possible."

Bix gave us all a quick look after making certain everything checked out on Booger. "Well, boys, we ready to go?"

Harry climbed wearily into his saddle. " 'Bout done in, but screwed down and sittin' deep."

I knew how he felt. Every muscle in my body ached. I could feel my saddle between my shoulder blades. But about ten minutes after we started south, the only thing

I could think about was Elizabeth and how I would get her back. Then about twenty minutes later, I'd made up my mind that even if it killed me she'd get back to Fort Smith safe and sound.

12

"I'VE HAD ENOUGH"

JUNIOR PINCHED THE bridge of his nose, leaned forward in his chair, and stretched like Black Jack Pershing after an eight-hour nap. "Well, much as I want to hear the rest of this, it's gonna have to wait. I'm wore out, Hayden. I'll see you in the morning." He wobbled out of Rolling Hills like a wagon dragging an axle in the dirt.

Maybe all those memories I'd hauled out for the boy caused the dream that night—old nightmare, one that hadn't bothered me since long before Elizabeth passed. Over the years, guess I must've dreamed it a thousand times.

She looked so far away. I could see her, but it seemed as though she stood in the bottom of a deep well. Her mouth moved and her faint voice trembled with terror. I followed her cries into the darkness. As I lowered myself, my skin began to crawl with the feeling of being watched

by thousands of eyes. Glistening globes, fastened to either side of flattened heads, snapped and hissed in the
gloom.

"My sweet Lord, they're snakes!" I screamed down to
her. The Winchester roared and bit back till a single huge
serpent remained alive. Its body coiled endlessly around
a Bible lying on Elizabeth's stomach. Attached to the tail
of the beast, a tiny pistol flashed and spit fire at me.

"I have a message from the Book," hissed the snake.

The pages of the Bible fell open. The faces of my
father, mother, and sister flew from its depths and rushed
past me into the darkness of the well.

"They belong to me," wheezed the serpent. "You cannot have them."

I swung the Winchester to arm's length. "Maybe so,
but she's mine. You'll give her back."

Flame shot from the rifle muzzle. The fanged head
shattered into millions of glistening slivers that fell to the
floor and set fire to the bodies of its dead disciples.

As I reached to help Elizabeth to her feet, she whispered, "Oh, my God, Hayden. Look!"

Behind us, and all around our feet, the glittering pieces
of the shattered creature squirmed and wiggled toward
one another until they fused together and formed an even
larger and more horrible marvel. Could still hear the big
rifle's roar when I sat up in my bed and tried to rub the
image out of my brain.

Hard to believe, but next morning a candy striper
named Nancy wheeled Carlton J. Cecil out. He started
yammering soon as his chair stopped rolling. "Thought
I'd give up my guitar, didn't you, Tilden?"

"No, Carlton. You're too ornery to die. If cussedness
was gold, you'd be the richest old fart at Rolling Hills."

"Well, that black-robed bony-fingered sucker tried to take me again, but I told him he'd have to wait till Franklin J. Lightfoot published my friend's story. Don't leave nothin' out, you hear? Tell it all. Even the worst of it." He smiled, leaned back in his chair, and nodded off. I knew he'd be looking for the checkerboard as soon as he woke up, so I arranged everything on the table the way he liked it and waited for Junior.

Got to hand it to Lightfoot. He showed up at exactly the same time and looked like a brand new penny. He dragged his chair over, pulled the cushion out, and fluffed it up, before he kind of squirmed down into his nest.

He flipped through the pages of his notepad and licked his pencil. "See our buddy's back."

"Yes, sir. Guess ole Carlton decided to stay with the living a while longer. But don't be surprised if he up and checks out while we're sitting here talking."

Black Jack Pershing jumped up in Junior's lap. "You mean he could die right here, right now?"

"Oh, sure. Seen it lots of times before. You'll be talking to one of these ole gomers and all of a sudden they get this funny look in their eyes like they need to go to the john or something. Then they kind of grin at you and flop right out on the floor—real eye-popping startler sometimes. 'Course, ole Carlton's fought death off thirty-five or forty times this week, so if he buys the farm today it shouldn't be any real great surprise."

The boy looked at me like I'd just presented him with a problem so complex the cosmic implications of the thing were just too hard on the brain so early in the morning. Young folks who read his account of my ramblings should be aware that old people have a way of doing this. It's a trick we learn just to confuse them.

He decided to ignore me. That's the trick young people use to keep from thinking too much about the death of someone they know or love.

"You had your breakfast already, Hayden?"

"Yep. Cookey can rustle up a mean bowl of grits here at Rolling Hills. Sticks to you like ivy on a courthouse wall. Not as filling as her oatmeal, which I have been known to use to repair sagging wallpaper in my room, but close. 'Course, I personally get a hankering for biscuits and gravy 'bout twice a week, but they only have them on Fridays. Seems there's some question as to the nutritional value of such basic Ole West food groups. Nurse Willet says I need to eat more fruit and stuff. But, I'm eighty-eight years old. I ought to be able to eat anything I please, don't you think?"

"Are we gonna get back to Bob Magruder's kidnapping of your wife sometime today?"

"Oh, yeah. Almost forgot. For about a minute there, Junior, fooled myself into thinking you'd just come for a visit."

For the next two days, we rode hard, ate in the saddle, and didn't sleep much. Caesar must've got a heavy dose of Magruder's scent, or maybe he just picked up on the urgency of it from all of us. He ran with such devotion, and for so long, we started to worry about whether he could keep it up. Old Bear went off into the woods one day after he tied the dog to a tree. Came back with a fistful of bark and tree roots. Cooked everything up in a coffeepot, and when it cooled off he poured some down the dog from a tin cup.

"What's that?" Billy stood next to Caesar and scratched the big dog's head.

"Medicine. It will calm him. He must slow down or die soon. Too good to die." The old man ruffed the dog's ears and put his face against its neck. "We find the Dark Man, maybe give him to you, Caesar." He stood and walked back to the fire. "Want him hot for the trail. Don't want him to give us away."

Late on the third day, Harry took the point behind Caesar. Old Bear fell back and rode with me. Just North of the Red River and west of the Clear Boggy, we came around a clump of scrubby brush in the middle of some light timber and almost tripped over an astonishing sight.

Handsome Harry sat slumped against a tree. Didn't realize he'd been shot, till we stopped. Just thought he'd taken time out for a siesta. Bix got to him first and started yelling for us to hurry over.

Harry mumbled like we weren't there. "Tha' ole boy wuz ... jus' as fas' uz ... everyone said. But I doan thank ... he's fas' 'nuff." His words stumbled over one another like drunks on a Saturday binge.

"Who're you talking about, Harry?" Bix pulled the bloody shirt back. A neat hole just below the ribs on his left side oozed life onto the ground. We pulled him over and found where the bullet came out his back. Ugly wound. Billy stuffed a wad of material he ripped from an extra shirt into the hole. Harry made a strangled, moaning sound and passed out for a minute or so.

When he came back around, first thing he said was, "You ... fin' him yet?"

I leaned over so he could see my face. "Who're you talking about, Harry?"

"Pike. Tollman Pike. You ... fin' him yet?"

"Ain't looked for him, Harry." Billy pushed a slab of cloth onto the spot under his friend's ribs.

"Should be oafer yonner. Should be oafer yonner." He lifted his arm like it had a boat anchor attached and pointed into the trees at a spot about a hundred feet past his resting place. Bix stood, stared in the direction Harry indicated, and walked toward it.

"What happen here, Harry?" Old Bear looked more concerned than I'd seen him since we met.

Harry struggled to bring his head up. "Came 'roun these here . . . bushes. Pike . . . waitin'. Dog . . . got 'tween us. Lips . . . all curled back. 'Peared to me, Caesar . . . 'tended to take him down . . . right here." He almost laughed, but coughed and groaned in pain.

Billy dribbled water from his canteen over Harry's lips. "I said, Tollman . . . you have 'lizabeth Tilden. I wan' her. Give 'er up . . . or there'll be hell to pay. He got real . . . nervous. Got to fingerin' the rifle . . . he had layin' 'crost his saddle horn."

Billy gave him a few more drops of water and I put a rolled cloth we'd wetted down behind his neck. "Pike said . . . he ain't got her. Said . . . he's jus' here to slow us . . . down some. Said if we'd jus' lay back a bit, he wouldn't shoot . . . any of us. Then he brought that rifle . . . 'round in my direction. All the pushin' I needed. Put a hole in him . . . 'bout the same place he hit me. We couldn'a been . . . more'n ten, fifteen feet 'part. Discharge from his weapon . . . knocked me righ' here where I'm sittin'. His horse reared up . . . an' spun 'round. 'Fore he took . . . more'n a couple steps . . . put two more in 'im . . . as he made for the trees."

Harry passed out again just as Bix ambled up from his search. He motioned for us to follow. "You boys gonna have to see this to believe it."

Old Bear made shooing motions at us. "Go. Go. I will stay with our friend."

Billy and I followed Bix toward the tree line. We hadn't gone but about fifty feet or so when he pointed at a hat on the ground. "Harry musta fired twice. First one went through Pike's sombrero. Second one did that." He stopped, and we had to move around him to see what he pointed out.

I walked it off. Twenty paces past where Pike's hat hit the ground, the man lay across the neck of his dead horse. We all stood there gape-mouthed, staring at the wildest thing any of us had ever seen.

Bix pulled at the collar of Pike's vest and raised the corpse up. "Second bullet went into his back just under the left shoulder blade. Came out his chest and hit the horse right twixt the ears. Guess the horse 'uz goin' so fast they both kinda flew to here. Then the whole shebang went down like a bucket of rocks. Don't know 'bout you boys, but this here is the damnedest pistol shot I ever seen. Man and beast rubbed out with one .45 slug. Glad y'all 'uz here 'cause nobody's gonna believe this when I tell it."

Billy stood there scratching his chin like a man who'd just seen leprechauns dancing in the woods over a pot of gold. Then he started laughing. Jerked a John Doe warrant out of his vest, dropped it on Pike's corpse, and said, "Consider yourself served, you kidnappin' bastard. Normally we'd bury you, but you just shot my friend, and we're gonna have to be away from here pretty quick. So you'll just have to sit here and stink. Be an example to all the others like you. Hope the wolves get you, you woman-stealin' pile of horse dung." He stomped away, but came back with his ink roller before we left, and slapped a gob on Pike's right hand.

Bix brought a bottle of whiskey over to where Harry still lay unconscious. He poured some on the wound, then pushed the neck of the bottle into the bullet hole and held it there. Most of it ran through the man and out the opening in his back. When the liquid mingled with all the blood pooled in the dirt, Bix and Old Bear nodded and smiled. Billy brought his kit over and bandaged the wounds about as well as any doctor could've managed.

We'd been stopped for over an hour when I said, "Well, one of us is going to have to take him to Fort Smith. This traveling circus has got to get moving, and we can't drag him around with us or leave him here. I don't know enough about bullet wounds like this to have any idea if he'll survive, but if he don't get to a doctor soon, I'd guess chances won't be good."

Billy squatted, picked up a twig, and snapped it. "I ain't goin' back. I love ole Handsome like a brother, but Magruder and his bunch needs killin', and I aim to see it done."

Bix fumbled with his hat and wiped sweat from his face with a red bandanna. "No need for us to argue about it. I'll take him back. You boys help me build a travois, and I'll get him moving toward help soon's I can."

I shook the old marshal's hand. I could tell his concern for our friend was deeper than he let on. "Thanks, Bix, I appreciate it."

Later, Old Bear, Billy, and I watched as they started north. Harry didn't come around before they left, and there was no chance to say good-bye. Then, Old Bear took the lead. We almost sucked the leaves off the trees getting back on the trail. Next day, we crossed the Red

River and turned west. They'd slowed down a lot, and
we gained on them.

We'd pulled up to rest the horses when Billy said,
"They've started to panic. Magruder must have thought
Tollman would stop us." He threw his head back and
laughed. "Liked to have seen the shock on their faces
when they all realized Tollman was most likely dead.
Need to get yourself ready, Hayden. I'd bet tomorrow
they turn back north, cross the Red again, and head for
the safety of the Nations. Magruder's smart enough to
know his chances are better over there than here in Texas.
Not many towns, even fewer people on the other side.
Don't worry. We're close. Lot closer than he'd like. Look
for him to throw another one of his bootlickers at us.
Likely it'll be Vander Lamorette. He's the most dangerous one left. Personally, I'd rather face Magruder than
Lamorette. Don't expect me to give either man any
ground. I'll kill 'em the first chance I get."

Billy Bird turned out to be the closest thing to a
prophet I've ever known. Next day, Magruder's crew did
exactly what he said they'd do. Before we knew it, we
were headed toward the Wild Horse River country and
the Arbuckle Mountains. Old Bear said he could smell
them.

He'd stopped to read sign when he scratched his chin
and said, "Elizabeth safe. No sign of struggle. No time
to cause her harm. Running for their lives now. We catch
'um, they'll use her for trade."

If I slept during that chase, don't remember it. Stared
at the stars and promised each of them Magruder
wouldn't slip through my fingers. Planned his fate a thousand different ways. If it's a sin to wish such things, I'll
surely burn in hell for the deaths I plotted for him.

Tracking got tougher on the Wild Horse. Thicker brush and rocky ground made the going slow. We had to lead the horses and scout every cut we went through for ambush. No one but Old Bear and Caesar could've stayed on Magruder's bunch the way they did. Every time I thought we'd come to a dead end and the outlaw had managed to slip away again, they found his trail, and my failing spirits returned.

Two days after we turned west along the Wild Horse, Billy and I came up on Old Bear seated on a rock overlooking a canyon carved into the earth by the river. He motioned for us to climb down and stay quiet.

He leaned toward me when I kneeled beside him. "You see it?" He pointed to a spot in the side of the riverbank.

I tried. Couldn't locate anything but a rocky ledge that jutted out over the river where time and water had cut through it and left half an arch that once stretched completely across the lazy stream.

"Look hard—at bottom of rocks. Near gravel bar."

A wisp of smoke I'd never have discerned if he hadn't pointed it out drifted along the sandy bank and rose silently into the trees.

"Where's it coming from?" I asked.

"Cave—at base of broken bridge. Can't see from here. But Elizabeth's down there, Hayden." He pointed to a spot where the arch curved into the ground. Nothing but the smoke moved. The heavy air dropped over us like an unwanted blanket, and the eerie quiet left me more anxious and unsettled than at any time since the chase started.

"We hide on this side of river across from cave's mouth. See scrub brush. Good place—river very shallow. Wait till dark then go down."

"What're we gonna do when we get there?" Billy sounded like a man who'd run completely out of patience.

Old Bear reached for my anxious partner and placed a calming hand on his shoulder. "We wait, my hot young friend. We wait, till we have a chance."

Billy squirmed around so we could both see him. "We're gonna have to take whatever gets throwed our way. If any of them sons of bitches comes out of there, I say we kill 'em right on the spot. Maybe they'll all show themselves at the same time. If they do, I want Magruder."

I couldn't believe what he'd suggested. "We can't just shoot whoever shows his face. Those left just might kill Elizabeth."

Old Bear smiled. "Not to worry, Hayden. They not kill Elizabeth. Magruder smarter than that."

"Maybe so. But that leaves the other two, and I don't see how any of us can predict what they might do." I tried to think of a way we could snatch up each man as he came outside, but it just didn't work. Billy knew his outlaws. We'd have to kill them any way we could. One at a time, all in a bunch, whatever chance sent us.

That night, I must've drifted off sitting there behind that patch of scrub. I had the nightmare about the snake for the very first time. When I snapped awake, Billy had his nose right next to mine and held his fingers over my mouth. The sun had just got high enough to throw some light into the canyon. Across the river, two men stomped back and forth along the gravel bank. They shouted and gestured at one another. The tallest wore a pair of silver-plated pistols.

"That's Lamorette," Billy whispered. "The short one's Crouch Albrect."

"My God, Billy. From here we could kill them with rocks."

He pulled his guns. "I'll take Lamorette. Albrect's yours. If either man makes a move, kill 'em both."

Slowly came to my knees and leveled the Winchester on the outlaw. The tip of my front sight blotted out his head. All I had to do was squeeze the trigger. I hesitated, but my partner didn't.

Billy stood. His pistols flashed up and swept the two killers into range. "Vander Lamorette!" he yelled. "I have a warrant for your arrest. Throw down your weapons and give us Elizabeth Tilden."

The outlaw's pipe dropped from his lips as his hands darted toward his Schofields. Billy blasted the man out of his boots. He thumbed off six shots faster than I believed possible. Lamorette almost blew his own foot off with his first effort. As he crumpled to his knees, his second shot punched a hole in the clouds twisting above him.

The sound boomed down the canyon. In a panic, Albrect turned, ran for the safety of the cave, and sprayed lead in every direction as he lurched in the gravel. Rock fragments splintered and fell around us. Billy ripped off another round of shots that chased the outlaw toward the sheltering entrance.

Albrect yelled something just as he got to the opening. My first bullet caught him. He grabbed his left hip and went down, but struggled to his feet and staggered forward as my second shot hit him between the shoulder blades. His pistol fired into the ground as he fell, and once more when he rolled onto his back.

After about a minute, the silence that followed crept up my spine and rubbed my nerves so raw I wanted to pull up the biggest rocks in the river and throw them at the cave.

"My God, Billy, if they've killed Elizabeth, I'm not sure I'll be able to live with it."

"She's safe, Hayden. Even men as stupid as these wouldn't do anything to her with us so hard on their tails."

His voice still hung in the air when I heard her call to me. "Hayden, is that you? Hayden! He's dead! I'm coming out. Don't shoot anymore."

The three of us jumped into the shallow water at the same time and had barely reached the far side of the lazy stream when she toppled into my arms. I must've kissed her a thousand times before I stopped long enough to run my hands along her arms, back, and neck—to make certain she wasn't harmed. I checked the joint of every finger. I noticed she had a bruise over her right eye and a dark circle under it, but, other than that, she seemed in good shape.

"You're sure they didn't harm you?"

She nodded.

I pulled her to a safe spot on the right side of the entrance. "Where is he, Elizabeth?"

She looked surprised, like I should already know the answer. "Gone. He left yesterday morning." The words hit me like a boulder dropped from the top of the broken bridge above us. My knees went weak. She grabbed my shirt to stop me from falling. It took every ounce of strength I had left to keep from running into the woods and screaming until all the leaves on the trees fell and buried me alive.

When the shock of my continued failure to rid the world of Saginaw Bob finally wore off, we searched his hideout. The L-shaped cavern burrowed into the stone for almost thirty yards, before turning to the right for another fifty or so. Bits and pieces of furniture stood in the first open area. Three horses were staked in the deepest corner of the second room. It was dry, comfortable, and, from all appearances, had seen plenty of use in the past. In some respects, Magruder's hideaway was nicer than many cabins in the Nations.

Elizabeth took a wide path around Crouch Albrect, wouldn't go near the man. "Filthy beast, that one," she said. "I was more afraid of him than any of the others. They made me stay back near the horses. Good thing, I guess. Some of your bullets hit this back wall." She waved at broken spots in the dark rock.

Billy brought our animals inside and started a fire for coffee. We were all exhausted. I couldn't imagine where I'd have to go next to find Magruder once I got Elizabeth back home.

That night as I lay curled around her, she wept and whispered the story of the ordeal I felt I'd brought on her. "They stormed into Papa's. Shot him right in front of Mrs. Hull and me. The man dressed in black grabbed me by the front of my dress and hit me between the eyes. Everything's pretty confused for a time. Next thing I remember, I woke up on this side of the Poteau. He held me in front of him on that big black horse of his, Satan. When I came around enough to fend for myself, he threw me on an extra animal. I knew things were desperate when I heard the others call him the Preacher. And once, when we stopped, that nasty Albrect said if Magruder ever turned his back he'd 'teach me a little dance he knew.' " She sighed and pulled my arms tighter around her.

"You don't have to talk about it, Elizabeth."

Her hand came up to my cheek. "Yes, I do. For the first few days I had trouble hearing. My ears rang constantly, and my eye almost swelled shut. My view of the world looked like the reflection from an old mirror."

"Did he say anything to you?"

"He told me if I screamed, or ran, or tried to talk with anyone we might meet along the way, or did anything to betray them, he would let Pike and Albrect have me."

When I heard that, the world behind my eyes went red, and I wanted to storm hell and bite the devil's horns off.

"Hayden, you're squeezing me too hard. I can barely breathe."

I tried again to get her to understand she didn't have to relive the whole thing. Looking back on it now, I'm not sure if I said it for her sake or mine. Didn't matter. She plunged on.

"Yes, I have to get it all out now, while I can remember everything. I don't ever want to forget what they said or did. And I don't ever want to face such a thing again." She turned over and faced me. "Magruder told the others if they touched me, or molested me in any way, the dead captain at Minco Springs would be nothing compared to the way he'd make them suffer. What did he mean by that?"

"It doesn't matter right now. I'll tell you all about it another time."

Light from the fire flickered across her face. She seemed confused for a few seconds then started again. "We rode so long, Hayden. One day, when we'd stopped to rest the horses, Magruder and the one he called Pike got into an argument. The longer they went at each other the louder and more violent they got. For a few seconds the prospect that they'd kill each other looked pretty good. But I knew if that happened, I'd be left alone with Albrect, and only God knew what he might do."

She sat up and poured herself a cup of water before going on. "Pike kept screaming about how no one in his right mind would go back and confront you and the other marshals. Said he wouldn't do it. Told Magruder if he wanted you dead so bad, he should be the one to go back and do the killing. Magruder's stare made my blood run like ice water. He screeched and slobbered like a madman. Then screamed about how someone had to go back and slow the posse down, and Pike was it. He said, 'Go back now, or deal with me here. If you desert me, or run off, I'll find you and kill you myself. Now, take your choice, but make up your mind to it.' "

"What were Lamorette and Albrect doing during all this?"

"They kept their mouths shut and stayed out of the way. Pike looked to them for some help, but they just stared at the ground. Eventually he said something like, 'I've done some awful things in my life, Bob, but I've never shot anyone in the back from behind a rock.' Magruder cackled like one of Satan's imps and started yelling again. He told Lamorette if he was squeamish about it, he could do it in the open. Fight you lawdogs toe to toe with a hatchet, for all he cared, but slow the posse down long enough for the rest of us to get to his cave on the Wild Horse. Magruder seemed to believe not even the best trackers alive could find his hiding place. Pike left right after that. When he rode past me, he looked like a man who knew he'd be dead soon."

She rubbed her eyes with the backs of her hands, pulled her knees up, and hugged them. "Then the quiet one, Lamorette, rapped his pipe on the butt of one those big pistols. I can close my eyes and remember almost every word he said. 'What we gonna do with the woman if Tilden don't come or if he's behind us and Tollman don't manage to kill 'im?' Then he talked about how they'd been on a downhill slide ever since the mess they left at Minco Springs. Now, Magruder'd sent Tollman back alone to stop a bunch of hard cases none of them would try to face down alone on the best day they ever had. Then he said, 'But I'll tell you one thing, if you try to pull this same trick on me, I'll drill you faster'n you can read scripture from that Bible you stole.' Almost scared me to death."

She stopped for a few seconds and rolled back into my arms. "It got so quiet. I just knew Magruder would kill him. But he just laughed and said, 'My glorious God! I wish Azel, Benny, and Cecil were still alive.' Started ranting about nothing going right since those boys got rubbed out. He told Vander to get on his horse and get moving, or he just might get a chance to make good on his threat. And he pulled his coat away from his pistols like he intended to fight."

She fiddled with the buttons on my bib-front shirt. "Lamorette just snickered and walked away. Few minutes later, we were running again. Pike never came back. Then yesterday, we'd barely settled here when Magruder tried to do exactly what Lamorette told him not to. They argued and Magruder got to screaming again and said he guessed any job worth doing, and being done right, he'd have to do himself. He told them to keep me safe or he'd kill 'em both. Then he rode away."

"That was the last you saw of him?"

"Yes, and this morning, when Lamorette and Albrect realized he'd probably left them high and dry, they were fit to be tied. They argued about what to do for hours. Then went stomping out toward the river. That's when the shooting started." All the tension suddenly went out of her body. "I knew it was you." She closed her eyes. "I never doubted you'd come for me. My goodness, Hayden, I'm so tired." In less than a minute she was sound asleep. Don't think Gabriel's announcement of the Second Coming could have awakened her.

Stayed beside her for as long as I could. When I drew away and she didn't awaken, I pulled the blanket up and tiptoed outside to talk with Billy and Old Bear. They'd taken care of the bodies, and Old Bear now sported a big grin and two silver-plated pistols in his belt.

Billy smiled when I walked up and sipped at a steaming cup of coffee. "Elizabeth seems in fine shape, from what I could see."

"She's doing well."

Never had much luck hiding my feelings, and I guess he could tell something troubled me. "What's wrong, then, Hayden?"

"I need you to do a big favor for me, Billy."

"Sure, if I can. You know I'd do pretty much anything you could ask."

"This one will be hard, Billy."

"How hard?"

"I want you to take Elizabeth back to Fort Smith for me."

His smile vanished as he pitched his cup onto the

ground. It rattled and clanged across the rocks. "You really know how to take the wind out of a man's sails, Hayden."

"I know."

"Why can't Old Bear take her back?" He kicked at the fire and sent embers spiraling into the night air.

"I need him, Billy. We can't track the way he can. And more importantly, he's better with Caesar. You're the one. I'm about to trust you with the most important person in my life. Can't think of anyone else I'd put such faith in. The trip back to Fort Smith's dangerous, and she has to be accompanied by someone who'd be willing to give his life to keep her safe. I know you're the one to do that, Billy."

"My God, but you do know how to put a man on the spot." He pushed the butts of his pistols forward and tapped his fingers against the lip of the scabbards, then smiled. "You've been takin' lessons from Handsome Harry, haven't you?"

"Does that mean you'll do it?"

"As God is my witness, Hayden, I've never wanted to kill a man as bad in my entire life as Magruder. You know that." His head bobbed, and the emotion of memories caused his voice to crack. "Even swore to do it in the name of my friend Dick Little." A long pause left us standing there in the quiet, listening to the fire crackle. "But I guess if you rub him out for me that'll work just as well. Besides, your claim on his worthless hide outweighs mine by a considerable margin."

"You still didn't answer me. Will you take her back?"

He gave the fire one final kick and sighed like a man who couldn't see any way out of the thing. "When do you want me to start?"

"Tomorrow morning Old Bear and I'll each take an extra horse, find Magruder's trail, and ride him down. You let Elizabeth decide when she's ready. I think she should rest here for at least a day or two then you can start back. She's not gonna like the plan at all, but that's the way I've decided it."

Not only did she not like the idea, it looked for a while like I might just have to tie her up before we struck out again. But in the end, she knew I was right. Before I could get away, she pressed herself against me and whispered in my ear, "I understand now why you want Magruder so badly. Do what you have to do and hurry back to me." Then, she kissed me inside out. My brain turned into something like cornmeal mush, and my head was still spinning when Billy slapped Booger's rump.

Well, it didn't take Old Bear but about an hour to find Magruder's real trail. Murdering bastard tried to fool us by running east for a piece. But a few miles past Tishomingo, he turned south, heading for Texas, and pushed that black horse like demons were chasing him. Just when I felt certain we'd have him in our sights, he pulled a trick the likes of which neither of us could've imagined.

On a bridge just outside the hamlet of Celina, a party of heavily armed men blocked our way. Leader of the group rode the biggest horse in Texas. He needed every bit of that animal. Just like Magruder, he dressed in black and carried a Bible in his right hand and a shotgun in his left. Although the others in the group didn't appear to be the handiest lot with firearms, the man in black looked fully capable of holding his own with just about anyone, armed or otherwise.

We checked up on the north side of the bridge and he let us know real fast how determined they were. He bellowed like a lion and waved at the men behind him. "Gentlemen, I am the Reverend Jeremiah Cobb. These men are a deputation from the Church of the Everlasting Redeemer of Celina, Texas. We were informed this morning by our brother-in-faith, the Right Reverend Robert Magruder, dangerous men were determined to kill him. We've come here to make certain your nefarious plans do not come to fruition."

Old Bear looked at me like he couldn't believe what was happening. "What now, Hayden? Big man that one. Good target."

"I don't want to shoot a bunch of real honest-to-God, Bible-thumping, churchgoing Texians. But I'll do what I have to." Pulled the Winchester and rested it across my left arm. "Sir, I am Deputy U.S. Marshal Hayden Tilden on the business of Judge Isaac C. Parker's court in Fort Smith, Arkansas. Gentleman on my right is my scout and also an officer of the court. We seek the arrest and return to Fort Smith of the outlaw Saginaw Bob Magruder. If he's the man you mentioned, then you should know that he is a killer, rapist, and thief of the first water. We aim to kill him or carry him back to Arkansas for trial and hanging."

Let that one set on them for a bit. The reverend turned in his saddle and got an earful from some of his deacons. Figured I had them going. So I forged ahead. "If you attempt to stop us, I will see to it that you are brought before local magistrates on the charge of obstructing a federal officer in performance of his duty. If you threaten us, you will be dealt with in a much more severe manner." Turned back to Old Bear and whispered, "Sound tough enough?" He smiled, pulled his rifle, and took a pose just like mine.

Some of the Reverend Cobb's congregation evidently didn't care for what they'd just heard. Two of them snatched at his sleeves and gestured wildly. The argument got fairly heated before he pushed back to the front of the group.

"Reverend Magruder told me you would try to lie your way around this. We will not be swayed from our duty as we see it. I cannot allow you to continue the pursuit and persecution of a devout member of our brotherhood-in-faith."

Old Bear turned in the saddle. "Want me to shoot the preacher man, Hayden?"

"No. I've had enough of this. I don't want things to get out of hand." Stood as high in the stirrups as I could and yelled, "Mr. Cobb, would you come forward and speak with me in private?"

"Careful, my friend." Old Bear pulled the hammer back on his rifle as I moved to the center of the bridge.

Cobb approached with some degree of unease and stopped a little more than a few feet away. He came up so close I noticed his old shotgun appeared on the verge of falling apart. Most of his company seemed similarly equipped. His black suit, so imposing at a distance, suffered from years of hard use. Most of the other men were dressed in the garb of farmers. They had no idea how dangerous a situation now confronted them.

I slowly raised my right hand. "May I reach into the pocket of my coat, sir?" Flattery never hurts, and it doesn't cost much.

"Of course," he replied.

I pulled a warrant I'd had Judge Parker's clerk specially prepare for me. Rather than the pencil-scribbled *John Doe* that appeared on most of my documents, this

one was carefully lettered in a beautiful inked script. Saginaw Bob Magruder's name looked like it belonged at
the bottom the Declaration of Independence. Inside the
writ rested the letter Judge Parker sent me after the killings at Minco Springs.

"I think you should take a careful look at these documents, Mr. Cobb."

He accepted the papers and eyeballed me for several
seconds before beginning his examination. He scratched
his gray beard while reading, and eventually removed his
hat and hung it on the saddle horn. His ability at deci-
phering the documents appeared sorely limited, but he
got the gist.

Eventually, he handed everything back to me and
glanced at the nervous men he'd left behind. "Robert at-
tended our church here in Celina two, three times a year.
Always donated heavily in gold when he came. Money
he gave has been invaluable to us in the continuance of
our ministry. I must tell you, sir, the charges listed on
those papers are beyond my comprehension. That is not
the man we know. As I said, he passed our way this
morning and begged for our help. We had to come, Marshal. You do understand, don't you?" His shoulders
sagged with the realization of how wrong he'd been and
how badly he'd been duped.

"Will you and your friends move aside, Reverend
Cobb?"

"Of course, Marshal Tilden. Please accept my apology
for the harsh consequences of our meeting. Godspeed and
good luck to you and your friend, sir."

The preacher stopped his horse in the midst of Magruder's most recent group of protectors. Found myself
amazed at the number of people willing to stand between

Saginaw Bob and those, like me, who would bring him to justice. Solution to that puzzle completely eluded me.

After some moments of grumbling and a few raised voices, the Cobb party moved away from the bridge and melted back into their drab surroundings. Kept an eye on them the entire time. Given my past experience with Magruder's followers, I didn't trust the self-proclaimed Bible-beaters any further than I could throw Booger.

Old Bear and I arrived at the Empress Hotel just as it got dark. I went to the front desk and told the clerk to fetch the owner. Missy swept into the room on a cloud of silk carried by a swirl of perfume so light it just kind of tickled the edges of a man's nose and made him aware something wild and expensive approached.

"Hayden, you do turn up at the most amazingly unexpected moments. I'm so glad to see you again, dear man." She slathered on the southern charm and brushed my cheek with a kiss. "My private parlor will be more comfortable. Do come in."

We followed her down the hallway and into a brightly lit room. Overstuffed chairs and a huge sofa dominated it. I'd barely got seated when a man in a dress coat offered me a drink on a tray. Felt almost like we'd been expected.

"Missy, Saginaw Bob Magruder is here in Dallas. I'm fairly certain he's at Gertie's visiting the twins or soon will be. Old Bear and I'll go there and take him or kill him. If Carter Caine's word is any good, he'll help. Should anything go amiss, I want you to promise you'll get in touch with Elizabeth and let her know what took place."

She looked absolutely thunderstruck as she slowly lowered herself onto the sofa beside me. "Of course,

Hayden. I'll do anything you ask. But let's take a bit more positive view of this and make up our minds that I won't have to deliver such a terrible message."

"We've chased the man all over Arkansas, Texas, the Nations, Kansas, and back again. At first, he didn't have any idea we were after him. Now he does. Most likely he's on the second floor of Gertie's waiting for me to show up. But I just might have a surprise for ole Bob. I want you to go to Gertie's with us and bring Carter Caine out so I can talk with him. He's the key to ending this, once and for all."

She smiled and kissed me again. Old Bear looked away and tried to pretend he wasn't there. "I'll help you any way I can."

"Have Samson get the barouche ready. We don't want to attract any more attention than necessary."

No griping or discussion from her that time. "Clarise. We're going out immediately. Have Samson bring the carriage around."

13

"Cut Him Down, Shoot Him, and Bury Him"

THE THREE OF us sat in Missy's carriage
across the street from Gertie's and watched the front of
the building. I described the interior in detail for Old
Bear. He agreed his best position would be just left of
the main doorway in a corner created by the pillars that
decorated the building's face. I would go to the back of
the house and wait for Missy to bring Caine out.

I'd barely had time to check all my weapons when the
back door popped open and a dapper Carter Caine danced
down the steps. "Most pleasant to see you again, Marshal
Tilden." He extended his hand and shook mine warmly.

"Where's Missy?"

"Don't trouble yourself, sir. I escorted her back to the
carriage and Samson's very capable protection. She told
me why you're here. Didn't really have to. Knew you'd
be along. Magruder came stormin' in late yesterday afternoon. Man threw enough money on the table to keep

me'n the girls eatin' high on the hog for at least two years."

"Is he upstairs now?"

"Yes, but he's edgier than a cornered wildcat. Gonna have to be careful, or we might all end up gettin' dead before this night ends."

"Last time I visited, you just kind of appeared in the corner of the twins' room. Figure you have a way in that most people don't know about."

"You are a smart one, Tilden. Didn't think you noticed that." He smiled, motioned me toward the door and spoke in a low, conspiratorial manner. "Come with me. I'll show you something no one else in Dallas has ever seen or even suspects."

I hung my spurs on the back of a chair just inside the doorway of the long screened porch. We entered the house through the kitchen. Caine went directly to what appeared to be a blank wall on the far side of the room.

"Fairly wealthy family built this house. But the neighborhood went south faster than they expected." He pushed on the wall, and it swung out like a door. "Servants used these back stairs to go about their work without being seen." He motioned for me to follow. "I had the original doors removed and put up false walls all over the second floor."

The staircase twisted upward and opened onto several different landings. He picked one that placed us in a room that contained a chair, crude table, and narrow bed.

He turned and whispered, "When the girls have overnight visitors, I sleep here." He pointed to a little hole in the far wall and said, "Take a peek."

Being half a foot taller than the stocky sporting man, I had to bend over to see through his secret viewer. The

room looked exactly the way I remembered. On the bed
farthest from us, Magruder and the girls rolled about in
a tangle of arms and legs. Muffled squeals, laughter and
giggles filtered through the heavy wall. A chair decorated
with piles of weapons sat next to the head of the bed,
within Magruder's reaching distance.

Caine leaned close and whispered, "I've been waiting
for the girls to move away from him. But he's been holding on pretty tight. Cagey scoundrel knows I won't let
anything happen while they're close by. Sent in a bottle
of laudanum-spiked bourbon 'bout an hour ago. He's
been hittin' it pretty hard. Won't be long 'fore he'll be
right where we want him. Once he starts to fade, the girls
will sneak out, and we'll take him."

"What if he can taste the laudanum?"

"I've been doing this for a long time, Marshal Tilden.
I know just how much to use." He pulled his pocket
watch out and looked at it. "He should start to wither in
about another thirty minutes or so. Trust me on this, we'll
have him in cuffs within the hour."

Sure as cows in Kansas, I'd just taken a break from
the peephole when Caine slapped me on the arm. "Now's
the time." He stepped to the far end of the bed and
pushed on the wall. Five seconds later, we stood in the
corner where he'd suddenly appeared on my last visit.

Girls had vanished, but the air still dripped with the
scent of whiskey, tobacco, and sweaty bodies. Magruder
was sprawled across the bed in his drawers and breathing
heavily. Caine's right hand dipped into the collar of his
coat and snapped forward like a whip. A gleaming bowie
flashed into his fingers. Its twin sprang from the top of
his left boot. He motioned me to the right side of the

room while he moved to the left. We crept across the floor like church mice with sore feet.

Truth of it is, to this very moment I'm still not exactly sure what happened next. It all went so fast and so slow at the same time. But near as I can remember, we'd managed to get less than two steps away from Magruder when he sat up in the bed and shot Carter Caine. The sporting man grabbed his head and dropped like a felled tree.

In the dying flash of that pistol's fire—a span of less than half a second—I had to decide whether to kill the most evil man I'd ever encountered outright or try to take him alive. Everything I knew of him screamed from the deepest part of my soul for the end of his sorry life. It would've been so easy. The Winchester had him dead center. A single trigger pull and a cavern the size of my hand would've exploded from his back. An eye for an eye—a tooth for a tooth—blood for blood. But a vision of him hanging from Maledon's Gates of Hell popped into my brain as he swung his pistol my direction. I stepped into him, brought the rifle butt around, and swatted the little pocket gun out of his hand.

He came off the bed like a panther with a red-hot poker up its behind. I didn't even have time to blink before he grabbed my wrist and jerked so hard the rifle went flying across the room. Tried for the pistol on my hip, but he latched onto my right arm with a grip that felt like it could have stripped bark off a green Texas cottonwood limb.

We were near nose to nose. "So nice to finally see you again, plow pusher." He hissed so loud spit sprayed all over my face. "Say hi to yore stupid, clod-kicking daddy for me when I finish with you." He smiled and winked.

But the sneer on his lips started to fade as arms that had busted Kentucky sod from the age of seven slowly forced his hands up till my fingers wrapped around his throat.

His right hand darted down between us and snatched at the pistol hanging against my belly. We grappled around the room for some seconds before the gun slipped from his sweaty grip and landed on one of the feather pillows from the bed. Ragged fingernails sliced across my face and left bloody cuts. I came down on him with a wicked lick that caught him between the eyes. Blow like that should have been enough to fell a Montana antelope.

He stumbled backward and dropped to his right knee. I grabbed a bar stool and caught him a glancing blow across his left shoulder. Splintered wood shot up the wall and destroyed an oil painting of one of the Hunter sisters. Men from all over the West must have admired that picture for its ability to arouse them. Naked, that red-haired gal was something to see.

Magruder screeched like a wounded wildcat and bounced off the floor like he had springs in his feet. I went down under the weight of him. Sweat and blood and spit flew in every direction. We rolled around on the floor for so long not a stick of furniture got spared. I finally bulldogged him onto his back. Hit him at least a dozen times with a closed fist that bounced off his head and sent flames of pain up through my hand to my elbow. He went limp for a second, and I hesitated. Then he came off the floor with another burst of screaming, bloodthirsty power. Sent us ricocheting off the walls from one side of the room to the other.

Just when I'd about given up any hope of success and begun to actually fear for my life, I caught him with an

awesome right to the jaw. Put him on his knees again.
Things got real quiet.

Then, out of thin air, Old Bear appeared beside me.
Held a piece of corner post from one of the beds. "You
havin' too much fun, Hayden. Rest, my friend." Never
expected to see a man get a beating with a piece of furniture. But, calm as a cow in clover, my old friend went
at Magruder with all the skill of a watchmaker. Started
at his feet and worked his way up. Ended it all with a
shattering blow to the head. Magruder went down like a
hog in a slaughterhouse.

Old Bear pitched his club into the corner and let out
a long, ragged breath. "Feel much better now, Hayden.
When I see him dead, think the spirits of Waxon and his
family will leave me in peace."

We pulled Carter Caine to his feet and discovered Magruder's bullet had put a nice dent in his skull, but left
his brains intact. 'Course, he bled all over hell and yonder. Old Bear wiped him off with a piece of rag while I
cuffed and shackled our bloodied killer.

Caine grabbed me by the sleeve. "Hayden, get him
away from Dallas . . . quick as you can. He has friends
here. If they find out he's been taken, could be trouble
aplenty. Go down the back way. I'll cover for you when
the local law arrives. Take 'em a few minutes, but, trust
me, they're coming."

We snatched up everything that looked like it might
belong to Magruder. Caine and I dragged him down the
stairs and threw him over my extra mount. Old Bear followed with all the clothes and weapons he could carry.
He did an ingenious rope trick on the outlaw. Said he'd
packed mules for the cavalry for a time. "This way, pos-

sible for us to run hard for home. Not worry 'bout losin' him."

Caine slapped me on the back and shooed us away. "Go, go . . . go now. The girls and I'll take care of everything. Get ole Bob to Fort Smith and hang him. Then, cut him down, shoot him, and bury him."

I jumped on Booger, then leaned down and took Caine's hand in mine. "I'm forever in your debt, sir. Should you need help in any way, just send word. I'll come to you as fast as horses can run. Be sure and tell Missy what happened and apologize for my hasty departure." He smiled and slapped Booger's enormous rump.

We left town like tomcats shot with a bootjack. Didn't stop running for two days. No sleep. No rest. Ride nearly killed Magruder. When we pulled him off that horse, he was black and blue from the roots of his hair to his ankles and could barely move. Had to keep a watchful eye on Old Bear the whole time. Kept remembering what he'd said about taking Magruder's heart.

We ran hard from Dallas all the way to Durant. Caught the M.K.&T. to Vinita. One time on the train I went to sleep. Magruder was all bloody again when I woke up. Old Bear smiled for hours.

Story about us catching the evil rascal must have been running ahead of us like a grass fire. Sizable crowd gathered at Vinita station when we got down. Locals seemed awestruck. But the possibility of losing him to someone bent on vengeance didn't hit me till we got back out on the trail.

Several times men rode up carrying rope already braided in a hangman's knot. One said, "Give him to me. No need to waste time on the son of a bitch. They's a likely limb just yonder. We'll see he meets the devil today."

A throng of rowdies formed up on the east side of the Arkansas next to the ferry landing. Things got to looking pretty hairy till Bix and some other marshals showed up. We were all relieved when we finally managed to get Magruder in a cell. The door clanged shut, and he looked back at me like an animal with his foot in a trap. Crowd stood around outside for hours. Long 'bout midnight, they'd managed to get pretty drunk and raised such a ruckus we had to go out and put an end to it.

I didn't get to see Elizabeth till the day after we got back. Near as I could tell she'd survived her ordeal virtually unscathed and gave no indication a deadly interruption of her life had even occurred.

She kissed me so hard it bruised my lips. Rested her head on my shoulder and said, "Handsome Harry's going to make it. We moved him from the doctor's office into a room over the store. I hired a nurse to take care of him."

"That's good to hear, Elizabeth. Feared he might be dead by the time we got back."

"He came close, Hayden. He came real close."

Went to see him soon as I could. He looked right pale and didn't talk much, but I could tell he was mighty glad to see me.

"Heard you caught the scurvy cur." He held my hand like he didn't want to let go.

"We caught him, Harry. He's in a cell on Murderers Row right now."

He leaned back into his pillows. "Good, I think I can sleep some now."

It's still an unfathomable mystery how life can step up

to the table and deal you out a hand you never in your wildest dreams expected. Elizabeth had moved all the things we kept at the Pines to our new quarters over the store. By her father's death, we now owned a bank, a general store, several plots of land on both ends of Towson Avenue, and rent houses all over town. Awful to think it, but when Magruder killed Jennings Reed he pretty much ensured me of a fine livelihood, no matter how I chose to spend my time.

First thing I did with some of my newfound wealth was buy Billy a model 1873 Winchester marked One of One Thousand. Elizabeth's father had the rifle hid in back of his gun case. No one around Fort Smith had been able to come up with enough money to purchase it from him. According to her, Mr. Reed hadn't done much to try to sell the weapon. She made me pay for it. Said it'd mess with her bookkeeping if we just gave it away.

About a week later, we took Billy out for the evening and presented our little gift to him. He was the proudest man I've ever seen, and the envy of all his friends.

Anyhow, Judge Parker's demand for efficiency was as strong as ever. Magruder's head barely had time to hit his pillow on Murderers Row when I sat in court and watched as jailers dragged him before the bench and he heard the words that sealed his fate like sour pickles in a glass jar. Judge set his trial date for six months from the first day of confinement. I can remember almost every word Judge Parker said the morning of Bob's arraignment.

"Normally I would not put the occurrence for such an event so far away from the present date. I do, however, want to give everyone who wishes an opportunity to offer testimony in this prosecution. Since your capture, sir, I have received communications from those all over Arkansas, Texas, and the Indian Nations who wish to publicly tell their stories of your sins against them. Highly unusual—in most cases, my marshals have to go out and drag witnesses in for the trial of a man with your background. It appears many of those you mistreated in the past can't wait to tell their stories. Additionally, it has come to my attention you have escaped from law enforcement officials and jails in the past. I therefore direct the chief jailer to keep you in shackles until such time as this proceeding resolves itself."

Magruder's face flushed. A stream of the hottest language I've ever heard poured out of the man. 'Fore the bailiffs could even think to respond, he jumped up on the table between the Judge and the station where those accused stood to hear rulings. Law books, evidence, stacks of depositions, and other related papers skittered all directions as he ran through them and sent himself flying headlong toward the double windows behind Parker's gigantic desk.

Quicker than any of us could have imagined, the Judge grabbed the soaring outlaw around the neck. They tumbled to the floor and wrestled about in the pile of law books and papers. Magruder screamed at the top of his lungs, but no one could understand him. Sounded like something foreign. Everyone in the court rushed forward to help.

Took two bailiffs and a marshal to pull the crazed outlaw off the Judge. Tussle got even more violent when Magruder managed to bring up a knife from his boot top and put some painful, but minor, cuts in the arms and hands of the men who eventually subdued him. After a few more minutes of his foul mouth, the bailiffs jerked him to his feet and pushed him back to his place. By that time, they'd shackled and chained him hand and foot.

When I glanced back at the Judge, it appeared as though absolutely nothing wayward had occurred. He was totally unruffled and even-keeled when he said, "Sir, this court has seen almost every form of human debris imaginable over the past several years. We have tried murderers, rapists, arsonists, child killers, deviates of manifold types, and almost every other kind of criminal imaginable. This is the first time any of the accused has exhibited brass enough to attempt an escape directly from my courtroom. Your conduct leaves me no choice but to keep you chained until such time as judgment against you has been rendered. I would like you to know too, all those who have attempted escape from this place, prior to your most recent effort, are now dead. Bailiffs, take Mr. Magruder back to his cell. Instruct all the marshals and jailers to watch him closely, and tell them to shoot him if he makes any other such attempt."

That afternoon Bix Conner strolled into the chief marshal's office, poured himself a cup from the pot of stout coffee that lived on the big-bellied iron stove, then dropped his sizable bulk into a chair beside me. "Hear tell Magruder done tried to fly out the window behind the Judge's desk."

"Yep. Judge himself brought the man down."

"You saw it, Hayden?" He blew and sipped at the steaming liquid.

"Saw it all, Bix. Trust me, Magruder would never have made it to the window. I had him in my sights as soon as he topped the table in front of Parker's desk. If one of his fingertips had touched a pane of that glass, we'd be digging a grave right now."

The old lawman grinned from ear to ear. "Now that would've been worth seein'. You gotta admit, though, the crazy scoundrel has a lotta hard bark coverin' his big arrogant self to pull such a trick. Tried to fly over the Hangin' Judge. Absolutely astonishin'."

Well, the *Fort Smith Elevator* couldn't print enough about Magruder, his evil deeds, and the coming trial. About two weeks after his birdman imitation, word got out that he'd sent for Marcus Aurelius Strawn. That's when the heavy-duty stuff really started flying.

In form and execution, lawyer Strawn came close to resembling a traveling tent revivalist who had deliberately set himself on fire and was in the process of trying to put the blaze out with his own voice. Some, who'd heard the man speak at public gatherings in the wilds of untamed Arkansas, held he could whisper loud enough to be heard from a hundred yards away during the passing of a mile-wide cyclone.

I met him over lunch in Julia's Café about a week after he arrived. He just pulled up a chair to my table and imposed himself on me. "Marshal Tilden, I'm Marcus Strawn." He held out a hand the size of a dinner plate and acted like it would be my privilege to shake it.

I refused and said, "I know who you are. Paper's hereabouts have been full of Marcus Aurelius Strawn lately." Took an immediate dislike of the flashy lawyer for a variety of reasons, not the least of which was that his arrogance knew absolutely no bounds.

The six-and-a-half-foot-tall man leaned back in his chair and eyeballed me like I was a dangerous bug he needed to squash. "You know, Mr. Tilden, I've defended Robert Magruder before. Got him off every time." He had one of those voices made it sound like God spoke through him directly to his audience.

"Mr. Strawn, he's going to hang this time around. Trust me on this one."

"I've known Bob Magruder for years and cannot believe the charges brought against him. He says he didn't do any of it. Said it must've been someone who looked like him or maybe the witnesses hate him for some unknowable reason." He brushed cigar ashes from the front of his white linen suit, a costume he evidently wore in the coldest of weather.

"Mr. Strawn, I saw Saginaw Bob Magruder shoot and kill my father. His men murdered my mother and sister. And he's rubbed out a good many others I'm aware of. By rights he should be dead and buried in Texas as we speak, but killing's too good for the evil bastard. I want to see his neck stretched. My testimony alone should hang the man. But I'm not unique. A score of witnesses have similar stories to tell and, like me, can't wait for the trial to start. Your backwoods fame won't help him, sir."

I leaned across the table and dropped my voice so low he could barely hear me. "And on top of all that, even if Satan comes straight from the pit and manages to help you get him off, you have my personal assurance he won't get out of the courthouse alive. Gave up my personal claim on his death once and won't do it again."

"That's mighty bold talk, Marshal Tilden. I might have to speak with Judge Parker about what you just said."

Sat and stared at him like I wanted to rip his head off somewhere around the neighborhood of his shirt collar. His bushy brows scrunched up in a knot over eyes so brown they were almost black.

"I met Bob Magruder in Mount Pleasant, Texas, ten years ago, Marshal. We shared a game of poker at the Lone Pine Saloon. Worthless piece of human dung named Logan Silvers argued with us over every card hitting the table that night. When Silvers finally branded Bob a cheat, the gunfire was in-stan-taneous. One shot from the Preacher's pocket pistol caught the loud-mouthed rube just over his right eyebrow. Silvers was dead when his head hit the table."

"You have a point to this story, Mr. Strawn?"

"I do, Marshal Tilden. Local law enforcement jerked Bob up short and put him on trial for murder. I testified on his behalf. Court found him not guilty. We've been friends ever since. Got him off several other times when similarly charged. I intend on using all the legal powers at my considerable disposal to get my friend out of your clutches."

"Your client shot my father in the eye, too, sir. Part of his brains ended up on my face. I intend to walk that murdering son of a bitch to the noose for it. And if, by some fluke of nature, you manage to get him off, I'll do what I should have done in Texas. And if I have to I'll come after you next."

Strawn's eyeballs looked like saucers. "Takes a lot of nerve to threaten a client's life right in the face of his lawyer, then threaten his lawyer too."

"You could be correct about that, sir, but trust me on this matter—I meant every word of it. You might be one of the more highly-thought-of attorneys in Arkansas—by those who don't know any better—but I'm sure you understand completely that even if you get lucky enough to win another one for ole Bob, a lot could happen between then and the day he walks away from jail again. Truth is, the two of you might just go out together. Not likely, but then you just never know, do you?"

He looked like a man who had just confronted his own mortality for the first time. "You know I might inform the court of that threat, Mr. Tilden."

"That's the second time you've threatened me with exposure, sir. I'll deny this conversation ever took place. Who do you think Judge Parker will believe?" He mumbled something else, pushed away from the table, and lumbered to the door. I tried to stay away from him after that.

He had arrived in Fort Smith accompanied by a fragile, gray-haired lady they introduced around town as the mother of Saginaw Bob. Claimed the old woman traveled all the way from New York City in order to testify on behalf of her wayward son. Local newspaper types managed to drum up considerable sympathy on her behalf and, indirectly, for her poor misguided baby boy.

Seems things haven't changed all that much over the years. Folks who ply the ink-slinging trade haven't evolved too far past freshwater mussels when it comes to thinking. Given the slightest chance they'll get all misty-eyed and weepy over the plight of anyone who can cast themselves in the role of victim. Strawn and that old woman did a hell of a job playing pitiful.

Few days after that gray-haired saint made her appearance, the Reverend Mr. Cobb and about ten members from the Church of the Everlasting Redeemer of Celina, Texas showed up. Didn't take me long to realize lawyer Strawn intended to make it appear Magruder spent most of his time singing hymns for his sweet, elderly mother—who wept profusely for reporters and local churchgoing ladies at the mere mention of his name. Billy warned me things would get a lot worse before they got any better.

All the local newspapers were roundly fooled by their pile of horse fritters. Hardly a day passed that didn't result in some new revelation about the innate goodness and upstanding citizenship of Robert James Magruder, itinerant minister and devout man of God. Some women in the community openly sloshed tears in every direction after reading about the terrible circumstances of poor Robert's untimely departure from the comfort and safety of his family home—and the numerous instances of other such charges against him that had also resulted in acquittals. By the time the Preacher actually had his day in the sun, I'd begun to fear he might appear in Parker's courtroom dragging a wooden cross and sporting a crown of thorns. Rubbed my nerves so raw, I finally had to stop reading the damned newspapers.

Judge named Noble Mason chief prosecutor. He worked like Hephaestus at the forge. Exact opposite of Strawn. Man of small physical stature, natty dresser, blessed with a legal mind some people compared to a crosscut saw. Went at his job with such single-minded devotion those closest to him sometimes feared he would ruin his intellect with such narrow dedication to duty. Hadn't been for him, Bob's trial for the murders of my family would have been held in the Eastern District Court of Arkansas. Mason got that changed.

When evil men found out that single-minded little lawyer would prosecute them, many automatically pled guilty rather than go to trial. Marcus Aurelius Strawn's overconfident and cheery disposition changed dramatically when he discovered who his opponent at the bar was.

14

"OYEZ! OYEZ! OYEZ!"

HONEST TO GOD, when the trial finally started people jammed that courtroom like sardines in a seal-tight. Reporters from Mississippi, Louisiana, and Texas had to bargain for whatever seats they could get. Hundreds of spectators milled around outside, and were kept apprised of the proceedings by informers who held the valuable window spots.

Reminded me of that first hanging I saw. Hawkers sold everything from roasted corn on the cob to hand-carved renditions of Maledon's gallows. Even the prisoners held in the cellar section of the jail got all the blustery details by way of messages shouted down to them by outside observers. Old Bear, Billy, Handsome Harry, and I had choice front-row seats so I'd be right handy when the prosecution called on me. Caesar flopped his big self in a spot on the floor right at my feet.

Court crier, Mr. Hammersley, almost blew our spurs

off when he announced Judge Parker's entrance. "Oyez!
Oyez! Oyez! The Honorable District and Circuit Courts
of the United States for the Western District of Arkansas,
having jurisdictions of the Indian Territory, are now in
session. God bless the United States and these honorable
courts."

Judge Parker took his seat, shuffled a pile of papers,
glanced around the packed room, and said, "Case before
the court today is the United States versus Robert James
Magruder—indicted for the murders of Jonathan, Mary,
and Rachael Tilden. You may begin, Mr. Mason."

Lawyer Mason believed so firmly in the ironclad nature of Bob's guilt for the crimes against my family, he
decided to limit my direct oath to that single incident.
Most everyone in Arkansas and the Territories had heard
of the killings.

Mason had said to me earlier, "Hayden, your story
contains such unadorned drama and awful tragedy that
the necessity of any prolonged ordeal might be avoided
by simply convicting ole Bob of the misfortune he visited
on you."

Despite the fact that Magruder had only been indicted
by the grand jury for the murders of my family, Noble
planned to follow my testimony with a speedy parade of
people who could also personally attest to the outlaw's
astonishing capacity for brutality.

Anyway, when he called me up he only asked two
questions. "Marshal Tilden, would you tell the court how
you know the defendant?"

Told it all in as even and emotionless a tone as I could
muster, given the gruesome facts. My tale had exactly
the impact Mason wanted. Virtually every spectator in

the courtroom had a cupped hand over his or her best ear in order to hear what I had to say.

When I finished, the prosecutor shook his finger ominously in Magruder's direction and said, "And that man, Robert Magruder—alias Saginaw Bob—is the one who killed your father and led the gang of assassins who murdered your sister and mother?"

"Yes, that's him. I tracked the man in Arkansas, the Nations, Texas, and Kansas. Captured him in Dallas with the assistance of a friend."

Tried to appear calm. For a bit it felt like I might explode. But when I sneaked a glance at Marcus Strawn's face, a feeling of peace I hadn't known in almost two years came over me. Honest to God, he looked like a man staring into a well where clearing waters rapidly revealed the face of doom. He didn't even bother to question me. Just shook his head. Magruder shot me a look that could have peeled paint off a barn door in Maine.

Far as anyone in court that day could tell, ole Bob would certainly hang for killing my family. But, like I said before, Noble didn't stop there and Judge Parker allowed all of it. Mason kept up the attack and called over a dozen others who'd witnessed the varied and terrible crimes of Magruder and his henchmen. Every time Strawn objected, the Judge simply motioned him back to his seat.

The testimony of that parade of God-fearing citizens had a visible impact on the killer. His arrogance and swagger faded. His belligerent attitude went into hiding. About halfway through the day he refused to look anyone in the courtroom in the eye. The public airing of his transgressions seemed to douse most of the fire left in the man.

Once Billy Bird turned to me and whispered, "I knew he'd cave when the full weight of what would surely happen hit him. The man can see his own hanging coming now. He's done. Even if he weren't hanged, he'll never be the same. He wouldn't get a mile away from this courthouse, now, before someone killed him. It's over, Hayden."

"Not till I see him swing, Billy. Not till I see him swing."

I suppose everyone who had a Magruder horror to relate thought his or hers was the worst. Percy Billings's account of the torture of Captain Roland Gatewood at Minco Springs stunned everyone. But not even such heartless disregard for a fellow man's life as Magruder showed at Minco Springs compared to some of his other criminal activity.

Several folks from Texarkana relived the death of little Suzan Moody. As Michael Moody described the broken body of his only child, tears streamed down the faces of even the most callous. Range-toughened cowhands, crime-hardened marshals, red-necked farmers, and tight-fisted bankers openly wept when Moody was so overcome with anguish he could no longer speak. Noble rested his case after Moody testified.

Later he told me, "I just didn't think the court could've taken any more horror."

Gotta hand it to Marcus Aurelius Strawn. He brought in a string of character witnesses who reeled off glowing stories about his murderous client. The Reverend Mr. Cobb and the deacons from his church recited individual experiences attesting to the Christian goodness of the man. And the sainted, gray-haired Mrs. Robert Magruder, Senior, hobbled to the stand and gave a weepy-eyed performance on the innate benevolence and humanity of her "kindly" son.

When Mason got an opportunity to cross-examine the old lady, he asked a single question. "Have you ever heard the name Bessie Stubbelfield?"

Color disappeared from the woman's cheeks like coffee running off a saucer. Strawn jerked upright as if he'd been hit by lightning. She dabbed her eyes and nose with an embroidered hanky and cast a nervous glance in the direction of the defense table. Strawn stared at his hands.

"Did you understand the question? Have you ever heard the name Bessie Stubbelfield?"

Turned out that sweet little old lady owned a whorehouse in El Paso, Texas, and every word of her widely circulated tales about her "son" Robert were nothing more than blackhearted lies. When her "testimony" ended she tottered out of the courtroom amid hisses and boos. Noble Mason noted that he might charge her with perjury sometime in the future. Heard later some of the "good ladies" rode her out of town on a rail.

Next day, people jammed the courthouse for the prosecutor's closing remarks. He reminded the jury of every detail of my family's murders and all the other crimes brought before the bar.

After describing each transgression in detail, he pointed to Saginaw Bob and thundered, "The witness identified that man as the person responsible for the atrocity."

Then, he attacked every inconsistency he could find in the testimony of the defense character witnesses. He used the perjury of Bessie Stubbelfield like a club and gave Marcus Aurelius Strawn a public whipping with it.

Mason finished with one final admonition to the jury.

"Gentlemen, you've heard all you need to hear. You know what is right and what is wrong. We expect a verdict of guilty. You know your duty in this matter. Go now and do your sworn duty."

Strawn's final statement turned out to be the most pitiful anyone could remember having heard from the man. I always felt he couldn't keep his mind on things there at the end. Probably thought the Judge just might throw him in jail for his part in Bessie Stubbelfield's obvious perjury.

Anyway, he said, "May it please the court and the gentlemen of the jury, you did indeed hear the evidence. The defense has nothing more to add."

Even old-time court followers were thunderstruck by the brevity of his remark. I have little doubt it ranked right up there with the shortest final plea for a defendant ever recorded.

Judge Parker presented the jury with a brief, but impressive charge. They retired for deliberation and it only took them about ten minutes to bring in a verdict of guilty for the murders of my father, mother, and sister. I heard later they never even got around to a written ballot.

Foreman Arthur Hunnicutt stood and read in a strong voice, "We, the jury, find the defendant, Robert James Magruder, guilty of murder as charged in the indictment."

Took Judge Parker just about two more minutes to sentence the murdering bastard. His words burned a spot in my brain like a brand on a steer.

"Robert James Magruder, stand up. You have been convicted by a verdict of the jury, justly rendered, of the heinous crime of murder. Have you anything to say why sentence of the law should not be passed on you?"

Magruder's head snapped up. "I ain't got nuthin' to say to you egg-suckin' sons of bitches. Go on and get it over with, you black-robed bastard."

Judge didn't even blink. "I do not relish the prospect of being responsible for the departure of any man from this earth at the end of a rope, sir. But, the verdict was an entirely just one, and, by God, you have justly earned such an end. The enormity and wickedness of your sins against mankind leave no room for sympathy for one such as yourself. Therefore, one month from today, between the hours of nine o'clock in the forenoon and five o'clock in the afternoon of the said day, you will be taken to the gallows under guard by the U.S. marshal, or his deputies, and hanged by the neck until you are dead. May God, whose laws you have broken, have mercy on your immortal soul and the souls of all those you've sent to him."

Courtroom erupted in a torrent of emotion. People whooped with joy and threw their hats in the air. Billy Bird put his arm around my shoulders to keep me from collapsing.

Old Bear smiled and fingered his huge knife. "It is near, Magruder. Your time with me is near," he whispered.

Those thirty days passed like molasses flowing in February. Oh, I went to work, did my job, and saw to the needs of my wife and friends. But when the time for his departure finally came, I must admit it surprised me. In my mind, he died the moment Art Hunnicutt read the verdict. The physical act of sending him to hell was little more than a formality. But, it was a formality I planned to attend. Forced Judge Parker and the U.S. marshal into letting me act as one of the party who escorted ole Bob to the gallows.

Met with the other five guards that morning. We waited outside the prison door until five minutes before noon. Strawn walked with him when the jailers brought him out. They'd dressed him in a brand spankin' new preacher's frock. The old fierceness seemed to have returned. Looked to me like the man planned to go to his Maker in just as defiant a manner as he'd lived his life.

When he stepped outside, and we started toward Maledon's playground, he swelled up and looked pleased with the size of the crowd. Bixley Conner said later he'd never seen that many people in town for a single hanging.

God gave him a beautiful, crisp morning to die. Few puffy, fast-moving clouds here and there. Huge throng of people gathered on the grounds. Hush kind of washed back through the multitude as we made our way past them and started up the steps of the platform. Reverend Mr. Cobb walked with us. Prayed loud enough to be heard in St. Louis. Maledon'd set up a single noose at the end of the scaffold next to the steps. U.S. marshal read the death warrant then gave Magruder the chance to say some final words. He waited so long Maledon stepped up with the hood. Magruder shook it aside then went on a hell of a rip.

Sounded like he was preaching one of his sermons when he said, "You biscuit-eatin' sons of bitches make me sick. For the past ten years, I've robbed men, raped women, murdered anyone I wanted, stole cattle, and done as I damn well pleased. If I had it to do over again, I'd do all that and worse. It took you sanctimonious, church-goin' bastards more than a decade to finally do something about it. You know why? You're cowards, every damned one of you. No more guts than a garter snake. You're average, and the average man is a yellow-bellied rabbit waitin' to get skinned. Decisive men, men of power, man killers who have no fear of the law, other men's opinions, or the prospect of death will always prey on such as you. You're sheep just waitin' to be sheared, cattle waitin' to be butchered."

Then he turned on me with a look that could have scorched the devil's doormat. "If I'd been a better shot, Tilden, you'd be dead, and I wouldn't be in this fix. See you in hell, boy."

Mr. Maledon got Bob's next verbal broadside. "Thought you were gonna hang me, you grave-ugly son of a bitch. Let's get on with it."

Executioner just stood there and smiled back. Shadow from one of those clouds crept across the stage and made Maledon's face look like a skull.

Some folks in the mob who had heard what ole Bob said started screaming, "Hang him, hang him, hang the son of a bitch!"

Magruder glared at me and winked as Maledon started to pull the hood over his head. I think the last thing he saw on this earth, when he turned away from me, was the smiling face of a child in the front row who sat on his pa's shoulders and held an ear of roasted corn.

Junior glanced up from his notes. He sounded eager, his questions more urgent. "You're sure about that? The last thing he saw was probably a child eating corn?"

"As sure as I can be. But if you're looking for drama, Junior, don't look to a towheaded kid with a roasting ear in his hand. You won't believe what happened next." I hesitated just long enough to let that sink in and build on the boy. He took the bait like a starving bass.

"What? What happened? Come on. Come on. Quit smiling like the Cheshire cat and get on with it."

"Well, during Bob's speech—and while Maledon slipped the noose over his head and cinched the knot up tight against his ear—a small black cloud split from those others, came across the Arkansas from the southwest, and stopped almost directly over the stage. Once everything looked the way Mr. Maledon wanted it, he stepped over to the lever and threw it. Platform disappeared under Magruder's feet, and the open hole swallowed him up. But, before his body hit the end of that piece of oiled hemp, a searing bolt of lightning fell from that cloud and shattered the right front corner of the gallows, not fifteen feet from where I stood. Resulting thunderclap rattled every window for miles around."

"Aw, come on now. Lightning hit the gallows?"

"Yep. Knocked me colder than January in Kansas. When I came around, Handsome Harry was slapping my face. I'd landed on the ground about ten feet from where I started. Harry pulled me back to my feet. Hundreds of people were on their knees praying. Reverend Mr. Cobb passed out and, for a while, people thought he'd died. Heard one woman say she felt God sure enough approved Magruder's exit from this world. One old man ran through the crowd shouting, 'He's cookin' in hell! He's cookin' in hell!' I stumbled back onto the scaffold. There was a black streak ran from the corner post to the trap and dove into the hole. Magruder's body was spinning at the end of that rope like a kid's top, and smoke poured from the sack covering his head. I looked up, and the sky was as clear as a glass of water."

"You're sincere about this? You know I can go back

and check the newspapers. You're not just telling the greenhorn a big stretcher here, are you, Tilden?"

"Do what you have to, Junior. Check the *Elevator* under 'Saginaw Bob Executed: A Remarkable Occurrence.' But that's not the end of it."

"Oh, my glorious God. What else? Come on, give me all of it."

"That night I went over to Grubbs' Funeral Home and sat with the body for over an hour. Just to satisfy myself he was gone for good, you know. Went back home to Elizabeth and—for the first time in longer than I could remember—slept like a man restored. Next morning, all the local newspapers carried the story of the execution. One had a side bar special a few days later that told of an odd happening at Grubbs'. Seems Clarence Grubbs claimed that when he went to embalm the body, he found a hole in the man's chest—the heart had gone missing."

"Oh, my Lord. Old Bear actually stole Magruder's heart?"

"Never really knew the answer to that one for sure. We buried the outlaw, minus his black heart, of course, in an obscure area of the graveyard. Someone planted a marker made from the upper half of an outhouse door. Thing just kind of mysteriously appeared a few days after the burial. People were so superstitious, at the time, no one had nerve enough to take it down."

"What about Old Bear?"

"He showed up again about a week after the hanging. I didn't question him about his comings and goings. We never discussed where he'd been. Didn't have time. By then, a renegade half-breed named Charlie Two Knives was leading a party of killers on a rampage across the southern half of the Territories, and Judge Parker wanted him caught or killed. Billy, Harry, and I got back out on the scout pretty quick. Old Bear and the dog shadowed us everywhere we went."

Junior fell back into his chair and groaned like he'd been poleaxed. "Oh, God. It's late. I've got to go. I'm going to spend the rest of this week writing all this up. First installment—or chapter—should be in next Sunday's paper, if I can get it ready in time."

He staggered to his feet. General Black Jack Pershing hopped to the floor, then to my lap. Franklin J. Lightfoot Jr. shook my hand. "It's been quite a ride, Marshal Tilden, quite a ride. Thanks for the trip."

"My pleasure, Junior. Don't be a stranger."

He wobbled down the hallway and waved absently over his shoulder. "I'll send you copies of everything that's printed."

Couple of days later, Chief Nurse Leona Wildbank herself wheeled Carlton out. He looked happier than a dog with two tails—had his head pushed back against that gal's extensive chest like it was a goose-down pillow.

When she strutted away he said, "Just love that big-boned woman. Wish I was sixty again." After his mind finally came back to reality, he realized Junior hadn't made an appearance. "Where's our pink-faced boy, Hayden?"

"Oh, he won't be back for a few days."

He cupped his right hand over his ear. "You say he won't be back?"

"Won't be back for a few days." Had to yell at him that time.

"You tell him everything? You tell it all, like I said?"

"Not quite everything."

"Tell him about Albino Bob Thornton?"

"Didn't get to Albino Bob."

"What'd ya say?"

"No, didn't get to the Albino," I yelled.

"How 'bout Three Toed Willie Thornton?"

"Nope."

"Colonel Black Jack Rix?"

"Didn't make it to Black Jack either."

"What about Smilin' Jack Paine, Dennis Limberhand, and Cotton MaCabe?"

"Sorry."

"Hell, old man, you didn't tell him anything."

"Oh, I told him enough. We've got a hook in him now, Carl. He'll be back. That boy's gonna become a permanent fixture around the Rolling Hills Home for the Aged, as long as one of us can manage to keep telling stories. The life and times of Hayden Tilden and Carlton J. Cecil are gonna end up being the only thing he can think about. Hey, he still hasn't heard about Gopher Riley, L. B. Ledoux, or Chief Buffalo Head Long Feather. Barefoot Johnson, Matthew Standing Elk, or Lowdog. They're all waiting for him."

"Always liked that story 'bout Oliver White Eagle, myself. Wasn't with you on that 'un, Hayden, but liked hearin' 'bout it anyway. Say, could you put Black Jack in my lap? He'll warm me up. I think I'll take a nap."

"I swear, Carlton, it's got to be over ninety already. Just don't understand how you can be cold." I dropped Black Jack in his lap and started for the lunchroom to get us some bowls of that green Jell-O Carl likes so much.

He gathered in the cat like it was more important than

gold. "You'll wake me up when Junior comes back, won't you, Hayden?"

"You bet, Carl. Soon as the boy shows that seriously shaved face of his."

He pulled his shawl tighter, stroked Black Jack's head, and nodded. "Good. Wouldn't want to miss any of Hayden's stories, now would we, Black Jack?"

I don't care what Carlton says, I still believe that old man hears a lot better than he lets on.

ABOUT THE AUTHOR

Jimmy Butts earned a Bachelor of Science in Education degree, with a major in English and minors in American History and Communications from Henderson State University. He taught seniors in public schools for thirteen years. An early flirtation with the military led to an eight-year hitch with the U.S. Army Reserve and a rank of sergeant upon discharge.

Jimmy left the teaching profession in 1981 to seek a career with IBM in Los Angeles, California. After six years with the company as customer relations representative to MGM, 20th Century Fox, Orion, William Morris Agency, and other well-known entertainment accounts, he left IBM and worked for a short time in the public sector before his wife Carol's continued relationship with IBM sent them to Kansas City and then to Dallas in 1992.

Golf, shooting, fencing, and travel comprise his extracurricular activities. For the past five years he has devoted all his time to writing and the pursuit of publication. He writes for the love of it and attends weekly meetings of the DFW Writers Workshop in an effort to hone the skills required of his accomplished authors. This is his second year as president of DFWWW.